A Novel

by

Sydney Schuster

Copyright © 2011 Sydney Schuster

sydney.schuster@gmail.com
www.deadspot-book.com
www.sydneyschuster.com
sydneyschuster.wordpress.com

Author's Note

Dead Spot is a work of fiction. The events and characters it describes are literary inventions. If you think you recognize anyone, don't flatter yourself.

The author wishes to acknowledge Susan Morrison, Graydon Carter, Kurt Andersen, Joanne Gruber, and Mim Udovitch for trying so hard to make a writer out of me a long time ago, in a millennium far, far away. If I'd never met them, this book would be a lot worse. Thank you for the ride of a lifetime.

Sydney Schuster's work has been published hundreds of times, mostly in magazines you'll never read. This is her first novel.

Prologue

"You want *WHAT*?" I screamed at Stacy.

I was not having a good day, for a change.

"Exactly *what does that mean*, Stacy — you'd like for Chris and Dana to 'meet' me?"

"You know," said Stacy coyly, twirling a strand of hair. "They want an introduction."

I confess I may have hammered Stacy with more than my usual opaque skepticism. But for once it seemed reasonable, given the circumstances.

Chris and Dana were esteemed cretins from Stacy's "adoring public." That's the generous handle the Met Opera crowd gave their rich groupies. It wasn't all they gave them.

Most of Stacy's fans were blue-haired worm fodder, but Chris and Dana were slightly less necrotic. They made handsome donations to Lincoln Center and Juilliard and Sloan-Kettering, just in case. They took big expensive trips for no reason and wore silk. They were legendary aficionados of classical music and the lost art of swinging.

I hate swingers who wear silk almost as much as I hate schoolgirl ingenuousness. I especially hate people with so much money, they don't know what to do with it. Dorothy Parker once said, "If you want to know what God thinks of money, just look at the people he gave it to."

"WHY do they want to meet me, Stacy?" I couldn't wait to hear the rest.

"They wanna see what you're like. I told 'em you're a hotshit author! Can I bring 'em over? PLEASE? They're dying to see our house."

Of course, Stacy meant MY house, the quaintly dilapidated historic property I was working my ass off renovating not quite as quickly as it was crumbling. It also meant Stacy had been talking about me to the wrong people again. We'd discussed this before, many times. I guess I wasn't shrieking loudly enough then.

Now don't get me wrong. I totally see the value of public relations and networking and all that crap. They can be good for business, and God knows I need all the career help I can get.

But this wasn't help. This was a very special personal hell. I'd have to underwrite a usurious trip to Food Emporium. I'd have to iron two shirts. I'd have to clean my gigantic house by myself, because Stacy won't. ("Makes callouses on the bow hand," Stacy insisted.) Then I'd be expected to check my temper while Chris and Dana parked their Ferragamos on the last of my antiques and dreamed up services I could provide them for free. I'd have to think of nonconfrontational things to say to them, smiling, as they sized me up and packed away all the nutritionally bankrupt food I'd charged at 20 percent interest. I'd have to plunge the toilet after they clogged my historic plumbing with their solid gold shit.

Long story short, it was one more been-there-done-that day with the bloodsucking Met gang. I'd long ago wiped my hands of that whole nest except for Stacy, the last holdout, who was becoming increasingly difficult to talk to lately. That's because anybody who's in the Met Opera orchestra is that much closer to God than everybody who isn't.

Did I mention I hate musicians, too? Periodically I swear off them forever, usually right after I give one the bum's rush. Next thing you know, I'm swan diving into that snakepit again. Fortunately it's still considered chic for hotshit authors to possess one tragic Shakespearean personality flaw. Mine happens to be musician overload.

Right now Stacy was dangerously testing the limits of my bullshit tolerance threshold, having just returned from a spa trip with Chris and Dana that I hadn't sanctioned. I didn't even know about it until the call came from a pay phone at a Catskills resort, which Stacy neglected to identify before cutting me off. When I found out who the other campers were, I plotzed.

We weren't engaged, exactly. But when someone hogs your blankets, eats your groceries, usurps your entire medicine cabinet, and rides on the back of your motorcycle like the queen of the bikers, you're at least going steady.

We had a deal, me and Stacy. There was one thing Stacy needed that I couldn't supply, but not because I wasn't game. I was a total sex slave to Stacy. My failure was the configuration of my plumbing.

"Yeah, yeah," I told Stacy in our tender beginning, "you need it? Go get it." And there were rules. "Use a condom. Don't give me any diseases. Don't let me find any third-party pubic hairs in my boudoir. And don't tell me who you're doing, 'cause I don't wanna know."

So sometimes Stacy would go to a sleepover. All very 1990s. Totally aboveboard, no messy entanglements. Everyone knew this going in. A bad pun indeed, and I'll just insert one more here about the biological masterpiece that was Stacy's teeny perfect butt. Poetically if not physiologically, Stacy's ass was mine. And since I'd only ever found the usual brown and auburn hairs in my sheets, this arrangement worked fine.

That is to say, it did until Stacy called from this spa thing with the Dynamic Duo and said something about roasting wienies with *both* Chris and Dana, which I didn't recall ever being an option in our deal. I'd been given to understand that the only one materially involved with Stacy was the half who peed different from me. So you can appreciate how I really didn't want to know Chris and Dana any better, unless it included modifying their hat size with a bat.

Stacy couldn't have picked a worse time to pull such a dumb stunt. Two of the magazines I write for — correction: wrote for — had just gone under and taken my steady gigs with them. The city I'm stuck in had just reassessed my slum dwelling and jacked up my property taxes, so of course my roof sprung a leak. And there I was, dead broke and strung out from damage control, with Stacy snuggling in a blue algae body wrap with two oversexed mummies who want me in their Shtup of the Month Club.

Suddenly I didn't want to know Stacy, either. It was painfully obvious that our ideas of a committed relationship, no matter how warped the working details got, would never overlap. Why I didn't actually just *kill* Stacy, I don't know. Maybe it's because I'm an expert at taking direct hits. Between dead-end relationships and publishing debacles, I had it covered. Practice makes perfect, say the Metsters. Or maybe it was just that I was awfully fond of Stacy. I'd been hoping our problems would evaporate. Unfortunately, what was evaporating was Stacy.

"So lemme see if I got all this straight. Chris and Dana want to see what *I'm* like?" I said, my blood pressure skyrocketing. "News flash for ya, Stace. I don't want those dehydrated old farts in my house. I don't want them poking around my stuff and leaving poodle hair on my furniture and hoovering my food. Tell 'em to slither back to their crypt and rot."

"But I already told them you'd go for it, you're so moderne!" said Stacy, giggling and leaping around as if making repulsive social plans on my behalf was a fun game.

Being a dedicated wordsmith with a vast and useless vocabulary, "moderne" isn't exactly the term I'd choose to describe my feelings right then.

I picked up Stacy's precious Guarneri and pitched it out a third-floor window. It was followed closely by all of Stacy's overpriced clothes, and promtime tchotchkes, and Ricky Martin posters, and new Macintosh Classic, all of which would've been followed closely by Stacy personally, had he not already bulleted down my semiattached stairs and into history.

Chapter 1

Dorothy Parker is my idol. Well, she's one of them, anyway. She was obnoxious and inconsiderate. She didn't give a damn what people thought about her. She hung color photos of cadavers over her desk at *Vanity Fair*. And she never, ever paid her own way. Grown men feared her.

Admirable qualities all, though not the main reasons she's my hero. *That* would be her singular talent for blasting straight through mountains of crap.

"What fresh hell is this?" was how she answered her phone. Of course, that was in the days before you could blow off pests with answering machines like mine.

To honor the auspicious debut of the shittiest (and mercifully, last) decade of the twentieth century, I offer this update on Parker's breezy Depression era wisdom: If it feels like you're in hell, maybe you are.

Yeah, I know. Thud. Crash. It won't win any free drinks at the Algonquin, but it *really* ticks people off good. Go ahead, try it on your friends. Next time things don't go your way, just bark, "Where the hell am I? In *Hell*?"

Parker also beat me to the perfect epitaph. It was published during the 1920s in the *New Yorker*: "That would be a good thing for them to cut on my tombstone: 'Wherever she went, including here, it was against her better judgment.'" Dot has since departed New York for some more ethereal place worthy of reconsideration.

I, on the other hand, am stuck in this suckfest. Like, not long ago I woke up strapped to a gurney that was being shoveled into an EMS meat wagon. A paramedic was on the mobile phone telling someone, "Yeah, this one's out. Definitely out."

If ever a mountain of crap needed blasting in a hurry, this was it. It was think fast or be on my merry way into the bowels of the public hospital system of the viral plague capital of America.

"I'm *not* out!" I yelled, kicking a paramedic in the knee with a steel-toed boot he probably wished he'd tied down better. "See? Not out! No transfusions!"

I struggled to rise but couldn't. "Untie me!"

He didn't untie me. "How many fingers?" he said instead, holding up three digits in my face. I would've ripped them from his knuckles had I not been trussed up like a holiday turkey.

"Quit with the fingers! Lemme up! Where's my damned bike?"

One of the paramedics held up a folded piece of paper. "Guy at the scene said they'd keep it inside for you 'til you could come get it. It's at the sugar factory on Cumberland. Here's his number." He slipped it into my jacket pocket.

"Factory? Cumberland? Where am I? This crate looks like hell."

"It's just an ambulance. You're in Brooklyn."

Of course. Brooklyn. I should've known. The swirling red disco lights. The sirens. The diesel fumes. I looked around for Tony Manero. All I saw was oxygen tanks and vermin scat.

"What about that stuff in the corner?" I nagged him. "Looks like rat poop."

"Looks like caraway seeds to me."

"It's poop, dammit. How do you know we're not in hell?"

With that, the annoyed medics popped me with a hit of Thorazine and I passed out again.

I dreamed about my precious goddamned bike being "warehoused" in a Third World sweatshop, and how I was on my merry way to purgatory with a concussion and a fractured jaw.

My head felt like a truck had driven through it, because that's more or less what actually happened. Some hoser had cut me off. I remembered locking my rear brake hard and pivoting the bike 90 degrees so I wouldn't break my fork or my neck, just before broadsiding him at 45 mph.

My brilliant plan worked, kind of. First there was the dreaded *whump*. Next thing I know, I'm rising from the asphalt unassisted and wondering how to pick up a quarter-ton bike that was rubber side up. I wasn't hurt so much as surprised. And slightly dazed. And a tad bloody. Mostly I was angry. My bike had a dented exhaust pipe that would cost three figures to replace. My expensive leathers were ripped. But I was fine. I ride okay, for a girl. Except for this.

I'd already peeled off my helmet and was assessing the damage when Driver of the Year came trotting over.

"Look what you did to my truck!" he screamed. I guess he meant that big me-shaped hole in the side of it.

"Fuck you," I said. The last thing I remember was his fist flying at my face.

When I came to, I learned many fascinating things from the medics. One was that they took an hour to get there. Good thing I wasn't *really* sick.

Some voyeurs who came by to snort my oxygen said the police had arrived only five minutes earlier than the medics. Since I was unavailable at the time, someone else gave the cops a complete plate number and a detailed vehicle description, and there was no shortage of eyewitnesses eagerly telling the officers exactly what happened in every language but English.

Best I could make out, being unconscious while all this took place, was that New York's Finest solved my case in record time by proclaiming I hit myself. I woke up just before they cut out to apprehend donuts.

"You aren't hurt bad enough to press charges," one of them actually said to me, "if there was anyone to file charges against, which there isn't."

Indeed, my dancing partner was long gone, thanks to them. I'm usually more persuasive about convincing uniformed retards to make an effort to catch hosers, but I was already strapped to the gurney.

"This one's out," they lied to the EMTs, then left me in the middle of Flushing Avenue.

The ambulance took me to Kings County Hospital, where the emergency room geniuses said I wasn't hurt bad enough to stay. "Whaddya expect *us* to do?" they said. "Put your head in a cast?"

I definitely had ideas about exactly what they could do. Unfortunately, I was unable to convey them since my jaw hinge was completely disconnected by then. My head looked like the Hindenburg.

That was a couple of months ago. I hardly stutter at all now. I got right back on the bike as soon as I could squeeze my head into a helmet again, and resumed my glamorous life as a deadbeat writer. It's all you can do. If you live in New York, this sort of thing happens to you all the time.

Of course, I wasn't always this aggressively nihilistic. Once I was an upper-middle-class Bible Belt girl who studied art and music, got chauffeured around in big American sedans, and was carefully groomed to booby trap a mate from a highly localized, inbred pool of agri-nerds and tractor retailers of tomorrow. But big Southern guys, I discovered the hard way, have big attitude problems. They yell, and they hit anyone shorter than them who can't get out of their way fast enough. After eighteen years of ducking and running, I rebelled against giant, dimwitted good ol' boys by becoming a woman who lives in a New York ghetto, drives motorcycles, and digs midgets.

Here in Nueva York, land of the eternal immigrant, the anthropological paradigm spins a full 180 degrees from the hillbilly archetype of the South.

At 5'10" I pretty much tower over any Yankee with both feet on the ground. The ones in trucks are still kind of a problem. But thankfully, New York is a place where being a pink ghetto-dwelling woman with a motorcycle (or with a midget, for that matter) inspires awe more often than pugilism. Total strangers ask me, "Aren't you afraid?"

Well, let's see. Hospitals? Afraid of those. Loose rabid dogs? We no likey. Spiders? Double ugh — ever get one of those things in your ear? But going out in a ball of gasoline-fed flames? Suits me just fine, thanks. That's assuming, of course, that I'm not already dead.

That's what I mean, about being in hell. What else would explain why other vehicles don't see me until they've hit me? Why do pedestrians step off curbs in front of me? Why do cars on the expressway cut me off, going half as fast? When I stop at red lights behind trucks, why do they suddenly decide to back up? Why don't I have a boyfriend? Or a job? Obviously I'm in some netherworld where every day I die horribly, only to wake the next day and do it again. Crash, wince, repeat.

It's only half as stupid as it sounds. Many cultures believe in continued existence after worldly demise, just not in an attractive way. And I certainly could've gotten dead at any time. You got your knifings here, your subway pushings, your drivings by, your cars with pothole-busted tie-rods flipping over with you in them, your crackheads in RVs. New Yorkers are the worst drivers in the world. They make U-turns over double yellow lines because they're too lazy to go around the block. They back up on the highway if they miss their exit. They drive at night with their lights off. They turn and change lanes for no reason, without signaling. They drive with their doors open and their hatches flapping and their brake lights burned out. It's like being inside a pinball machine. A pinball machine in hell.

They say ghosts are dead people who don't know it. So yes, it would appear I'm in hell. And no, I'm not afraid. Dorothy Parker wouldn't be afraid. What could possibly be the point?

Chapter 2

"Nona, your ship's docked!" Darryl shouts as he compulsively bisects and rebisects the *New York Times* classifieds into an origami-like production. If he hadn't stopped when he did, I would've had to pound him.

"Listen to this one," he says, reading out loud. "'Wait staff wanted, eight dollars an hour.' C'mon, Nona! Let's go! I got gas in my car!"

I was pretty close to killing Darryl. "What else?" I say instead. It's his lucky day.

"'Delivery work. Light lifting. Must know South Bronx. Eight dollars an hour. Drive own vehicle.'"

I took a conservative sip of the last tequila I'd be able to afford until the check from the *Voice* came, if it ever did. Darryl picked an argument with the bartender in a noble attempt to finagle a free round. Something about losing his original drink and needing a replacement.

"We don't replace lost drinks," said the bartender.

"But that drunk over there slammed into me and now he's wearing my beer."

"Then get *him* to pay for it. That'll be eight bucks for the last round."

Darryl and I did this a lot, got blasted together and complained about work. Or more accurately, we complained about not having any. Jobs had become impossible to find, unless you wanted to be a drug mule or an $8-an-hour office temp.

You'd never know it to look at us now, but Darryl and I used to be hot pooh in advertising. Before the industry spat both of us out, I lived in a privileged, parallel universe of Yellow cabs, expense account steaks, and designer clothes. I ran the print production department of Dancer Fitzgerald Sample, a gargantuan New York advertising agency that doesn't exist anymore.

We won a ton of industry awards when I was at Dancer: Clio; Graphis; The Creativity Award of Distinction; Glammies. Toadies. Phooeys. Whatever. My point is that you could open up any issue of *Time* back then, and on every other page was an ad I'd assembled.

Mine was a hard job, deciding if colors looked right and comp work was clean, and constantly ordering someone to eradicate supermodel cellulite. Everybody at Dancer had a problem only I could solve.

"Nona," the traffic manager would say, "there's a whole panel missing from this Chanel ad."

"Nona," the ad salesman would say, "the *Miami Vice* people are on the phone about the rush four-color double-truck — you know, with the contours and drop-outs and 3-D insert and all that, the one we already sent to the printer. They wanna change it."

"Hey, Nona, the printer's on the phone," the customer service rep would say. "He says the color separation negs we sent him for the Pan Am job aren't."

"Aren't what?"

"Separated."

Navigating the minefield that was Dancer was how I hooked up with my
pal Darryl Colletti, before his graphic arts career was disrupted into oblivion by
Macintosh.

We met when we joined forces on the now-defunct Billowform account. A friend had told me he was an awesome retouch artist, so I got Darryl's number and told him to stop by my office at Dancer with his portfolio. He did, and he was so good I hired him immediately to nuke the supercurds on Gia Carangi's bum.

After Billowform, I called Darryl often to do freelance retouching. There were a zillion other retouchers in town, all of them hungrier and cheaper than Darryl was. But he was fast and clean and understood exactly what I wanted, with a minimum of whining. And frankly, his stock really went up with me when he won honorable mention in a "New New York" slogan contest. His entry was: "New York — The Bathroom Is Broken State."

Dancer was our Golden Age. We shared countless corporate card lunches, viciously dishing everyone we knew in advertising. We attended glittering film premieres and yammered all the way through them. We went to black tie events where we poked luminaries in the butt and pretended it was an accident. We even got thrown out of The Palm once after Darryl ambushed Jerry Della Femina and demanded Tums. A lot of people were quite glad when our careers were ruined.

My star rose and fell fast, in a pathetically straight line. It was a longer, squiglier trip to the bottom for Darryl. He's just like one of those wind-up toys that hits a wall, turns around, and keeps going until it hits another wall.

Darryl's my age, a Queens homeboy who tried lots of things and was infuriatingly competent at all of them. "Hey, Nona, I got the stylist job for the Calvin spot!" "Hey, Nona, guess who's on the bloody-nose-and-entrails crew for *Terminator*?" "Hey, Nona — Jon Bon Jovi wants *me* to teach *him* to play jazz!"

Back when I was still an assistant ad production manager, Darryl's concurrent incarnation was lead guitarist for Migraine, the second hottest bar band on the East Coast. He quit cutting hair at Sassoon to join Migraine. Then he quit Migraine to play the American tour of Delroy Prince, King of Blues, right before His Majesty was deported over an import/export misunderstanding. Darryl was not thrilled when the tour got canceled, especially after he found out Migraine had replaced him. Then he noticed his beautician's license had expired. Or as he explains it, "Twelve hundred fucking bucks for a fucking replacement license in fucking New York!"

That's when he backed into photo retouching. Things were going great, too, until the venerable art of airbrushing was unexpectedly automated into a cellulite-blasting cyberrealm beyond his skill set, and he was on his butt in the street.

Nowadays Darryl cuts my hair for free and plays guitar for bands you've never heard of for pocket change. The latest of these is the recently defunct Phlegmtones.

Back when both of us toiled in advertising, before the Great Crash of '87, we were rolling in green. Me, I was a twenty-something on the express elevator. Whenever people at Dancer left for better jobs, I moved up; next thing you know, I'm queen of the glory hole.

The agency paid me grandly to yell at people seventy hours a week. I had a nice office with a view of the UN. It came with a cushy chair that spun, a giant ficus nobody watered, and a free Midtown parking space I didn't need because the company paid my carfare. Instead of saving my money, I spent it all on yuppie candy like a motorcycle I didn't have time to ride. Black Monday fixed all that.

In October of 1987 there was that little 500-point stock market dip the Reagan administration blew off as a "correction," except for that it was one third of the volume of the whole New York Stock Exchange. A month earlier, half of New York was complaining about their bosses and microscopic apartments as usual; a year later they were maxing out all their credit cards and filing for bankruptcy. Dancer's board of directors grabbed their golden parachutes and ejected. The company was swallowed by a bigger company that already had a production department, and my operation became redundant.

"We're sorry to have to tell you this," was how it was stuck to me by the HR hatchet waver. "We always hate giving bad news to a loyal, valued employee such as yourself. But..."

And that's how the middle class and I parted ways. Outplacement wasn't a fully realized concept in Reagan's shining scrapheap on a hill. It slowly and painfully became clear that I'd never find another advertising job, or any other kind. The same thing that happened at Dancer was happening all over town. A job became a thing you needed connections to get, like contraband or backstage passes.

It's a gross understatement to call the '80s depressing. Half my friends died of AIDS, and most of the rest moved out West where the jobs were. Me, I'm a thirty-something who crawls around in oil pools with wrenches. I eat Spam tacos and take out 4x4s. By golly, I'm the Mrs. Peel in an Australian's nightmare.

Chapter 3

And so began the circuitous and weird trip through career retooling hell that made me the magazine writer I am today — an angry, broke, bitter magazine writer, with dangerous heavy machinery. It seemed like a good idea at the time.

"I may be forced to take some underpaid, entry-level job," I reassured the clerk at the bodega where I buy all my beer. "But don't worry. It's gonna be a *hip* underpaid job!"

Writing was more like a no-brainer, being my only option. I'd already been doing it for years anyway. Originally it was a lark, a part-time sideline to my go-go advertising career when the money didn't matter and the travel was a bonus. Plus it didn't hurt that publishing credits were priceless on a resume.

"I see here that you're a very accomplished professional, Ms. Gold," HR drones would gush. "We always have room for versatile talent like yours here at Grubs International."

Early in the Reagan regime, magazines had great steaming gobs of cash to throw at freelancers like me, especially those willing to skewer important people. And being in advertising, I personally knew many showbiz sycophants with access to highly confidential information of a sensitive nature that they blabbed freely.

"I've got a major unflattering scoop about Jerry Falwell," I'd call some editor and say. Bam, I had an assignment.

One thing never changes: Everyone loves a train wreck. Once Dorothy Parker was taken to view a raging wildfire that she watched through her fingers, with her hands over her face. "Think how frightened all the little animals are," she said to the people who took her there, "the little squirrels, the little rabbits, all the little birds. Do you think we could get any closer?"

The '80s were synonymous with "closer." That's how I got sucked into the inexplicable media flurry surrounding Chola, the badly aging Andy Warhol star. During her endlessly discussed comeback (comeback to what was never made clear), she got paid way more than real journalists to go on about herself in print. First the *Village Voice* ran three repetitious Chola features by Chola about Chola. Then three more identical features appeared in *New York Woman*, an annoying magazine that, happily, went under right afterward.

Money in the bank, I thought, *sign me up!* One of Chola's "investigations" involved a surrogate-for-hire whose post-utero change of heart led to a high-profile custody battle. It ended with her losing her kid and commercial surrogacy being outlawed in New Jersey. Six months before Black Monday, I reported on Chola's reporting for *Spy*:

> In her touching paean in the *Voice* to tragic surrogate mother Marybeth Whitehead, Chola crucified her own ex-husbands for not paying her enough alimony. She mentioned her own children 27 times, detailed six totally unrelated vacations she took, and plugged six professional services she was selling. The moving tribute to Whitehead featured a quarter-page portrait by the author's daughter of the author.
>
> In two other *Voice* articles, Chola pounded on her father, who still supports her, and took sole credit for Warhol's filmmaking success even though she only worked with him for a year. One piece included nude photos of Prima Gravida Barbie along with her home address, in case you were thinking of sending a check.

It was a spectacularly distasteful decade, except when I was cashing a check or writing about motorcycle racing. I got sent to see 1982 World Champion Franco Uncini collide with future 500cc champ Wayne Gardner at the Dutch Time Trial. I went to Bike Week in Daytona, the 24-hour races at LeMans, and historic beach racing in South Australia. I spent my vacations from Dancer hanging out with cute guys in tight leather pants and couldn't believe I was getting paid for it.

Shiny trousers aside, the most gratifying thing about crafting great journalism isn't the product. Trust me when I tell you that nothing is more fun than snooping through famous people's yearbooks and criminal records. I adored asking unwary celebrities invasive questions. "Ivana, *Cosmo* wants to know what you're wearing under that Valentino." And I especially enjoyed seeing BY NONA GOLD prominently typeset in the largest possible letters, preferably near a wildly flattering photo of Nona Gold.

That was pre-Black Monday. This is post. All the editors I'd worked for in the '80s — in some cases, whole magazines I'd worked for in the '80s — are gone, just like all those nice trips I used to take. A lot of my old editors are processing words for $8 an hour. All of us were dragged kicking and screaming into a universal reset. Do not pass go, do not collect $200, at least not very often.

The good news was, I had a place to live. In the '80s I'd been a good enough muckraker and supermodel curd eliminator to buy a house I can't afford anymore. The bad news was, nobody else could afford to buy it from me when I put it up for sale, and the bank wouldn't take it, either. So making the mortgage payments became my ultimate challenge.

I sold nearly everything else I owned. My antique kilims, my Nikon collection, my Accord. Who needs a car in New York anyway? But I kept the Beemer, in a final stupid act of yuppie defiance.

My bike is 800 CCs of pulsating Krautish horstpower. The only negative is a big dead spot at 4,000 rpm in fifth gear. It's almost as if the thing's cut out on you, except you can still hear the engine thumping away mightily, doing nothing. That's German engineering for you. There are two things Nazis do efficiently. One is build bikes.

Mine happens to be all that stands between me and getting mugged on the C train. It also makes a great conversation starter, once new acquaintances overcome their horror at a woman operating it.

Eventually I got pretty good at fixing the thing, too, seeing as how the services of a mechanic cost sixty dollars an hour that I didn't have. As the bike got older and parts wore out, it broke down in increasingly inconvenient places and my skills improved exponentially. I could rebuild the engine with a rock.

Normal wear and tear aside, just being in New York is hard on a bike. No matter how good of a driver one may be, everyone else isn't. A frightening proportion of New York's motoring population was driving camels and rickshaws last year. The rest are legally blind, unlicensed or uninsured or both, and/or looking for a Tito Puente tape instead of where they're going.

Ours is indeed a diverse culture. If you drop your bike in Manhattan, traffic stops all around you while hunky guys jump out of trucks to help. If you drop your bike in Brooklyn, you help yourself.

Nobody remembers or cares that I was tooling around on this thing before Mickey Rourke and Jay Leno made bikes fashionable. They don't even remember that *I* used to be fashionable. No biggie. I just pretend it's an angle of my new cool-rebel lifestyle that I'd give up in a second if I could find another advertising job. But like I said, I'm a writer now.

Chapter 4

The '80s beat the Holofil out of all of us. Many New Yorkers were reduced to grate dwellers. Me and Darryl, we had game.

We stayed friends after Dancer self-destructed. For a guitar player, he's okay. Not like all the other musical geniuses I know who are as reliable as Lucas ignitions. Darryl has never left me on a street corner to go off with some tramp. He'd steal the jewelry off your grandmother at her own funeral, but he'd give you a finder's fee.

Not that Darryl isn't adorable in his own civil-servant sort of way. Behind the golf shirts and permanent press chinos lies the basic infrastructure of Nona's Type: a diminutive, wiry guy with an impossibly cute little ass. As anyone who bothers remembering the erstwhile Stacy may recall, Nona prefers her bikes big and her men compact. Like the motorcycle racers say: It's not size that matters. It's what you do with it.

Our relationship is about many things — money, fun, torture — but not sex. Darryl has a couple of girlfriends for that, and probably a couple of cowfriends, too. God knows where he's been. I wouldn't touch him with a barge pole. What Darryl had that mattered was a lucrative sideline.

The thing Michael Milken did to junk bonds, Darryl does to used instruments. He buys stuff cheap and sells high, in volume. A lot of it's made of parts that didn't start out in the same guitar together, much less in the same factory.

He also keeps a smaller revolving collection of fine vintage guitars, mostly Gibsons on account of he's the blues king. He plays with those until he gets bored, then dumps them for a nifty profit.

Recently Darryl bought an original, unrestored Flying V for $8,000. He swore he got it at the 25th Street flea market, but the case had a luggage tag that read If Found, Please Return To Leslie Weinstein. I thought eight grand was a lot of money for a beat-up ax, but Darryl said no. "Gibson only made a few hundred Flying Vs. They were so radical, nobody wanted them in the '50s. They do now." Darryl turned his around for $25,000. Tax free.

He likes it when I help out. "Are you still trying to sell hack garbage to magazines? Forget about it!" He says this *FuhGEDabowdit*. "Get over here and help me sell this Frankenstein for more than it's worth. Put on some leather pants." I learned everything I'd like to forget about guitars from Darryl.

"Come over tonight. I'm cutting your hair," he says every time we talk. Then he gets drunk, forgets my hair, and stumbles off to his closet or bed and hauls out a guitar case.

"Look what I got! Like my new Martin?"

"I always wanted a Dreadnought. Get *me* one," I say as he finally starts clipping my overgrown mop.

"Can't. All the good guitars got shipped to Japan."

"So I'm not getting a Dreadnought?"

"Sure you are. Go to Japan. They're all in basements there, nailed to walls." Big chunks of my hair crash to the floor.

"Okay. Get me an old Les Paul then."

"I already told you. Forget about it, unless ya got fifteen grand. Coulda got you one cheap a while back. A good Les Paul *used* to go for six thousand. Back before the Japs came in and started paying ten, 'cause they didn't know the market."

"According to *Kiplinger's*, the Japanese *own* all the markets."

"They're army ants!" Darryl snorts. The angrier he becomes, the fluffier my hair gets. "I had this one piece, sold it to a store for twelve thousand. The store sold it to a Japanese guy for eighteen. He sold it for forty in Japan. Most American dealers, they saw all the good stuff disappearing overseas, so they stopped selling to the Japanese." Of course,

Darryl would sell *his* guitars to a Martian if it waved enough dead presidents in his face.

"Once they're out of the country," he said, "they're gone — Les Pauls, Firebirds, Stratocasters, Telecasters, D'Angelicos. Say goodnight, Gracie."

Despite this regrettable state of foreign affairs, Darryl always has a choice lineup. So I tapped out the cash advance line on my gold card and gave him my last $10,000 to invest in the rock'n'roll grey market. It was the only way I was going to keep up with my mortgage, freelance journalism being the remunerative font it ain't.

Chapter 5

"Get *off* my bike!" I screamed at the teenaged bottom-feeder using my ride for a lounge. Great — another new drug customer on the block, scratching up my paint with the brads on his Bugle Boys.

"I'm gonna call the cops!" he shot back.

"You do that!" I yelled, grabbing a wrecking bar even though I was too old to catch up.

"Ma! She hit me!" he screamed to no one I could see as he sprinted off down the block.

I went back to plastering ceiling holes and waited. Soon there would be sirens, and angry unwed mothers, and dumb-as-stumps uniforms assembling on my crumbling stoop to lynch me for assaulting someone's 6'2" baby. It's a nice enough neighborhood, except for all the belligerent juvenile delinquents messing up other peoples' property in baggy-ass pants boosted from Wal-Mart.

I was living, or trying to anyway, in the brownstone row house I'd bought at city auction, some luckless Brooklynite's repossessed tax burden that I'd transformed from a ghetto hovel into an artist's hovel. The historical society says the architectural style is called Greek Revival. I call it Greek Tragedy.

My fake temple is four once-elegant stories of masonry that need repointing, plaster that's failing, stairs that are disengaging from their stringers, and appliances that should be in a museum. It has a magic roof that always leaks no matter how many times I fix it. My house was nicer once, when I had money to fix it, before the crash of '87.

It has way too many rooms for just one person. Instead of furniture they're full of things like skis and racquets that I can't afford to use anymore, and boxes of research from magazine assignments that got killed halfway through. You could say my legacy adds up to my decor: stacks of broken junk and a bunch of great writing no one will ever read. And many dust bunnies. Maybe a couple cockaroaches. There are no treasures here anymore, because I sold them all. Who needs them? Jumeau dolls are for losers anyway.

My decor is the story of a life. It's a consistent life, a life they use for setting clocks in hell: wrong place, wrong time, over and over.

My neighborhood is perfect for me. We are both crusty, antiquated appendages of Manhattan that devolved in a long and ugly decline. My turn-of-the-century 'hood was briefly reborn in that '80s real estate boom distinguished by mass displacement of poor people by yuppies like me. This phenomenon is what New Yorkers euphemistically call "gentrification."

Following the market correction of '87, the area submerged into the urban decay whence it sprang. Strapped homeowners split. Halfway houses appeared overnight. Unfocused crotch scratchers, junkies, and hookers walked the streets at all hours, arguing loudly with their associates or themselves. Sometimes they had guns. I waited until I started finding crack vials in my yard to put my house on the market. No reasonable offer refused.

Great timing, that. The banks started redlining my area, and now I'm stuck in it.

Hardly anyone ever comes over, not that I blame them, so I felt free to furnish the place with old lady settees and horrible prints of landscapes I found on the street. One day I acquired a genuine Eames chair, the label still intact, left out for the trash collector on Lexington Avenue. It always amazes me how people will fight over dumb shit like dents in their trucks, then go and throw away a $200 chair. I carried it home via train at rush hour. It's the last time I remember having a subway seat.

As you can tell from my decorator bill, my career was really percolating. I'd been recruited as a contributing editor by a motor sports magazine no one seemed to read, and was sending them lots of invoices that would never be paid. The only places they ever sent me were industry shows. "Somebody take my pulse" I'd mutter as I shlepped past vendor after vendor shilling the same chrome-plated drek nobody needs. I guess you can call that a career, if that's all ya got.

My sole pleasure in life was my bike. I was game for any assignments requiring road trips, especially ones as far away from New York as possible. No proposition involving a ride was too ridiculous to consider. That's how an entertainment magazine editor suckered me into doing a where-are-they-now celebrity feature on spec.

The spec part was bad enough. I really do like knowing whether I'll be paid. But damn, I hate celebrities! I hate pretending to be fascinated by their boring, self-centered existences. I hate having to make their meatheaded introspections sound profound. "*Really*, Mr. Vellechaize? Tell me more about overcoming your vertical challenge to conquer Hollywood." But unfortunately, that's what magazines pay writers for. And apparently, it's what Americans prefer to read.

Anyway, the shitstorm I drove into for this spec gig was a fortyish one-hit wonder named Lane McCarthy. His historic contribution to Western culture was a freakish record with Hitchcockian pretensions, cut just before he rightfully vanished from MTV's radar screen forever.

Right after Bruce Springsteen made *Nebraska*, a concept album about the Starkweather murder spree, Lane barfed up *Itasca*, a concept album about a transvestite serial murderer in Texas named Nelda. The press couldn't stop disparaging *Itasca*, resulting in the immediate sale of six million units.

In the eight years since, Lane was unable to reprise his success and had slunk back to the suds pits that begat him. Why any rag wanted verbiage about *that* beat the hell out of me.

But far be it from me to give a damn. *Money in the bank*, I thought. Probably somebody owed somebody a favor. And I never met a has-been who wasn't desperate for publicity. Lane McCarthy would be good for a heart-tugging unbosoming that would be a cinch to fact check. A fast write for a quick buck, complete with a road trip and free beer. And he was easy to find. The dead, they walk among you.

Chapter 6

"Aren't you scared?" the New Jersey Turnpike toll booth clerk asked when I pushed up my visor to ask for a receipt.

"I'd never let *my* wife drive a bike," said the one on the way back. Gad, I hate Jersey.

The first time I ever saw Lane McCarthy with his band, Love Dinghy, was in a Long Branch shore bar, right after accepting what I now affectionately refer to as my last fucking spec assignment ever. I hadn't been to Jersey in ages, and now I was forced to recall why.

The drive to Long Branch was distinguished by an interminable string of boring industrial parks, all lit up like carnivals without any of the good stuff. The turnpike was straight and wide and endless, its surface strangely damp and glasslike. I spent most of the time watching for my odometer to turn over 55,555 miles. The most interesting part of the trip was the cars swerving all over the place for no reason.

My destination was a boardwalk clip joint packed with squealing, drunken women reeking of White Diamonds and peppermint schnapps. All of them were either frightfully skinny or fat, and wearing shiny synthetic-fiber outfits that clung in all the wrong places, with standard issue megahair. The State Hair of Jersey, Darryl calls it. I wished he was here to see this.

Darryl wouldn't be caught dead in a place like this. But all the original Love Dinghies were here, proudly dressed like fugitives from the '80s. Except for Lane. He was dressed like a gay dockworker from the '70s. I half expected him to burst into "Macho Man." As I was to discover, Lane McCarthy had many influences, all of them in mortal combat over control of him.

The rest of the band was a blur of Aztec prints and leopard spots, big gold neck chains, and Western shoe boots made in Sri Lanka. I was astounded they could draw a crowd this big, even one as ignorant of current styles as this one. Some wore the most bizarre costumes I ever saw, with ruffled aprons and big fake scythes.

This band was more than a tribute to classic rock. Much more. It was like the Mummy. You couldn't kill it, it wouldn't die by itself, and the faster you ran away, the quicker it caught up.

Lane's stage persona seemed vaguely about connecting with regular people. Two songs into the band's first set, he launched into a Cougar-like, rebel-dude intro to a power ballad about the Vietnam draft, or something. It didn't make much sense to me, but then not much does.

"We all know things ain't goin' so good. Lotta people losin' their jobs and houses," Lane intoned grimly to folks who'd come to dance. Slow, meaningful drumroll in background. "Factories closin' down. Businesses goin' under." Signature guitar riff starts and repeats. I'm telling you, this crap made "Patches" sound like gospel. "Where I'm from, government froze the credit unions' assets so no one can get at their savings." *And I'm a millionaire and you're not. That'll be a twelve-dollar cover, please.*

Spokesman for the masses, you bet. All the regular types who came to forget their problems got up and left. The ones in the idiotic costumes ran out to their cars for a toke. The place cleared out so fast, you'd have thought there was a bomb threat.

Maybe Lane really *was* lathered up about the plight of downtrodden wage slaves and all that. But when Mellencamp was headlining benefits for bankrupt farmers, Lane was playing wet T-shirt competitions at Harley rallies.

A couple of other things about him stood out that shouldn't. By the second set, the stage was littered with empty Dos Equis bottles. It sort of forced one to conclude that the greatest of his talents wasn't necessarily the most obvious. Who can drink that much gas-inducing swill and still be able to sing?

And our conversation is one I'll never forget, for all the wrong reasons. After the show I found him where he was holding court, signing autographs in lush, voluptuous cursive. When his three fans went back to the sanitarium, I introduced myself.

"Hi, Mr. McCarthy. My name's Nona Gold. I'm a reporter. I've written for *Spy* and *Smart*."

I handed him my card. He looked at it like it was a parking ticket.

"I'd like to do a profile on you and the band," I said, and waited. I hoped he'd be impressed, like everybody else. Plus, I'd artfully avoided naming the lowbrow rag that actually sent me here.

He agreed immediately. Or anyway, he made sounds like he was agreeing. "Yeah, great! Okay! And call me Lane. Please."

He sounded sincere, and he was so short and wiry — I love that in a guy. He had a Harley can opener on his keychain. I wondered if he had a bike to go with it.

"I'm finishing up another project now," I lied, "but I'll be ready to start this one in a week. How can I reach you then?"

"Gimme that," he said to my notebook and grabbed it away. "Call my PR guy. He'll set it up. Got a pen?"

He scribbled the name of the New York company that tried to manage him, in incongruously blocky and childlike hand that was miles different from his pretty autograph script. I wondered why a loser the world forgot needed someone to manage his press schedule, and why I couldn't just call him at home like I did with everyone else.

"I don't remember their phone number," he said. I believed that. "But they're in the phone book. And, uh, I can't remember their address. It's one of those number streets." That certainly narrowed it down. Thanks, Lane.

"Don't worry. I'll find it." I said, stopping just short of saying *I can find anybody*, although I can. Easily. I keep it to myself. Don't like to scare people more than I already do without trying.

I already knew the town where Lane lived. He'd casually shoehorned it into his stage patter, right after the guano he rearloaded onto the blue-collar crowd about being just like them. Lane lived in an impoverished Connecticut burg called Groton.

Lane parked his excellent butt on a Super Reverb amp, balancing my notebook on his knee while he struggled unsuccessfully to recall fundamental business data. As he frowned down at the pen that refused to cooperate, I noticed he had a lot of hair for a dinosaur. It wasn't fake like I'd guessed, herded the way it was into a style last seen on Warren Beatty in *Shampoo*. He had a mullet the size of Ohio.

Darryl will flip when he sees this, I thought. Lane's 'do was black with lightning-white stripes, floating like a buoy over gigantic greying muttonchops. All way too big and high-contrast for my taste, though it seemed to meet the standards of the local fatgirls just fine. They appreciate beauty school improv.

Lane's eyes were a coordinating slate color. He was still pre-bifocal: I could see the rims of his contact lenses. His lumpy nose was an unexpected counterpoint to all the overwrought hair artifice. Apparently it never met a fight it didn't like. I liked the fact that he never fixed that; it wasn't as if he couldn't afford to. I heard he'd invested well.

So I didn't know if not fixing his nose indicated self-confidence — like any American male who's 5'4" is drowning in that — or brain damage. It's a toss-up. He may have charted, but this is a guy who sang about being sensitive and misunderstood with a sock stuffed in his crotch.

Not that I was any hipper myself in the Me Decade. I stopped listening to the radio in 1980, the year I started working seventy-hour weeks in advertising, fast-tracking my way to welfare. I'm afraid I missed Love Dinghy's one-round Top Forty invasion. I was therefore obliged to go to extraordinary lengths to unearth a Nelda album. I finally found one, by accident, inside a Johnny Mathis jacket in a slush bin at Bleecker Bob's. I promptly regretted it.

Lane was an idiot savant. Granted, an idiot savant who was allowed to make three major-label albums, but nobody bought two of them. The Nelda album, however, they picked clean from the stores. *Itasca* featured eleven perverse, sexually ambiguous immortalizations of insufferable debs and the homicidal stalker who loved them. One became a Top Ten single. "What Are You Looking At?" went like this:

> How's my make-up, honey?
> Do you think my butt's too flat?
> I hate singles bar ladies' room mirrors.
> They make us look so fat.
>
> Are you searching for the right man?
> Do you think you've found him yet?
> Oh, it's that time of month for moi,
> otherwise I'd sweat.
>
> Did I say my name is Nelda?
> Are my seams straight? Am I pretty?
> Honey, what are you looking at?
> Doesn't every girl pack a machete?

How people can pull shit like this out of their asses and face anyone again is baffling. And honestly, Lane did seem like a lot of things, but misogynist wasn't among them. He didn't sweat as we spoke. He shook my hand firmly. He looked me in the eye. He asked me for a dollar for the cigarette machine. I was sure he pissed in the shower and tested candy bars in the grocery store like everyone else. There *was* that power tube tucked into his shirt sleeve where a normal person would've stashed cigs. But unless he was hiding something in a body cavity, he was unarmed. Come to think of it, so was Ted Bundy. Nevertheless, I dismissed the Nelda songs as the fruit of a pharmaceutical binge.

Darryl and I bought Lane's other two albums for four bits at a garage sale in Staten Island along with a 1955 Kremo-Kustom Doubleneck. Those LPs were far more conventional, with occasional bursts of exquisite poetry — about conmen, barflies, street trash — that would blow your doors off. But most of the cuts were trite slop about motorcycles, scratch'n'sniff babes, and blue-collar blues, typified by hackneyed lyrics about working "on my daddy's farm" in one song with a father who "worked the mines" in another. Oy.

In Lane's defense, those are certainly more romantic phrases (and way easier to rhyme things with) than dirges about spare parts and fertilizer. Came to find out his real dad was a lifer at the US Agriculture Department Fruits and Vegetable Division, Northeast Headquarters, in Johnston, Rhode Island. The only actual job Lane himself ever held was in the summer of 1972, stacking car parts in GM's Detroit factory on Clark Street. The two McCarthys never worked one day together, in any mine shaft or chicken farm or anyplace else, ever.

I got the Detroit information from a reporter who'd interviewed Lane years ago. He called Lane a pill and couldn't believe anyone was still interested in him. A letter to the government invoking the Freedom of Information Act took care of Pop. It was easy dirt to shovel. Most of Lane's dirt was.

After meeting Lane, I went home and looked up Groton in the *Places Rated Almanac*. Just a humble village full of working-class stiffs! The town's big industry is nuclear sub building. The US Navy outpost there is the largest submarine base in the world. Median house price is $159,000. Only 2.5 murders per 100,000 population. And no state or city income taxes, unlike the hole where I live where they tax everything including the smog you breathe.

Call my manager, my ass. I wrote to Lane via his agency, like he asked, about the interview he agreed to. The response was a form letter stating they forwarded my letters to him.

The agency abnegating its press-wrangling responsibilities wasn't much of a surprise. Probably Lane couldn't remember their address enough to pay them. I called the agency a few times anyway and left messages, but still no Lane.

Chapter 7

"Freshen your drink, m'am?" said the bartender.

M'am? Who came in?

"More peanuts, m'am?" *Help you across the street, m'am? Give you a hand with that heavy blunt instrument, m'am?*

I definitely needed to find some other bar to squander my money in. It was time for a new office anyway.

* * * *

My income from guitar deals with Darryl wasn't staggering, but it did guarantee two things: I could afford to keep my luxury dive, and I could still practice the writerly discipline of slouching around bars, drinking.

In between those activities I somehow had some articles published. One was a toxic waste expose about everyone who was dumping stuff they shouldn't in downstate New York. Some of it went like this:

> **FRUMP CITY, WEST END AVENUE BETWEEN 59TH AND 72ND STREETS,** *boorish condo peddler Ronald Frump's latest plans for the site of his defunct NBC relocation scheme.* According to the Environmental Protection Department, someone furtively removed 1,700 truckloads of PCB-contaminated soil from the site without a permit. Coincidentally, an unofficial delivery of 1,700 truckloads of soil was reported by a witness at the Fresh Kills landfill in Staten Island the same week.

The other piece I wrote was about professional sports and the dubious achievements enquiring minds don't ordinarily get to read about — wrecked support vehicles, camera cable pullers falling down air shafts, covered-up drug casualties, whole teams incarcerated. Things like that.

The good news was, my phone was ringing again. The problem was who was on the other end. Often it was some hyperventilating zine teen panting, "Babe, you *gotta* write for us! We pay beer money and retain all rights."

The other calls were usually worse. Merger mania was clobbering the publishing business, and my editors were enjoying another round of musical chairs. They never knew who would end up without seats, or when. Every time a masthead changed, I lost an assignment.

"Assignment? What assignment?" replacement editors always said. "Really? Well, we don't have any record of your contract. What? Kill fee? Not without a
contract."

Without Darryl and his musical hardware carousel, I wouldn't have survived. Here's how the magic worked:

Some guitar dealer would call Darryl. He'd be looking for a particular model, for a customer he'd just told, "Yeah, I think I have one in stock! I'll call you back after I check." Then he calls Darryl in a panic and says, "Darryl, you still got that guitar?" "Sure!" says Darryl. Then Darryl calls me. "C'mon, we're going to the
Guitar Show. Don't wear a bra."

The New York Guitar Show is in an old East Village church. Everything's dirt cheap. We shove through winos outside and hirsute crowds inside to beat Ric Ocasek to a perfect Danelectro, the quintessential piece of space-age masonite crap. But man, do they ever sound sweet! Then Darryl wanders off to buy twenty-five-cent guitar strings he'll complain about later.

Sometimes we visit one of our many unemployed friends' attics and go home with whatever hippie relic the dealer specified, plus anything else that looks marketable. Tube amps. Speakers. Signed posters. If it was underpriced, we were buyers.

Once we picked up a resprayed Stratocaster that turned out to be a rare early '60s model, its original sunburst intact underneath an exuberant Earl Scheib paint job. A professional restorer could've easily made it worth thousands. Darryl just wanted to turn it over fast, so he sold it to a guy in his building who was in a Who cover group. We passed on seeing his musical stylings.

Darryl preferred more subdued entertainment, like blues clubs. I had to trick him into going with me to see Lane McCarthy and Love Dinghy.

"*All* they play is blues," I lied, sealing it with a promise of free pints I had no money for.

I was still hoping to get my interview with Lane, and I wanted company while I ambushed him. I figured Lane with a couple hundred beers in him and the false security of his posse would be an easier score than if I rang his doorbell or called his unlisted phone.

Darryl only went along because he hoped to get some business, maybe find a gig or pawn off unsellable leftovers on the band.

"Working bands," he told me, "they always look for cheap instruments to gig with. Too much of a risk to take your good stuff — never know what might happen." One time Delroy Prince was waiting for a limo with his upright bass in a huge road case. He remembered he'd left his shoulder bag in the hotel and ran inside to get it. He got back just in time to see his $10,000 bass being crushed in the maw of a sanitation truck.

So Darryl and I saw Love Dinghy together for the first time at a fine Long Island venue, O'Toole's. It was two blocks of bar filled with every neighborhood inebriate and countless misanthropes in Nelda costumes. "The Woodstock Generation in all its glory," said Darryl.

We waited to get in with a large man in seamed stockings and a hatchet. When the door troll ran off to break up a fight, Darryl and I ran in without paying.

"Hey, Dar — let's check out Lane's goods!" I said, trying to delay the purchase of the pints I promised.

We shouldered our way through the sodden audience to the stage. Lane had brought a cheesy new Japanese Tele, a Brand X acoustic ("worth altogether about twenty-five cents," said Darryl), and a blond Strat Darryl said was worth five grand.

"It has to be a mid-'50s model, because of the clay dots and the one-piece maple neck," Darryl whispered in awe. "And the neck's curly maple, which wasn't standard. The color makes it *real* rare, 'cause it was reserved then pretty much for Telecasters." He said only an idiot would bring a guitar like that to a place like this.

We were still yacking loudly, our elbows on the stage, when the band lumbered onto it wearing platforms they should've junked decades ago. Darryl stopped appraising their equipment and stared at Lane.

"Lookit his sideburns!" Darryl squawked loud enough for the dead to hear. Pretty much the whole band shot him a look.

Lane returned fire by sizing up Darryl, who looks like an accountant. Deciding that was probably its own punishment, Lane went looking for his guitar.

We found him fascinating, but not for any reasons he would like. His taste in guitars was one. And he saw nothing ridiculous about being a Baby Boom dwarf dressed like Stanley Kowalski.

Like his repertoire, Lane's retro physiognomy had miraculously defied the structural settling of middle age. You could rely on him to overstate the obvious with skimpy sleeveless shirts and jeans that were tight. Real tight.

They had to be, because he couldn't wear a belt to hold them up. A buckle would've scratched up his precious Strat.

But tonight something was different. Something very unLanelike.

Complementing Lane's regulation wifebeater shirt was a tiny black leather motorcycle jacket. I wondered why he wore it. He didn't have a bike. I checked. The weather was too warm for leather, the stage lights too hot. He couldn't have been comfortable. Plus it obscured the miniature biceps whose definition he worked so hard to make perceptible to the naked eye.

But what Lane lacked in authenticity or common sense, he made up for in serendipity. The jacket was scuffed and buttery and perfect. Not too many zippers. Just enough snaps. There was a steel truss rod wrench sticking out of one pocket.

As Love Dinghy plunged into a Nelda song called "It's Not What You Think," Lane whipped off the jacket dramatically. Or anyway, he tried to. The right sleeve snagged on one of those asinine wristbands he insists on wearing, and he spent the next ten bars trying to get it loose. When he finally succeeded, the jacket went flying. It subsequently landed on a klieg light and caught fire. The truss rod wrench took a different trajectory, into the bass player's ear. O'Toole's staff sure had their hands full tonight.

Darryl mumbled something about profit potential and went to the can.

We barely survived two sets of Nelda chestnuts, with retards in Nelda drag doing chorus lines on the dance floor. They were kicking especially high tonight for "It's Not What You Think." Here's how it goes:

> I've had it with women,
> They all want one thing.
> I'd just as soon kill them
> as buy one a ring.

They drove me so crazy
I needed a change,
so I gassed my last date
with her Westinghouse range.

Love is a strange thing, it's different each time.
You have it your way, I'll have it mine.

I wore a Lacroix fake,
I picked up a man.
He got mad when I showed him
the surprise in my hand.
Don't hit me, big guy,
I said with a wink,
I was only kidding.
It's not what you think.

Darryl was amused for the first couple of Nelda numbers, but then I practically had to sit on him to keep him from fleeing. Blues this was not.

"Forget about it!" he shrieked.

"It's almost over."

"No, I'm outta here! Get off me!"

"You're staying, Dar."

"No! Let go!"

As a writer, I am trained to observe patiently, to analyze the essence of human experience and rehash it into lowest-common-denominator pulp. Granted, I do have a lower bullshit tolerance threshold than most people, and I did consider taking poor Darryl home. But — and this is embarrassing to admit — I was genuinely mesmerized by Lane's singing tonight. Sit, Nona, stay.

Last time I saw Love Dinghy, they did their best just to get through the show. Tonight Lane delivered the usual order of homicide and sweatshop anthems, but this time he ground his voice like a hasp on a metal pipe. To further enhance the effect, he'd run offstage and smoke whenever the band took over a tune, jockeying for solos. Cloud puffs would rise from behind speaker stacks like Indian signals as he indulged in nodular exacerbation.

Sure, he was an asshole. But what a voice! And there was a bonus. When he was really into it, he'd get this look on his face, like he was having the lalapalooza orgasm of all time. It was novel to watch that sort of thing from a distance, with a tequila. So much tidier.

His bogus persona was fascinating, too, but not in the way he meant. A tragic misfire in his bid for heartland rock immortality, it was certainly entertaining. But logical? No. Why cling to bad songs about gory murders if he wants people to believe he's a surfing farmer? Why the patinated country boy act, the corn pone accent? Give me a break — the guy's from North Smithfield, Rhode Island (or "Nawt Smitfeel," the natives call it in a mouthful more reminiscent of Canarsie than Sunnydale Farm). Why *bother* with all this shtick when he could sing like that?

As I maintained my death grip on Darryl, I digested a bitter truth: Lane was a big fat phony with a great ass and the voice of a god who'd never add up.

Of course, the real Lane was here, too. He was the one with the visual acuity of a vulture, the radar capability of a bat. What wasn't obvious to the casual observer of his drawl-faking, beer-swigging, wife-correcting act was how Lane always paid attention to absolutely every little thing — his band, the sound guy, the entrance, the head count, even the time, though I never saw him wear a timepiece. But by god, he knew *exactly* when it was time to go home, where the waitress was, what his door take totaled before it was counted. He was a colossus of micromanagement. And he watched certain people who were watching him. Probably he was just gauging their cup size, or their x-y coordinates so he could avoid them later.

He was so sneaky about it, they usually never realized they were being scrutinized. And it's damned spooky, especially if it's happening to you. Or, in my case, to me. Which it did, and he looked away every time I caught him.

I struggled mightily to reconcile Corn Pone Lane with Nazi Lane and the Lane with the anguished face whose life or whatever was so hard. I got zip. And no, I didn't get my interview, either. Looked like I'd have to try again.

* * * *

Darryl stayed home the night I went to Lane's gig at Toad's Place in New Haven. I like a nice long bike ride, so I can talk to myself. I need smog in my face, car exhaust in my lungs, bugs in my teeth. The romance of the road. An excuse to wear leather.

New Haven is a perpetually drunken college town, strategically located a block from the Yale campus. Dorothy Parker once noted that "if all the girls who attended the Yale prom were laid end to end, I wouldn't be a bit surprised."

Toad's Place is roughly the size of a dirigible hangar, with none of the charm. Two-story ceilings, see-through floors, no back door. It's old and built entirely of wood, the kind of place where rational folks don't light matches.

The room that night was filled with smoke and people, at least a million over the legal capacity, and many not an hour over seventeen. A fiftyish guy with a combover told me he "came to find Nelda." I doubt he ever did, but he bought me a tequila so who cares?

By now Lane had effectively convinced me he really *wanted* the fawning attention of the fourth estate. He just didn't want to get any of it on him.

I planned to march straight into the green room after the show and tell him it was his last chance to not give me an interview. Until then I'd somehow have to peel off all the Neldaheads rubbing up against me and overlook Lane's unfortunate habit of cribbing Dion moves.

It was a good thing Darryl stayed home. He'd be having a panic attack by now. All these dumbass costumes. All the line dancing, and the drunken fight picking. Sheesh!

Tonight in this mob scene I was no one to everyone, or so I thought. Amid a roiling mass of adolescents with fake IDs, Boomers with no shame, and drunken Yalies with no clue where they were, I stood in the darkest place I could find. I staked my claim where anonymity was assured, safe in a lake of beer. Vast quantities of stale brew lapped at the insteps of my Dan Posts as I pondered the wisdom of having come here.

When the band walked onto the stage, I finally looked up. Lane was staring dead at me.

Now, in New York, no one looks anyone in the eye. It can get you killed. I couldn't remember the last time anyone had looked at me so hard, or for so long.

I could be overreacting here. But I mean, how did he spot me in the first place? And was this a good kind of stare, or a bad one?

This sort of behavior strikes Nona as a tad deranged. What can I tell you? He knocked me over like a DUI plowing into a traffic cone.

Chapter 8

The very specialized research required for journalism of sociological importance always includes a stop at Nick's Videorama. Nick's is located one shabby landmark district over from mine, a block down from the new prison.

Nick almost never has any movies I want to see, especially if they're older than Michael Jackson's latest surgery. What he lacks in stock, however, he makes up for in resources.

"Nah, um all outta dat, Nona," Nick always says to me, no matter what I ask for. "But I can get it. No problemo. Gimme a week. How many ya want? Need a standee to go wid dat?"

Which is why you go straight to Nick for a forgotten eight-year-old tape of Lane McCarthy and Love Dinghy performing their single hit single, "What Are You Looking At?"

I never saw it when it was boring everyone else to death in MTV's regular rotation. Brooklyn, cultural bastion that it is, doesn't have cable. Not any kosher kind of cable, anyway. There are always those guys in hoodies flogging your doorbell when you have company, hawking illegal descrambler boxes. So actually you *could* have cable, if you want it more than sex and enough to do time, and then later you can watch it all nice and legal at Rikers.

Judging by the heated arguments at the bodega over the hardware of the week on Madonna's boobs, I'm apparently the only Brooklynite uninterested in backdoor cable service. I may even be the only one who never wants to hear "What Are You Looking At?" again as long as I live. God knows it's now hardwired into my memory and will never go away. But this particular bootleg I asked Nick to get was shot live at CBGB, and I jumped many curbs hustling to Videorama to collect it. I'd heard that if you were on the ball, you'd see a sot with his pants around his ankles, spinning on a bar stool and pissing like Bethesda Fountain.

Anyway, it was a balmy May day. Videorama's front door was propped open with a gas can. Plenty of browsers were in the aisles. Nick was on the phone with his supplier of fine custom cinematography when I arrived.

"Nick," somebody said, "a rat just came in."

Everyone looked just in time to see a dog-sized rodent race into Nick's humor section. Salesvixens Andrea and Shanikwah, who mere seconds before had been testing Julio Iglesias tapes on the store's monitor, now squealed fetchingly atop the counter in their miniskirts and cropped Ts. Nevertheless, the customers fled en masse to check their meters.

Nick chased the rat with a baseball bat as it ran in and out of his displays. Video boxes spewed like bullets out of an M-16. Julio was singing "Mona Lisa."

I didn't get my tape that day. Not that it was an urgent matter. When the editor who'd requested the Love Dinghy piece smelled trouble with the Lane interview, he stopped returning my calls.

So what? I can still sell it to some sucker, somewhere, I kept telling myself. It wasn't exactly the type of material for which timeliness was a factor. God knows Lane McCarthy was a living fossil and people were still paying to see him, sometimes. Mediawise, he was barely breathing and everyone knew it but him. But if the world still has to read about Cher and Suzanne Somers, then why not Lane?

So I tailored different versions of my story to suit the editors who weren't too young to remember, who then held onto it forever before rejecting it. "It lacks the requisite heartfelt blather about roads not taken and regrets quoted out of context to be commercially viable pathos," said one. "Not fresh anymore," said another.

I persevered. I made shit up. "I met Lane McCarthy," responded one editor, "and he's not a quadriplegic."

My article got leaner, tighter, and sharper with every revision, until it was like a stave. Best goddamned work I ever did. And it never sold.

And that's how Lane officially wrecked my story about him and any chance of me ever getting a car. Okay, a used car. A very used car. But if I ever caught him, I'd throttle him. I'd wrap an E string around his nuts and yank it so hard, he'd have to go back to Detroit to find his dick.

* * * *

And with that, Lane moved directly to my back burner. My plate was full of other stuff, as I had recently gone to work for a new magazine called *Motorhead*. It was to be the iconoclastic connoisseur's bible about classic bikes.

Motorhead's CEO was an industry sycophant named Jean Poule. The only thing French about him, besides his name, was how often he bathed. Jean thought he smelled all sportsmany. We thought he smelled all dumpster-behind-Key-Foody. In the time-honored tradition of entrepreneurs with family money and no job skills, he went into publishing.

Against ample advice to the contrary, Jean established *Motorhead*'s office on the fringes of Newport. Actually it was a suite of offices, in a creepy, half-rented concrete shopping center that was like a ghost town. The only restaurant in it was Japanese, and there were always trays around the *Motorhead* office with bite-sized mounds of Nessie. I always passed. Nona does not eat raw slimy things. Not dead ones, anyway.

Bad enough the headquarters of a motoring enterprise were on a tiny island, much less one with wicked bad traffic during prime driving season. But Newport is also on an island where it always seems to rain. You *could* road test a bike there, on the other side of Narragansett Bay, if Jean remembered to give you the cash for the tolls (which we always asked for, since it was all the money we were ever likely to get from him), and if you could then get the bike across a wet steel-deck bridge with gale-force crosswinds without wiping out.

Motorhead started up during the darkest period of disenfranchisement of magazine personnel, so Jean was able to assemble a crack staff that he never had to coddle. One of them, Don DeRosa, was an editor for whom I'd freelanced years earlier at *Kickstart*.

Kickstart was a popular bike magazine where I'd diligently carved a reputation as the house malcontent. DeRosa let me write columns, features, personality profiles, travel guides, you name it, in which I took the art of complaining to new and dizzying heights. I was so cynical and disapproving of just about everything, Don once got a letter from a reader who wrote: "Nona Gold sounds like a big fat guy." I enlarged it ten times on the stat camera at Dancer and nailed it to my office wall.

I left *Kickstart* in a snit after it was bought by Nathan Reubenfeld, a mogul-wannabe who systematically bled the magazine dry to fund his colossal stable of loser publications like *International Beach Volleyball*. He seeded *Kickstart* with money from the string of porno theaters he owned before becoming a publishing maggot. Oopsy, I mean magnate. He'd never owned a bike himself. His first and last act as my new boss was to ship me a stack of old *Kickstarts*, with his fulsome criticisms blackening the margins of two years' worth of my brilliant journalism.

"Play up the leather angle," he wrote. "Can't you quit carping about civil rights? So what if the rules are different for women? Get over it!"

Well, one of us did. Not long after that, Nathan was waiting for a light underneath the 23rd Street overpass of the FDR Drive when it fell in on him.

His creditors liquidated *Kickstart*'s assets and Don DeRosa's job faster than you can say "electronic ignition." That's how Don ended up at *Motorhead*. Just when I thought I'd never get a magazine job ever again, he called me about enlivening *Motorhead* with the PMS point of view.

"Write about anything you want, any way you like. You wanna bitch? Go for it, babe! Make me proud!"

When there was a backlog of editorial work or a surplus of bikes to test, I stayed in town. DeRosa let me sleep at his house in Middletown, where his Labrador graciously shared a hair-covered couch with me ("no, no, I *insist*," said DeRosa). And so his fake antique saltbox saved me from any more of the hotel bills Jean always promised he'd reimburse, but never did.

The best part of my new job was how it required many motorcycle trips to Rhode Island. It was four hours from Brooklyn to Newport. Or as I preferred to look at it, four hours with nobody bothering me.

Rhode Island is a nice enough place, an impossibly scenic fairyland where the roads are perfection and police are afraid to write tickets because everyone is Mafia. So everyone speeds everywhere, careening down the highway shoulders they think are exit ramps, yet observing each other's personal space by minding their own lanes at Mach speed. By contrast, invading Massachusetts drivers are so mindlessly aggressive, the mild-mannered Rhode Islanders call them Massholes.

Rhode Island is a little quirky, too. There's no sales tax on boats. Prostitution is legal. And it may be the only place on earth with a historical monument to a chicken. It's in Adamsville. It's seven feet tall. I am not making this up.

But it's the natives who make Rhode Island truly special. They're are all so cheerful, so helpful. Never get directions from them. I spent a lot of time lost in Rhode Island. People there eagerly draw incredibly detailed maps of a state that doesn't exist, a place with high spots in the road for landmarks instead of buildings or water towers. They say, "When you come to the hill, go up the hill, then go down the hill, then go straight, and then turn left at the stump." Sometimes they cite history for landmarks: "Bear right where the Sinclair station used to be."

There are no street signs, either. I lost count of how many times I got told to turn at something called Hoxie Four Corners. Stupidly, I thought that meant there was a Hoxie Street somewhere, or a town, or at least an office building called Hoxie. Nope. There was no town or building or anything else named Hoxie that I ever saw, except for the top step of the Westerly Library and a dirt road in South County — another place that doesn't actually exist. Eventually I learned there *used* to be a Hoxie Four Corners Restaurant at an intersection in Warwick, but it was razed decades before I ever needed to turn there.

Don Imus, the radio guy, once called Rhode Island "the state that's in the way." I think he meant between Connecticut and Massachusetts. Still, there's something to be said for any place where everyone's not aiming at you.

Chapter 9

"Nona!" the bartender at the Narragansett Cafe yelled. "Call for you."

I was in my favorite office of the week, a Jamestown neighborhood bar, soaking up some live R&B. My new routine included darkening the *Motorhead* office by day, and brightening Rhode Island bars by night. Inasmuch as you could call this a schedule, it gave my life a structure it hadn't had for some time.

Surprisingly, Little Rhody has a big music scene, probably due to it being the unlikely spawning ground of many famous musicians — The Cowsills, The Talking Heads, The Beaver Brown Band, even some performers without "the" in their names, like blues poobah Duke Robillard and Bill Conti, the guy who laid the *Dynasty* theme on you.

That's why there are plenty of clubs like this one, drawing three states' worth of slackers with a few bucks to burn and no place else to go. There's no shortage of bands, either, most with unfortunate names that sound like pyrosclastic jism. Love Pump. Soul Shot. Rhythm Juice. There oughta be a law.

But far be it from me to cast stones. I tried to get my *Motorhead* coworkers to go drinking with me, but they had real lives to go to after work.

"I gotta get home tonight, Nona," DeRosa would say, "or else the little woman's gonna disembowel me."

"Sorry, Nona. Got a date tonight," Joe the art director would say. "So many men, so little time!"

Darryl was useless, too. He flat refused to come to Rhode Island. "Sorry, Nona, I gotta cut hair," he'd lie. Sometimes it was, "Can't go with you this time. Gotta pick up stuff that fell off a truck behind Matty Umanov's."

I had exactly one non-work friend in Rhode Island, and she was the lucky winner who I conned into slumming with me.

"Oh god, not this again! You wanna go *where*?" Nat whined every time I begged her to go clubbing with me. She always gave in. She just liked being begged. And seeing me grovel. She had a laugh like a garbage disposal.

"C'mon. It'll be fun!" I'd always reply cheerily, if not accurately. Nat was used to that from me. We had history.

A long time ago, in a suckfest far, far away, Natalie Bryant and I shared a Texas-sized nightmare we'd both rather forget. It was a colorful time, filled with relationships from hell and illegal abortions, abusive families and squidlike bosses, and easy access to the McSmorgasbord of as-yet unregulated recreational pharmaceuticals available between 1967 and 1972.

After high school we veered off in totally different directions. She sold herself into slavery with the US Postal Service. I beat it to Cooper Union and the infinitely more attractive world of conceptual art, East Village junkies, and Hell's Angels.

I was inexplicably happy in New York, in a shoebox-sized tinderbox on East Third Street where I painted until I was blind, and then hung with fat, tattooed Harley nuts who constantly diddled the loves of their lives, namely their bikes. No way was I ever going back to Texas.

The dwindling stream of shorter and shorter letters between me and Nat was inevitable. I didn't even know she'd moved to Rhode Island until the day we collided in Pep Boys. We rekindled our sisterhood right there in the motor oil section, and the rest is herstory.

Turns out a year ago she was transferred by the USPS from Arlington to Providence, where she'd been enjoying a stress-free life until I started calling. Once again she was my last, best, and only chance for girl talk.

We picked up right where we left off. She wasn't looking for a man, she insisted, just some fun. She'd had enough shitty marriages, thank you, and needed a break. She was like a free ticket to an E ride. She was my foul-mouthed Stella Maris, holy mother of beer.

Sure, there were other women who'd barhop with me, in New York. They only bought drinks for themselves, even after I paid for rounds. I never understood why they were so cheap and self-involved, especially around dollar beers. They'd spend hours in the bathroom removing impossibly complex manbait outfits to pee, and painstakingly reassembling them afterward, then bouffing up their hair and retroweling their warpaint. Then they'd chase guys instead of talking to me, which actually was a blessing since they were always so grumpy from dieting. When did women blow off the revolution to do armed battle with each other over gainfully employed sperm generators, so they could pop tax dependents in the suburbs?

Somehow the world had changed without Nat. She was only humping her job, she said, and only until she was geriatric enough to retire from it with her full pension. Then she could *really* live. For the time being, she was a curious visitor in my strange world of big bikes, tiny men, and endless rejection slips, unburdened by the tyranny of fashion or the needs of post-apocalyptic spongers.

We weren't picky revelers. If a club in Rhode Island had music, we had a seat at the bar. We watched the social scene around us with great amusement and much arm punching. "Who's in charge of wildlife here?" we'd hoot. The local mating customs and regional costumes cracked us up. "Incoming at six o'clock!" we'd scream, and punch each other some more.

Was being a full-time life-support system for helpless, goo-spewing blobs of protoplasm and beer-swilling mess-makers really worth sacrificing a good time?

Together, we never figured it out.

Chapter 10

"Find your glamour helmet," I'd tell Nat over the phone. "And wear one of your Cyndi Lauper outfits. I'll be there at seven."

Whenever we went out, I always tried to talk Nat into a fun bike ride. This worked often on warm nights, which was lucky because otherwise we had to go in her company car. It's a rolling ashtray. And Nat drives it like she's in a Dodg'em. Traffic devices are just rough guidelines to her.

The post office assigned her some new wheels every three months, or about as often as she tried to squeeze them into someplace they wouldn't go. "Mail delivery is dangerous work," she'd tell her district manager. He'd just sigh and issue her another blue American sedan with an unnecessarily large engine and a strobe, which was especially handy for Slurpee runs.

Nat swore she preferred my bike to her car, usually after a few vodkas. "Your bike is aweshum!" she'd slur.

She'd even dress specially for these occasions, improvising road gear out of ski outfits and rodeo chaps left behind by ex-spouses. She'd wear an ancient pair of cowboy boots with engraved silver toe guards, and fingerless pink gloves covered with sharp studs. I gave her one of my old helmets with a "Die young, stay pretty" decal on it.

"You're gonna have to beat guys away in that get-up," I'd say.

"Shweet!" she'd spit. "Fashter, Pushycat!"

We'd strap her mammoth shoulderbag to my bike rack, because I didn't want that thing swinging around and throwing me off balance. And off we'd zoom, hopping curbs and speeding, leaning hard and laughing and torturing confused men in their cars at every stop light.

Nat and I spent a lot of time in one particularly isolated Rhode Island beach bar. We never ran into anyone we knew there, which is one reason we liked it so much. It's called the Gar.

To get there, you turn off Route 1 in the middle of nowhere, onto a road you'd never guess is paved, there's so much sand on it. You drive along this road toward the ocean, with nothing but corn fields and marshes and absurdly starry skies around you for another mile. The air smells like evergreens and dead skunks and fertilizer. You feel like an apartment dog with its head out the car window. And then boom! There's a village. Another fifty feet, and you're downtown. It consists of a pizza joint, a gas station, a convenience store, a bait shop, a little bar, and a big bar. The big one's the Gar.

That was an appropriate name, we decided, gar being a notorious trash fish and us being just trash. Our Gar was all atmosphere. The sheetrock was insouciantly tapeless, with plenty of code-defying electrical cable draped from it like crepe paper. The bar was strung with Christmas lights. A big sign over it announced Tuesday was Ladies' Night; underneath that was a smaller sign announcing a sale on dog chow. The unpainted plank floor was covered with sand and beer stains.

The Gar is a resort bar. No kidding. There are lots of beach bars like it in Rhode Island, officially making it the last place on earth where musicians can make a living playing music.

Because of that — and because Rhode Island was where they lived — it's where Love Dinghy got stuck working most of the time. Things weren't any better in the music industry than they were in publishing. That's how Love Dinghy became the house band at the Gar that summer.

The club was refreshingly free of Neldaheads, possibly because it was too difficult for them to find, but probably because Love Dinghy was ordered to not play Nelda songs at the Gar. The management was trying to beef up business. So the Stones were okay, and Freddie King and Eddie Cochran, and the Temptations, or even any original material the band's braindead record company vetoed. Anything but vintage arias about evisceration.

This bold experiment had mixed success, resulting in the Gar attracting two distinct flavors of oldies fans. In the daytime there were trucks outside and unemployed construction workers inside, drinking Buds with women dressed like Times Square hookers. At night the place was overrun by tourists in Benz ragtops with out-of-state vanity plates, wearing novelty print Bermuda shorts and sucking candy-colored blender drinks. Sunset was a magical time, when the natives and tourists overlapped. I often defended a spot outside the restrooms, just to watch the fashions and brawls.

There was always live music and exuberant bad moonwalking. Many of the men couldn't keep time at any hour, so they played pool ineptly or arm wrestled, or stood around gaping at skinny women in tennis whites dancing with each other. Sometimes they watched buzzed vacationers act out golfing while they frugged.

One night we all watched a well-lubed music lover wiggle and squeal on a billiard table. She abruptly ripped off her top and leapt onto the stage, where she resumed wiggling and squealing in what looked like her underwear.

Dear god. All that whining women did for so long about being taken seriously — Equal pay! Equal rights! Now they're air golfing and playing snooker with their butts.

Love Dinghy tried to act real cool by pretending not to look at the mostly nude wiggler sharing their stage. They're experts at pretending not to look at anything. They watched her through the corners of their eyes, and would make fun of her on their way home.

I knew this because they all talked to me now, except for Lane. The rest of the band found my interest in them flattering and often told me things they shouldn't, especially after I started bringing Nat along in her miracle stretch motoring outfits.

One time we sped over in her company car with the strobe going like it was a ten-alarm postal emergency, and burst into the Gar wearing nothing but raincoats. We flashed Love Dinghy, who never react to anything. But Lane subsequently had a hard time remembering the words to his own songs. The band was *really* friendly to Nat and me after that, not counting Lane.

We all pretended not to watch the wiggler now. I sat impassively at the bar as a bouncer dragged her away screaming.

"I thought panty dancing died in the '70s," I said to my date.

"Really, it's no big deal. It's a bathing suit," Nat said. Well, we *were* at a Rhode Island beach bar. For all I knew, this happened every night.

"How can you tell it's not underwear?" I pressed.

"Trust me. I shop for swimsuits *way* more than you do." Indeed, her coffee table had disappeared under a pile of Victoria's Secret catalogs.

The reason was Nat's new guy, Bob. He was a fiftyish, potbellied appliance salesman for a plumbing company. Or as Nat liked to put it, "Bob's into sewage."

Business was good. He'd bought a cabin cruiser they'd been spending way too much time on lately. Nat was all "Bob's boat this" and "Bob's boat that." When the Queen Elizabeth II ran aground at Martha's Vineyard with 815 shuffleboarders stuck on it, Nat and Bob couldn't resist sharing the love with a captive audience. They anchored a loogey away from the helpless QEII and boffed on his deck.

I'd met him once and wasn't impressed. I thought she was wasting herself on him, partly because his priorities seemed skewed toward getting her to clean his house. There were many other things I didn't like about

Bob. He was cheap, and he kept looking past her to see if something better was coming along.

When Bob wasn't milking Nat for free dinners, she and I would go to the beach, or to discount malls for irregular deck shoes and idiotic jewelry that looked like fishing bait. As long as she was willing to hang with me, I kept silent about her incurable bad taste in men.

I was grateful she didn't force me to socialize with Bob, especially when we'd go listen to music. There were plenty of good bands playing around: NRBQ, Los Lobos, Roomful of Blues still billing themselves as "direct from Chicago!" even though they've played New England gin mills every night since the beginning of time.

It was a no-brainer that the Gar became our regular hangout. Love Dinghy got us in for free, and it made Lane mad.

"Alright! No and Nat in the house!" they'd all yell as we rumbled in.

"Yo, No and Nat, get in here!" they'd call from their dressing room. "We got something to show you!"

They'd buy us drinks and talk about their gig adventures. They always had a new anecdote about what an ass Lane was.

Nat and I became the Gar's best customers. We'd lounge on pleather chairs with exploded stuffings, our feet on the bar as we laughed like donkeys at our own jokes. We got rip-snorting drunk and made requests Love Dinghy never played. One night we pissed Lane off good by demanding "Tiny Dancer." That was the night Alvin, the world's shyest bass player, came over and told us all about his Pez collection.

As for the Gar's other customers, an alarming percentage of them seemed to be related to Lane, a fact they felt compelled to tell us. He had a thousand cousins. A million. All of them were short and hairy and had beer guts. Nat and I were horrifyingly cruel to every one. Most of them were too drunk to feel hurt.

Nat is street smart and curvy, pretty and funny and, near as I can tell, the only natural blond in Rhode Island. Her crazy biker outfits were just gravy. Everyone likes her. She was flypaper to the flotsam at the Gar. That's how we came to be acquainted with a *real* celebrity, Richard T. Klegg, III.

"My friends call me Dick," he said. We already guessed that.

"That's my cous up there! Band sounds good tonight," Dick said knowingly to Nat, ignoring me. "You know, people usually come to listen to the group. Me, I like to hear a good sound man." Nat's elbow found my ribcage. "Like this guy tonight — he can make a room come alive with a Parametric."

Our eyes followed Dick's finger to some poor schmuck fumbling with the Gar's console and cursing. What the fuck was a Parametric?

"It's harder than it looks to work the board," Dick went on, and on. "Used to be a sound man myself. Worked with Aerosmith."

Wow. Nat and I tried to contain our enthusiasm. I looked for the bartender. Nat stifled a snort that Dick apparently didn't hear.

"Yep. Designed Aerosmith's PA," said Dick. "All the power amps were Crown. We were tri-amping them into JBL K-150s, K-130s, and horns. Full stereo. Needed ten roadies to set up *that* one! Had to supervise it every night personally, in every town on the whole tour."

Speaking of setting up, my glass was still empty. Time to find a refill Dick could buy. Where the heck was the bartender?

"But then it got too crazy, with the drugs and all, you know?" he said, shaking his head. "So I gave it up. What I really want to do anyway is produce. Hey, you like Joe Perry? I could introduce you. If you give me your number..."

By then Nat and I were gone.

Me, I attract a different type of clubgoer.

One night it was raining; I had a bad case of helmet hair, sticky leathers, and a drunken pipefitter humping my leg. Must be that new-car smell.

"You're the biggest dyke-otomy I ever saw!" he snorted at me. Obviously, any woman who didn't want him had to be gay.

"Go piss on a hydrant," said little Nat, but he didn't.

"Drink?" the bartender asked me over my new beau. Suddenly I was having three conversations at once when all I wanted was a shot.

"Gold tequila, straight up."

"Baby, did you bring the whips?"

"Get lost!"

"What?!" said the startled bartender.

"Not you."

"Oh. What'd you say you want to drink?"

"Gold. Tequila. Straight up."

"You oughtta watch more TV, Billie Jean, see how real girls dress."

"Did you say 'Sprite'?"

It was hopeless. I turned to address my enamorato.

"Just stop it. You don't want to make me fight you, now, do you? It wouldn't be ladylike."

"Since when are you a lady?"

"I was talking about you."

Furious, he tried to make himself bigger by getting between me and the delivery of my drink. Bad idea. I reached up and laid my hand on his neck as if to stroke it. He looked pleasantly surprised. Then I slammed his head down on the bar.

"You oughtta have that swelling looked at," I said.

I pushed him away like a Bowery bum. From the uncharted depths of her boodle bag, Nat produced a stun gun. We didn't find out how he was related to Lane before he tore out of there like a bottle rocket.

I finally got my drink. The band took a break. Nat and I watched Lane as he trotted in our direction. I figured we were about to receive a royal Munchkinland flogging for whacking his kin. But no. He dived for Nat's ashtray and ran off with it.

We watched him hit on two twentyish bottle blondes with beer handles. He stood with his back to us for a long time, showing us his good side as he wrote something down for them. He was scribbling for a long time. It wasn't his autograph.

"What the hell is he writing?" I asked Nat. The name of his agent?

"Directions. Hey, your friend McCartney, he has a real cute ass." Nat's boyfriend was fat and old and sold cesspools. He had an ass like two sacks of cement.

"Go over and grab it!" I said.

"You grab it for me, okay? Gotta go soon. School night. It's probably got pimples all over it anyway."

I confess I gave serious thought to Nat's suggestion — for half a second, before deciding I'd already wasted enough time trying to get to the bottom of Lane. Sometimes he'd stare at me across the room like the old days, but I was more interested in gossiping with Nat or losing money at pool. He blew his big chance to meet cute when I clobbered his cousin, and anyway he'd already made it clear as Stoli that I'd never catch him — not for an ass grabbing or an interview or anything else.

After all this time I still wondered why. Underneath this cartoonish facade beats the heart of a red-blooded girl who likes knowing where she stands, even if it's in a pile of shit.

It occurred to me that Nat might know the answer. Her ex was a school bus driver who used her for a punching bag, and her other ex was a minister who knocked out her tooth. She can read losers like a racetrack handicapper, despite a short circuit that causes her to mate with them.

"So whaddya think about that guy? Is he gay?"

"Nope."

"A sociopath?"

"I doubt it."

"He won't give me an interview. Everyone else gives me an interview. He always just lies or runs away. I can't figure him out."

"Maybe he thinks you're the biggest dyke-otomy he ever saw."

She had a point.

"So you're saying, shy is out?"

"*Puh-leeze*. Look at the guy! His pants are so tight you can tell if he's circumcised."

"I know. They're cutting off his circulation so bad, he can't pick up a phone."

We studied Lane as he flexed for some snockered barflies across the room. They looked young enough to be his grandchildren.

"He reminds me of my ex-husband."

"The bus driver?"

"The preacher."

I laughed. "Dig it — what's up with his sweatbands?"

"What is this? *Women's Wear Daily*? Jeez, Nona. I'm not a fashion critic. I just deliver mail." Nat laughed and drained her glass of vodka.

The band's break ended then, and they resumed playing too loudly. We twisted around on our barstools to watch Lane doing Dion doing "Shout."

Nat lit a cigarette with a Rambo lighter — "This? All the postal smokers have them" — and gazed at the door, which mentally she was halfway out.

I wanted her to stay. She wanted to go home to Bob. I amused her by devising clever scenarios starring Grandpa: Lane practicing Dion moves in the mirror in his underwear; Lane telling fatgirls they should be models before he groped them; Lane telling the IRS "but I use all those kilos in my business!"

She'd be gone within minutes. "I want your professional opinion as an ex-fashion critic," I said to her. "Check out the knees of his pants."

The dual holes in his Levis nagged at me like the collection department at Macy's. They were ridiculously perfect ovals. Were they a recession chic thing? Blowouts from extruding himself into sausage casings? "What' up with the holes?" I asked her.

"Easy," she said. "From praying."

"Figures. He seems overly depressed for a rich guy. He even stopped writing those lame-ass songs he's so proud of."

"*Rich*? Why's he playing dumps like this?"

"Because of the temporary eight-year lull in his career? Penance for screwing up a sure thing? Beats the crap outta me. Careers and guilt aren't my thing. That's what I have *you* for. You're a skilled Catholic. What do *you* think?"

"Me? I think he's straight as an ugly stick. I think he's a horny narcissist who spent all his money on blow and runty gold diggers with giant boobs and tiny brains. Smart women with big motorcycles probably scare the shit outta him. All that's enough to give anyone a writer's block bigger than Hoover Dam. That's why he needs the wristbands — c'mon, if you were him, wouldn't you sweat like a pig, too?"

"Well, what about all the dead-girl songs? You think he ever really killed anyone?"

"Only his audience." And with that, Nat stubbed out her cigarette, wrestled her shoulderbag off the bar, and shuffled off into the Rhode Island fog.

Chapter 11

"Nona, you got that lubricant review ready yet?" called Don DeRosa from his office down the hall.

"No. The sample exploded in the mail."

"What about the interview with the striking stitchers at Vanson? Didja make it to Fall River?"

"Got every word on tape, Don. It's all in Cape Verdean."

"Then just tart up that press release from Arrid, will ya? I gotta get this shit to the printer."

* * * *

A magazine start-up is heady business for the players, especially *Motorhead*'s. Unfortunately, ours was the longest start-up in the history of the printing press.

Everyone was restless. Half of our little family lived a whole continent away and phoned in their jobs, a minor technicality that didn't keep everyone from clawing each other's eyes out. You never knew who was intercepting your deliveries of SWAG, or reading your mail.

We also had a bunch of "contributing editors" contributing something that was a mystery to me, but they were always in *Motorhead*'s garage taking apart bikes that didn't belong to them. The first issue wasn't printed yet, and already there was so much infighting you'd think it was *Vogue*.

The rides to Newport were the best thing about working there. I'd zoom along blissfully for four hours, inhaling the outdoors while listening to a Walkman cranked all the way. I'd be singing and laughing at perfect shingled gingerbread houses with fake sheep in the yards, clearing my head, only to arrive to the unhappy sounds of *Motorhead*.

"Where's the exhaust nut wrench?"

"Dunno. Haven't seen it in a week."

"It better turn up soon, or Jean'll have another cow."

I'd run through the garage and into the offices before anyone could ask me about missing tools. I'd say hello to the bookkeeper, who always pretended not to know me because the magazine always owed me money. I'd stop and commiserate with Joe, our hotshot art director imported from LA at great expense, who was growing increasingly fretful about delays in his compensation. "Hi Nona," he'd greet me. "Jean stiffed me again!"

I'd wave to Ralph, our intrepid classifieds salesman who was selling lots of prepaid ad space for future issues, even though the first had yet to be published. Jean Poule told the advertisers he was printing twice as many of the grand premiere issue as he was ever likely to sell, so he could charge them twice as much. He was depositing all their checks into his personal bank account and didn't think anyone knew. He wasn't around much. Don DeRosa tried his best not to notice all this.

"Here," Don would say, handing me a stack of turgid prose fresh from the transom. "Edit this down to one paragraph."

We editors did plenty of product reviews. The guys got to test an Estrella, a Honda GB500, a Vincent Rapide, and a 1954 Squariel that miraculously remained crated for four decades until its moron owner decided it would be nice to drive it to work. I, Girl Editor, got to road test a chain mail brassiere and a coffee mug. I did the most damage I could with what little I had to work with:

> According to the manual, the mug is made of NASA-tested ceramic matrix molded to allow precise modulation of the acceleration of the liquid contents in the first known use of the Bernoulli Principle on a cycling-related product. But don't expect miracles. The manual goes on to caution: 'Do not use this mug to drive nails.'

Naturally, some California motocross kamikaze who was a drinking buddy of Jean's was crowned "guest editor" and given three pages and a big check to complain about an antique motorized bicycle. But since I was in Newport with Don and the other "editors" weren't, DeRosa let me edit all their stuff with a chainsaw.

I was proud of the first issue of *Motorhead*. I couldn't wait for people to see it. And I don't say that about every magazine I write for. This baby looked slick and had plenty of ads, which is what pays all the bills. Well, that's how it works at real magazines. At *our* magazine, Don, Joe, Ralph, and I did hard time and barely got paid diddly.

My primary revenue that summer was from guitar deals with Darryl and two interviews for *Newsday*, with Brooke Shields and Ed Koch. It was no big deal. They'd give interviews to *The Advocate*.

When I was needed at *Motorhead* I'd stay in town for a few days at a time, working twelve-hour shifts and fighting for control of DeRosa's hairy couch with his Lab, while Darryl fed my cat. Don had guitars, and after I dropped off Nat, he and I would stay up all night yodeling camp songs with his kids. We always showed up at work the next day with a full set of luggage under our eyes, giving everyone plenty to titter about.

The other days of the week were earmarked for field trips with Darryl. I still needed the money, plus I was kind of addicted to the schadenfreude of fleecing ex-hippies out of their treasures. It was a refreshing turnaround on the position I usually assumed, bent over and taking it up the wazoo with a hot poker.

I had this fantasy about introducing Darryl to Nat, and them hooking up. Bob was stupid and annoying, and she'd started bringing him along on our dates. I tried everything to get Darryl out of New York. I told him Nat was hot. I promised he could name the state hair of Rhode Island. But

Darryl was too busy putting together another band. "I'm calling it Hung Jewry," he deadpanned.

He'd been interviewing and interviewing an endless procession of hopeful musicians, none of whom was ever good enough to work for him for free. I was glad he still had time to shop for junk with me.

One of our better acquisitions was a 1971 Rickenbacker 331. The top was clear plastic, and it had colored bulbs inside that pulsed when you played it. It was supposed to be like a psychedelic light show. Its ex-flower child owner was ashamed to still own it, so we relieved him of his Rick for a couple hundred bucks. "You guys are nuts!" he yelled as we waved goodbye. We sold it to Richie Sambora for a couple thousand.

Two things about hanging with Darryl: You learn a lot about guitars, and you see the insides of famous people's car trunks, whether you want to or not. Christ! Handcuffs. Chains. Nude fan photos. Deformed fetuses in jars. I saw it all. Who knew you could buy a gross of Vaseline?

But now I can talk dots and logos, headstocks and skunk stripes. Before Darryl, my experience with guitars was limited to a Japanese twelve-string I owned in college. It had a short and sad life, thanks to a cokehead roommate who was boinking Mick Jagger. When she wasn't selling my things to buy drugs, she was talking about hiding from Bianca. She was always crawling home at dawn with her clothes torn and her purse missing. Her suppliers were the scariest people I ever saw, and nasty if not paid promptly. I came home one day to find my twelve-string exactly where I'd left it, with the top bashed in. I replaced the roommate with a cat and the twelve-string with a Yamaha bass I never learned to play.

Speaking of douchebags with bad attitudes, I came home yesterday to find a message on my answering machine that made me apoplectic. It was from Lane McCarthy's management. "Regrets he'll be unavailable indefinitely for interviews," or some shit.

I called Darryl. "Six months!" I shrieked. "Six months I waited for that retarded dwarf to talk to me. For christssake, Darryl — I'm in the same *room* with him, like, twenty times a week! Couldn't he just tell me himself?" I guess treating me like a fart in an elevator is the same thing.

"That and a buck-fifty will get you on the train!" Darryl said cheerily when he stopped laughing. "You're in showbiz now, babe! Welcome to my world."

It was easy for Darryl to laugh about it. He didn't need a car.

"Serves me right for being nice," I said.

"What do I always tell you, Nona? Repeat after me: Nice DOES NOT PAY."

Darryl was right. An article like mine was worth thousands at some magazines, especially if Lane ever succeeded in any of his tiresome comeback attempts. I never should've abandoned it. I didn't even need Lane, who clearly didn't understand that I don't need permission to find out anything about anyone, least of all him.

Now I was sorry I went easy on him — never materialized on his doorstep, never pried into his tax records. Now *there's* a motherlode of humus. I felt stupid to have believed he had talent or something — something that was worth some ink, even if it was only ink from a soulless hack writing about him to get a car. I regretted ever thinking he was more than a bag of neuroses with a cute butt.

Worst of all, I couldn't believe he was such an egomaniacal sadist that he'd string me along for months, just so he could pound me into the ground some more.

No way would I give that wackjob the satisfaction of seeing a feature about himself in print. Not even the cruel, vituperative drubbing his has-been ass so richly deserved, not even if someone offered me a shitload of money for it.

That little motherfucker made me mad. So I made him my project.

Chapter 12

"Jean did *what*?" I blurted to Don DeRosa.

"He bounced all the paychecks," Don repeated, with scary calmness.

"You mean he makes us wait all this time to get paid, and then he *stiffs* us?"

"Well, not all the paychecks bounced. The bookkeeper's cleared."

* * * *

In September, four days before the breathlessly awaited first issue of *Motorhead* was due from the printer, Jean Poule announced he was flat out of money.

DeRosa and I marveled at this masterpiece of skillful timing. The printer had been remarkably accommodating; he needed the work, and he hadn't demanded the whole $75,000 up front. He just wanted to see some scratch in escrow before he cranked up his Heidelberg. DeRosa and I didn't think this an unreasonable request, considering Jean had somehow spent a third of a million dollars with nothing to show for it except a lot of new drinking buddies and a one-station desktop publishing system. It became *Motorhead*'s sole asset by default because Jean, ace moron, paid cash for it instead of leasing.

Motorhead's publisher sent emergency funds, about $20,000, and Jean's mother lent him her IRA. Jean paid his bookies with it instead of his staff. The printer held the magazine hostage and nobody blamed him, because he was already out of pocket for the color separations.

The publisher was threatening to sue Jean. The advertisers were ringing the phone off the hook. Jean's mom was gonna shit.

I zoomed to Newport to help DeRosa mope while Jean went through the motions of putting together eleventh-hour financing. A dozen deals were born and collapsed with dazzling dispatch.

"You know, the issue's already on press," I heard Jean lying to someone as I sneaked up to his door. "Yeah, you can take my word to the bank. Just front me 'til the printer delivers." A pause. "No sir, I don't think you just fell off a truck."

I dutifully reported my findings to DeRosa. "Don't spy on Jean," he said. He'd been trying to think good thoughts. Jean and I weren't making it easy for him.

"How many publishing executives does it take to screw in a lightbulb?" I teased Don.

Don put his hands over his ears.

"Ten: One to twist it up the backer's ass, and the rest to hold him down."

Don tired of my gallows humor and chased me out. I didn't have anyplace else to go, so I drove straight to the Gar. Maybe I'd get a chance to torment Lane. That would definitely cheer me up.

In the meantime, I stayed busy discouraging two fishermen who never saw a woman with a motorcycle before. Together we watched Lane wish he was someplace else until 1 a.m.

The band had brought along all their own illumination junk so they could try out new lighting schemes for the classier venues they'd probably never work again. The band and the bar's six patrons found the whole thing fascinating. I ordered another double, parked my Justins on the unplugged jukebox, and looked out the back picture window at the dark ocean.

Between songs, the house went completely dark except for an upstage string of red floods spectacularly backlighting Love Dinghy. The aesthetic of the moment was sublime, in an expired-use-by-date way. The band stood silently in silhouette, eerily aglow. Lane's black, shaggy head was encircled by a dramatic fuchsia aureole.

And then someone farted into an open mic.

Whenever I pitied myself having to start a career from scratch in middle age, it comforted me to think of Lane having to start from scratch every week.

To be fair, although it beats the hell out of me why I should, he did his best to face it head on — the sidemen who would never take his career as seriously as he did, the would-be managers, the undressers, the autograph collectors who wanted him to endorse their butts. God gives you lemons, you make lemonade. Or try to.

Then again, what were his other options? It wasn't like he could go back to school and learn a trade. What was he going to do, sell insurance? Deliver mail? Be a jockey? What self-respecting horse would take his crap?

My resolve to make Lane suffer melted a little when I saw what a good job of it he was doing by himself.

The room had gone dead silent. "Now we're gonna do a love song," Lane said into a mic he didn't need to be heard, and they started a Nelda tune about a doomed glue-sniffing session at 40,000 feet. Only an insane person could compose lighthearted verse about cashing out in a Virgin toilet. But you gotta give props to anyone who would rhyme "mucilage" with "fuselage."

A tourist chose that moment to peruse the musical selections under my boots on the jukebox I was using for a hassock. I was having too bad of a day to make conversation with anyone who drinks Coors. I moved my feet, pulled out my notepad, and pretended to be very busy writing something important.

Too late. He appropriated the empty barstool next to mine.

I avoided looking at him. I studied my watch. I acted like I was waiting for someone. I added to the list of stuff I needed from Duane Reade. None of it worked.

"You come here a lot?" came the inevitable stale line in a drawl I recognized. I didn't answer. "Saw you talkin' to the band earlier. You know 'em?"

Band? I supposed he meant Alvin, telling me to watch out when he almost beaned me with an armload of mic stands. I should've stood up and walked away.

Instead, I put down my pen. "I come by once in a while," I said, and turned to face him. "I talk to the guys in the band, sometimes. Everybody here does."

"You *like* this band?" he said.

"They're okay." I resumed scratching on my pad.

"I'm partial to the Allman Brothers myself," he said.

"Uh, yeah. They're real good. Too bad about Duane."

I looked away then to see Lane across the room, stamping around the stage, pretending to adjust things while squinting at me and my companion, and looking away every time I glanced at him. He lit a cigarette, looked at it like it had stung him, and threw it on the floor.

Me, I was having a much worse day than Lane. All I wanted now was to drink quietly and listen to fishermen talk about tide levels and chum. Instead I found myself wedged between an angry troll and a shitkicker who stunk of Stetson. I didn't think anyone actually wore that stuff.

My new best friend was blond and tall; he wore Levis and a chambray work shirt that never saw an honest day's labor. There was a Leatherman fold-up tool in his pocket, the big model with the saw. His drawl was viscous as swingarm grease.

"Where're you from?" I asked him, just to see whether I'd guessed right.

"Austin. Up here on business." He pronounced the last word *bidniss*. At least he wasn't Lane's cousin. "Name's Roger."

He held out his hand. I ignored it. He reached into his pocket for a pack of cigs and lit up a Marlboro. My nose filled with sulfur from his match. I sneezed.

"You from here?" he said, and hung a smoke ring in the air.

"Nah. New York."

"What's yer name?"

"Nona. Could you not sit so close?"

I should've given him a phony name, but I figured I'd never see him again. I hoped that happened soon. Being a Texan, it was only a matter of time before he started swinging or shooting or something.

He still wouldn't leave, and he sure wasn't making any moves to buy me a drink. I wished Darryl was here. Dar would've scared Roger off with a Queens-sized fart by now.

"Why you wearin' them leather thangs?" Roger nodded toward my clothes, like I might not know what he meant.

"I drive a motorcycle."

"You come all the way ou'chere? On a *motorcycle*? Damn! I don't know no women in Texas that ride motorcycles. Kind of a long trip just to sit at a bar, ain't it?"

I sighed and tried to think of something to say, something that would inspire him to go away. What I should've done was left. But I was here first. Plus Lane didn't like me talking to this dode for some reason, so I stayed put.

"I'm a writer," I settled on telling Roger. "Working on a magazine article about the band. A big one." Whatever. It beat the hell out of saying I was unemployed.

At that news, Roger's face became alarmingly animated. Tell civilians you're a writer, and they transform into starstruck, slobbering suck-ups. I was sorry I'd mentioned it. I envisioned an evening of sliding from stool to stool to evade him.

"Oh, yeah! *Now* I know who you are! I seen your stuff in, in ..."

"*Reader's Digest.*"

"Yeah! That's it!"

There was still time to run away. I drained my glass and collected my gear.

"Hey, you know much 'bout that li'l singer?" he said, his eyes dancing.

Ohmigod. So that was it. A Lone Star Mary with a boner for Lane. Raise your hand if ew.

I was relieved it wasn't me who interested him, but his intense gaze made me fidget all the same. Hillbillies keep eye contact way too long.

"Yeah, I know more about him than I'd like. That guy's a mess of personalities so pathological, he makes Dr. Jekyll look like Debbie Gibson."

It was a good bet Roger didn't know what a pathology was, or Debbie Gibson either.

"I gotta go see a guy about a dog. Excuse me," I said and bolted.

When I came out of the restroom, he was gone. The band was taking a break. Charlie Vitelli, the keyboard player, was collecting free drinks at the bar. Looked like he needed my help.

We collected a couple of comp pints, and he'd just started filling me in on Lane's latest infuriating deeds when a Neldahead rudely interrupted us.

"I've got a very special message for Lane," she told Charlie. "Be a sweetie and give it to him for me." She put something on the bar next to Charlie's beer.

They shared some animated talk about red tide and boogie boards. No one introduced her to me. She just yammered at Charlie as if I wasn't even there. He acted like she was the most fascinating person he ever met. Then she ran off to organize a line dance. He swore later he didn't know her.

Lane, meanwhile, was hiding somewhere, giving mouth to mouth to a beer, or Roger. I hoped he and the Neldahead connected. She was just his type: short and tubby, wearing more ruffles than a Sicilian wedding party and a thing around her neck that looked like a flowered tourniquet.

The important message she'd brought for Lane was written in smudgy pencil on the back of a two-foot long grocery receipt that was now a bleeding mess of cash register ink and mixer stains.

"We shouldn't look at it," Charlie said.

"Yeah, right. Give it to me." I swiped the note from the bar and read it aloud.

"'Dear Lane, your songs are so deep. Where do you get your inspiration?'" Charlie and I shot each other a look. "'"Just About Impossible to Tell" always makes me want to go on one more day.'"

Charlie and I burst out laughing. A song about padded bras? I couldn't read any more, I was laughing so hard. Even the bartender was laughing.

"Charlie," I managed to force through my snorts, "why the intellectual pretensions? Why doesn't she just grab Lane's ass?"

"That's not the part she should grab!"

I never saw the actual handoff of the note, but Lane disappeared in a hurry when the show was over. The Neldahead did, too.

I walked out of the Gar, unlocked my bike, and packed to go. The band busied themselves in the parking lot, loading up their equipment and complaining, except for Lane, who was probably servicing his adoring public.

Charlie saw me unlocking my bike and came over. He'd changed into a polyester shirt with a long pointy collar that didn't come from the vintage store. Original owner, we call that at *Motorhead*.

As I suited up in my bug-covered leathers, he fondled the handgrip on my bike.

"You know," he said, "you look like a model."

He said that to all women. It was sort of a band tradition. I just wanted to go home.

"Charlie, why won't Lane talk to me?" I asked him point blank.

I thought he'd leave as soon as the conversation stopped being about him, like every other musician. But instead he stood there, thinking. Finally he said, "Well, he *would* talk to you if you wrote for *Rolling Stone*."

"Charlie, I *did* write for *Rolling Stone*." Once. It was an interview. They changed every question I asked Del Shannon to make his innocuous answers sound lascivious. I didn't know what they'd done until I saw it in print. Next thing I know, he's Swiss cheese. Talk about guilt.

Anyway, the only way Lane would ever get into *Rolling Stone* was if he died in a plane crash. And even then, they'd just blame him for it.

"Is Lane afraid of me?"

"No! He kinda just doesn't like reporters. And, uh, he's upset."

"*He's* upset? *Why*? Charlie, I've barely met the guy!"

"He doesn't like you asking around about him." Charlie's eyes darted wildly.

"Jeez, I'm not believing this! If he talked to me like he *said* he would, I wouldn't have to ask around about him, would I?"

Charlie started to sweat. There was yelling, mostly by me. By the time I got away, with him mooing "I'll call you!" at my back, I was so rattled I didn't see the sand in the hairpin turnaround to Route 1 South until I'd angled into it. The bike just kept leaning and leaning, until it was sideways on the ground. I must've been really torqued, because I picked it up by myself and the damned thing weighs 450 pounds.

When I finally got going again, my headlight was pointing at Jupiter — not on the night's itinerary. Putting it right was a simple matter: Loosen two bolts, re-aim the headlight, tighten the bolts, and you're off.

There was a wrench in the handy tool kit under my saddle. Only problem was, the saddle had to be removed by being unlocked, and my key chain had twenty-seven keys on it thanks to me being a New Yorker, and the whole business required some light. So first I had to find some light.

The night was opaque. No street lamps, no reflectors, not even a Botts dot. Nothing but fog. I had two choices: stay where I was in the road and be an accident waiting to happen, or leave. When the next car came by, I ducked in behind it. The car's headlights were better than none, until I ended up in someone's driveway. I waited for another escort. He turned at the next light. I limped like that all the way to I-95, where I wanted to pull over and wait for the highway patrol on the shoulder but couldn't, because I couldn't *see* the shoulder.

So I drove all the way to Groton chasing truck taillights. It was very educational. I wondered why I bother with a modern bike with crap electrics when I could just drive a Norton.

Finally in Groton there was a highway rest stop. I pulled in and almost kissed a towering mercury vapor lamp. In no time my helmet was over here, my saddle over there, my tool kit spread everywhere as I wrenched the headlight. The mess made it look like a far bigger project than it was. I never thought I'd say this, but I couldn't wait to get done and go home to Brooklyn.

Things were going pretty well. Then out of nowhere, an elderly woman appeared. It was 3:30 a.m.

"You're as bad as my grandson. Always working on his bike," she said to me, looming. Wasn't she overdue at the glue factory?

"It's just the headlamp," I said to my dashboard as I worked. "No big deal. Be done in a minute." But not nearly soon enough.

"Well, I hope someone comes along who can help you."

"I don't *need* help. It's just — "

I looked up. She was gone. So was my thirteen millimeter wrench.

Even without the wrench, the headlight surgery took less time than buttoning up everything afterward. It's a great bike until you have to put gas in it, change the oil, replace the battery, or find the tool kit. Then you have to take it all apart.

I needed caffeine to make the rest of the trip back to Brooklyn without an ambulance. I headed to the rest stop's McDonald's. As I passed by the front window, I looked in and stopped dead. Hot damn — there was Lane!

In journalism parlance, such a phenomenon is known as plain dumb luck. By jiminy, there the little jerk sat, in a family-friendly red vinyl booth, arguing animatedly with some poor schmuck whose face I couldn't see.

The two were surrounded by half a dozen ecologically sound paper coffee cups, piles of greasy, wadded-up napkins, and a bunch of papers and photos I couldn't make out. They energetically puffed on cigarettes and talked at the same time. The stranger waved his hands as he spoke. His back was to me; he seemed bigger than Lane. All I knew for sure was that he wasn't a Dinghy. Maybe he was the agent who got Lane all those deluxe gigs.

It would be fun to embarrass Lane in front of him. My impish imagination shifted into overdrive. But Lane looked plenty agitated already.

Whatever they were doing, they were very busy. Lane never saw me.

I went back to the parking lot. There was Lane's shit-brown van. I let all the air out of his tires.

The remainder of my trip was well-lit and uneventful. So nice to have a clear view again.

Chapter 13

Brooklyn — A Great Place to Visit, a Wonderful Place to Live!

That's what the billboard says, the one on your way in, the one that should read: Brooklyn — a pleasure to come home to. Highways like junkyards. Sidewalks full of vomit. Smog that makes your eyes burn. Oh yeah, and the roads suck. Jiggity jig jig.

While I was gone, my block association's two officers decided, without actually asking anyone besides themselves, to throw another block party. That's when they cordon off the street, force the homeowners to park where they can't hear their car alarms, and install a volleyball net directly over Nona's bike.

The city sells them a special permit to do all this, because the city doesn't see anything wrong with random destruction of personal property as long as there's money in it for the city. That, and block parties provide a wholesome diversion for my street's hyperactive, lead-poisoned little spazzes who have 350 Brooklyn parks to play in, but can't seem to find any of them.

Thanks to them, I'd already replaced three mysteriously demolished rearview mirrors and a gas tank, which nobody around here seemed to know anything about. "Nope, sorry. Didn't see nuthin'." Someone could back a van up to your door and no one here would see it.

On account of the block party, there was a lot of low-pitched grumbling from everyone who had to carry a trunkful of groceries for a mile and struggle with it through a bacchanal they didn't want. A louder discussion ensued about the volleyball net strung over my yard, after I offered to remove it with a chainsaw if I got to it first.

I was sawing away at the net when the block association president called the cops. They came, and then left in a big hurry when someone parked a giant woofer disguised as a Dodge Swinger in front of my house, blasting "Cop Killer."

I went inside my house, up to my third floor. I faced my nine-foot Voice of the Theater speaker to the open window. I loaded a Gene Autry tape loop in my stereo, turned all the knobs to ten, and left.

I met Darryl in Jackson Heights. It was a typical September day, hot and damp as a steam grate. First we went for greasy pizza on Main Street, then we headed over to Sam Ash on Queens Boulevard to enjoy the air conditioning and mess up any too-neat guitar displays.

"This new stuff is crap," Darryl said, changing all the settings on a purple John Reed Smith. A pair of hands flew up to every pair of ears in the store when he plugged in. After the manager threw us out, we loitered outside the store, waiting to intercept anyone famous sneaking in to sell something.

After a while we sat down on the curb, next to the Beemer. It was dirty and the tire treads were full of little stones.

"When are you getting a new bike?" whined Darryl.

"I like this one."

"It's old."

"So are you."

"You need a new one."

"Okay. You pay for it."

"With what?"

That's when we had a brainstorm. We took off for Long Island, to O'Toole's, where Love Dinghy was appearing.

We missed the load in, but Lane's battered van was out back, right next to a filthy rental truck big enough to transport three generations of wetbacks. It must've been the only truck left at the rental counter by the time anyone remembered to get one.

Darryl stood on his toes to peek through a parkway window on Lane's van, while I crouched to copy the plate number for later. He laughed and pulled me up by my collar.

"Look at *this*!" he said so loudly, I couldn't see the point of us sneaking around. Inside the van, safely illuminated by the club's security floodlights, were a big pile of packing blankets stamped "Beacon," a stuffed armadillo, and a hundred cannabis roaches.

We laughed so hard we were spitting on each other.

"That was so refreshing. Thanks!"

"Sshh!" Darryl squeaked out amid convulsions. "We'll get busted!"

"Who's out there?" came a voice from the club's back door.

"Sshh! Sshh!" Darryl kept shushing me and cackling and pushing me toward the street. "There's no beer in jail. You'll hate it. Go on! And sshh!"

"Stop hitting me, Dar!"

We finally snuck out of the back lot in tears, we were laughing so hard.

We strolled the block, making fun of the locals while looking for loose bricks and a cover-free entrance. If anyone said anything, we told them we were looking for our car. Nobody seemed to find that odd, even though I was wearing motorcycle leathers and we were both carrying helmets. Along the way a couple of street lamps accidentally broke. Shame about the infrastructure.

Meanwhile, Love Dinghy was cranked so loud we could hear their greatest hits all the way down the street. Attendance that night at O'Toole's was underwhelming. The club gave up collecting covers early, because who's gonna pay for something they can hear from home? We went in the front door for free, where a party who'd just been told who was playing turned around and left.

Lane had his usual battery of hardware: his new Tele with the mother-of-toilet-seat pickguard, a chintzy acoustic, the bitchin' Strat. Mostly he used them to play rhythm and ear-slamming power chords. He had Wizard Rodriquez to handle leads.

Wizard's real name is Ernest Pickens, which is why everyone calls him something else. His primary value to Lane is freeing him to fake orgasms and climb speaker cabinets like a chimp. Jerry Lee Lewis had nothing on Lane, except more talent and a bigger dick.

Darryl and I were standing at least a mile from the stage, chugging shots and joking about Lane in the dark. I knew he knew I was there. I'd swear he could see me. He kept looking in my direction, as if he expected something there to explode.

But something else was bugging him, too. Every so often he'd throw a pained look toward the emergency exit. The only life in that vicinity was some dude leaning against the fireproof door jamb. It was dark and hard to tell, but he kind of looked like that hick Roger, from the Gar. Lane's biggest fan. Or maybe he was just some South Shore ten-watt blocking a door Lane could've used to get away from me.

Whoever he was, he was clearly no New Yorker — too tall, too blond, too relaxed, and he wasn't doing anything threatening. He just stood there, in jeans and a too-tight T-shirt like everyone else in the club. He held his right bicep with his left hand, blowing smoke rings with a cigarette in the other as he watched the band play. There was some kind of tool sticking out of his hip pocket that looked like a shrub clipper.

I looked back at Lane. A magenta spotlight caught on a ribbon of sweat rolling down his cheek. The room was freezing.

Having wiped out O'Toole's supply of tequila trying to stay warm, Darryl and I staggered to the dance floor. We tirelessly screamed out retarded requests. "In-A-Gadda-Da-Vida!" "Mandy!" "My Zelda!"

Lane ignored us, but I had to punch a humorless Neldahead who threw her beer at me. She grabbed a handful of my hair. I grabbed a handful of her polyester shirt. She screamed and started swinging. Darryl put a headlock on her until the bouncers could get there, but they couldn't be bothered with a catfight. They had bigger fish to fry.

Apparently we'd started a riot. All around us, sodden O'Toole regulars were Heimliching each other to the floor. Out of the melee a thong flew onto the stage. The band just looked at it solemnly and kept playing.

Fully exposed now in the strobe-lit bedlam, Darryl and I had no hope of skulking around unnoticed. Lane homed right in on us.

"Hit Me With Your Best Shot!" Darryl yelled extra loudly at him.

"Hope you don't fall down," Lane responded to us personally, through a mic so loud Darryl turned carmine. I thought Lane meant "don't fall down on account of being utterly sloshed and getting bodyslammed." Darryl thought Lane was calling him too old to take a punch.

"Hey!" Darryl shouted back. He didn't need a mic to get personal. "I was rockin' an' rollin' when you were still shittin' in diapers!"

Now we had a problem. Darryl is three years younger than Lane. In terms of technical accuracy, his statement is what we veteran news journalists call a wideload. But it ticked Lane off anyway.

He was taking it out on his Tele, and glaring at us and stomping on a cable that had the bad sense to get in his way. Next thing you know, Lane's mic goes dead.

Bupkis was coming from his speakers, but he could still hear himself through his monitor so he kept banging his air-conditioned knees together and singing his heart out. Or rather, the ice cube where his heart would be if he had one. Meanwhile, the sound man was shaking his head wildly and making slit-my-throat signs at Lane. The band hesitated, then stopped.

If you believe in divine retribution, then I was wrong about Lane's salutation being toothless and Darryl was right, though this is highly unlikely.

Lane looked like he wanted to crawl into a hole and die. Darryl and I went to the men's room together. Six stalls, no waiting. I refuse to waste my whole night on a line for a women's room toilet awash in piss. Women — they piss on the seat, they piss under the seat, they piss on the floor. I don't even know how.

In the men's room there was a guy with a crack rig, shooting right out in the open. Nobody stopped him. O'Toole's would do anything to be like a Manhattan club. We completed our assorted businesses and all left the head together. The band started playing again. Back on the dance floor, Crack Guy got with the groove by hurling chunks at a security gorilla.

Four more missing links were now stationed around the elevated stage. They seemed more interested in peeling potted Islanders off each other than in protecting the band from overenthusiastic fans, not that this was a big danger. The band took a break. Darryl and I went for a walk. When the next set started, Lane couldn't find his $5,000 Strat.

Chapter 14

My writing career wasn't going any better by the fall than it had all summer. I was reduced to writing for the *New York Post* about the inspiring birth of the Barbie doll, on the occasion of one of her many tedious anniversaries:

> The toy juggernaut known as Mattel Corporation had its humble beginnings in a Long Island suburb. In 1959 entrepreneurial duo Ruth and Elliot Handler returned from a European vacation with a very special souvenir: the 11-1/2" plastic shiksa-goddess who would become Barbie. They set to work cranking out copies in an unlikely cultural ground zero — their garage. Hundreds of millions of sales later, the rest is history.
>
> The prototype Barbie was actually a promotional statuette of a cartoon character named Lili, star sexpot of the German newspaper *Bild* and a novelty item sold in bars to men. *Bild* Lili was a cross between Marilyn Monroe and Elly May Clampett. The Handlers thought she'd make a swell Mattel doll, especially since the *Bild*'s design wasn't copyrighted.
>
> Jack Ryan, Mattel's then-creative director, warned the Handlers that reproducing Lili was potentially actionable. Besides, she looked like a hooker. Who'd let their kids play with *that*?
>
> Undaunted, Ruth Handler hastily patented the virtually unaltered design — right down to the dominatrix makeup, suicide blond 'do, and bordello skivvies — and named it after her daughter. Lili wasn't vulgar to Handler, a woman clearly not averse to a little industrial free license.

I also completed a huge sports magazine assignment. I was confident it promised prime exposure and better paydays ahead. I was thrilled to get it. That was before the editor put his girlfriend's byline on it and never paid me, which he apparently thought I wouldn't mind.

First I sued him and won the money he thought I wouldn't miss. There was no way to get my byline or exposure back, but nothing to stop me from snooping. I got the county assessor after the magazine's publisher for nonpayment of taxes. I sicked the Audit Bureau of Control on them for accidentally on purpose misstating their circulation figures and illegally inflating their ad rates. I wrote disparaging letters about the magazine to the state attorney general, the Better Business Bureau, the Chamber of Commerce. Then I left them a chicken bomb.

A chicken bomb is a tightly sealed Mason jar filled with giblets and milk. After about a week, it ferments and explodes. The smell never comes out of anything it slimes. All you do is plant it, and wait.

It didn't take much to get the magazine's receptionist to leave her desk. "Hey — Tom Cruise is out in the hall, waiting for the elevator!" Then I left a present in the communal coat closet.

Unfortunately, it was going to take more than a chicken bomb to fix things in Newport. *Motorhead* was held hostage by the printer for the duration of September while Jean Poule hustled for money no one wanted to give him. Many potential investors sounded interested, then looked at his books and laughed. His disgruntled staff wouldn't continue working on the second issue without being paid for the first.

It wasn't yet public knowledge that *Motorhead*, the biggest buzz in the sports journalism world, was in a tailspin. To head off any suspicions, Don DeRosa talked Ralph the ad guy and me into attending the annual motorcycle industry show in Baltimore. "Everyone will be there," DeRosa said. "You should be, too."

"Why?" I asked him.

"For appearances' sake," Don said. "C'mon, Nona. Be a team player for once."

"I dunno, Don."

"I'll introduce you to Freddie Spencer."

"Already met him."

"Okay. You can test that old two-stroke for the next issue. The H2. A hundred-twenty mph. Two gears, stop and go. Alright?"

"What next issue?"

"The hotel room in Baltimore has a jacuzzi."

And so I went to the big trade show, hoping Bates would give me new leathers to review that I could forget to return. Ralph heroically announced his plan to sell ads at the show for our next issue. Nobody said it, but we all wanted to put our ears to the ground for new jobs.

Indeed, Jean had somehow finagled hotel rooms for us — we were sure he didn't pay for them — *and* a booth, ostensibly to give away the flashy *Motorhead* posters he swore he'd had printed, and genuine copies of the grand premiere issue he'd assured us would be ready in time.

When I got to the Baltimore Convention Center, Jean had already been there and gone. There was Ralph in front of a magnificent, and no doubt costly, ten-by-ten foot multicolored satin *Motorhead* banner hanging over an empty table. Poor Ralph told everyone who stopped by that everything was "at the printer's." He was glad to see Don and me. We stuck Ralph with the booth while we walked around the show, handing out our business cards and trying to get stuff for free. Jean never came back. The jacuzzi was awesome.

After that I only went to the Newport office to see if my paycheck was there. Like Dorothy Parker said, "The two most beautiful words in the English language are 'check enclosed'." Mine never was.

But it meant a road trip, and Indian summer is my favorite time of year for a drive. The leaves make a fabulous show of dying, all red and orange and gold, floating about like flaming angels, until the wind blows them into my cylinders where they stick and burn.

It's called Indian summer because on one spectacular fall day, right after the first colonial frost, the Indians knocked on the gate of Whitey's fort. "Come on out," the Indians said, "winter's over!" This being their first winter in America, the settlers had no point of reference for shit like this. So they piled out of their fort, and the Indians massacred them.

On a glorious November day, when it was 78 degrees and the sun shone and every leaf in New England lay dead and moldy on the ground, I dropped by the Connecticut Department of Motor Vehicles in Stamford to run Lane's plate. Their records showed he had a 1978 Chevy Jimmy the color of a mud dauber's nest that couldn't go fast enough for speeding tickets. I already knew that. The computer also said Lane's address was a fancy one in Groton. I got out my maps and took the route to Newport that ran past Lane's place.

His house was easy to find. It looked just like his van: nice once; now, not so much.

His rock star palace was a grimy white stone thing with four bedrooms at most, wood trim that needed paint, and a roof missing many terra cotta pantiles. The grass was unmanicured and brown. I tried to imagine Lane, The Fake King of Heartland Rock, on a riding mower. I laughed. All those farmer's kids starving in Indiana — too bad you can't feed them bull.

A black Range Rover cluttered the driveway that circled to the rear. It was the luxury model, the yuppie package with all the bells and whistles. Figures. The second he makes some money, Mr. America First goes out and buys foreign.

I had to check out the Rover, especially since it appeared no one was home to stop me. The doors were unlocked. The parking brake was on. I climbed in and released it. The Rover rolled promisingly into Lane's flowerbed, crushing his azaleas, only to stop an inch shy of the dirty stone wall.

Way in the back of the property I could see the top of a satellite dish bigger than NASA's. The garage wasn't visible at all from the front. I wandered down the drive and found it, locked up good and tight. He probably saved that for his fine van, which probably wasn't waterproof. Rain, rain, go away, wreck my amps some other day.

The staggering view of Long Island Sound was the one nice thing about the property, but there was nothing I could do about that. I thought about feeding Lane's garden hose through the mail slot and turning on the water, but I was in a hurry to get my check from *Motorhead*. I'd make it up to him later and leave a chicken bomb in his Rover.

An hour later I pulled into *Motorhead*'s garage, dripping a muddy puddle of New England rain onto Jean's immaculate concrete floor. Good thing I'd rushed. No one else had bothered coming into the office that day except Ralph. He was answering the 800 line, trying to get callers off it as fast as possible. I noticed the fridge was gone, and all the racing posters, too. All that remained of the test bikes was oil stains on the office carpeting. There were no paychecks, either. Nothing like a little encouragement to brighten one's day.

Chapter 15

"Yes, m'am!" the grinning Cumberland clerk in North Kingstown said as he took $3.11 for my three-gallon fill-up. Half of it was pennies. "No, m'am. Always glad to have change."

It sure beat the Brooklyn equivalent. "Hey, mama — you a bitch! Wachoo givin' me these pennies for?" Back home they couldn't even count change, much less be nice about charging $1.70 a gallon for watered-down gas.

I wasn't ready to go back there. I stopped by the Narragansett Pier and watched rich people in wetsuits dive-bomb geese with their Jet Skis. The water in the bay was turquoise and frothy, like SaniFlush. A Del's lemonade truck was making out like chicken robbers. As the sun set, the sky turned vermilion and aquamarine. I watched the rich people trickle home. When it started to get dark, I swung by Providence and loaded up Nat.

We had a new downtime project going. Her dumbass boyfriend Bob lived in a tract house, drove a standard economy truck, and worked six days a week for someone else, so of course he told Nat he was some kind of blueblood. She believed him. I didn't. Anyone with a Sears card can buy a boat.

Lately he'd been dragging her to yacht club festivities. These events were too upper crust for a Texas redneckette; Nat didn't have a clue how to behave, and Bob was usually too sauced or busy ogling other women to be instructional. At dinner she'd order vodka and iced coffee in front of snotheads asking tuxedoed waiters about the vintage of the port. She'd cram whole rolls directly into her face and then blabber about Bob's boat without swallowing. The only aspect of her evolvement showing growth was her can, from keeping up with Bob's drinking. He started with undiluted scotch right after breakfast.

"Guess what?" she said to me more than once, "I'm getting hitched!"

"Wow, that's great!" I always replied, envisioning my puce bridesmaid gown with airbags for sleeves. "When?"

"As soon as Bob sells his house," she said one time. "As soon as he gets a promotion," she said the next.

They set some dates that came and went. They shopped and shopped for a diamond, but they never saw one *he* liked. Cheap son of a bitch. Of course, his expired mother's flawless two-carat Tiffany engagement solitaire languished unused in a safe deposit box, but he told Nat it wasn't like he could just give away a family heirloom.

Inexplicably, he was the best she thought she could do, and she was therefore determined to outrun a bunch of second-string yacht clubbers to keep him. The Boat People, Nat and I called them. They weren't good enough to clean her toilet, and I couldn't bear the thought of them using her for target practice. So I endeavored to arm her sufficiently to keep them at bay, at least until the Bob thing blew over. Sometimes I wished he'd stop fucking around and hit her already, so she'd dump him. And thus was born the Etiquette Project.

At this particular lesson, Nat and I were test driving a choice poully fuisse in some twee bistro, where I was demonstrating sophisticated social comportment in Guatemalan paratrooper fatigues. Nat was wearing one of her drip-dry post office suits accessorized by ear chandeliers.

Our indentured servant du jour was Andre. It said so on his name tag. In true Gallic tradition, he made no attempt to conceal his amusement at us, a couple of American crackers out on the town. With a flourish he presented the cork from the vin blanc we ordered, confident we had no idea why. He waited for us to *tout foutre en l'air*.

"Just look at the cork. Don't pick it up," I whispered to Nat. "See if it's wet. That's how you know the wine was stored right. You can't send it back unless it tastes like urine. No! Don't smell the cork!"

Andre stood slightly out of earshot and tapped his foot. He was sure we were whispering about him. Who wouldn't?

The cork was well up Nat's nostril by the time he came back.

"Well?" said Andre.

She threw the cork on the tablecloth and buried her face in the menu.

I sampled the wine myself so Andre would go away. "It's fine. Fine," I told him. "Je n'ai jamais goute telle merde. *Please* leave now."

Didn't have to ask *him* twice. After he flew off in a snit, Nat tongued her wine to see what I'd gotten her into this time. She held the glass like it was a bowling trophy.

"Hold it by the stem, not the round part," I said. She was used to Schlitz cans and Bob's highball glasses.

"Why?"

"So the wine don't get het up," I said in my best exaggerated drawl. We shared an earsplitting howl in our usual girlish manner. Andre thought we were laughing at him and shot us a look.

Nat and I think Texas talk is funny, being Easterners now, but sometimes we still say "Pull the door to" and "Ah'm fixin' ta gwanna the 7-Eleven."

She pointed to the menu. "What's *cervelle*?"

"Brains."

"Gross!"

"It's good. Try it," I said, only because it would require ordering a bottle of red wine, and she was paying.

"No way. Mmmm! What's *ris de veau*?"

"Veal glands."

"Yuck!" She located a tissue in her thirty-gallon purse and honked her nose luxuriously into it.

I was starting to want to be elsewhere. "Everything come out okay?"

"Better out than in. Why?"

"If you do that in Japan, they put you in prison."

"Good thing we're in Warwick, then! What do you think the boat people would do?"

"Act even more obnoxious. If that's possible," I said, remembering our last encounter with them. We were supposed to go to lunch at a Mexican restaurant. Instead, she drove us to the Wickford marina in a panic. The emergency turned out to be she wanted to neck with Bob.

I should've guessed something was up when she spent an hour dressing in a fussy lime silk get-up, which apparently she considered appropriate for a nooner. It certainly wasn't necessary for an enchilada special. I had only just arrived in town on the bike and was still wearing exploded bugs.

At the marina, we got out of her blue muscle car and immediately were met by two boat people. We were not the type of visitor to whom they were accustomed.

They deliberately blocked our progress toward Bob. I didn't know whether they meant to intimidate us or just get a closer look, but sizzling fajitas were calling my name and I didn't want to drag this out. I had to shove one of them to get by. It was not pretty.

"I have something for you," Nat said now in the fake French bistro in Warwick. She hoisted her two-ton pocketbook onto Andre's table. Glass and silver quaked. She pulled out a rubber-banded bundle of printed pulp.

The outside piece looked like a Laura Ashley catalog. Figures. It would be just like Nat to buy dainty flowered dresses designed by a klutz who crashed down a flight of stairs and croaked.

Nat handed the bundle to me silently. I knew Bob had complained about my appearance, which never bothered her before she met him. I figured this was a hint, a patronizing stack of prissy self-improvement material.

I opened it anyway. To my surprise, it wasn't a makeover kit at all. It was a bundle of mail. Lane's mail.

Recently a carrier had left his Jeep running while he stopped to empty some street mailboxes in Groton. As he was collecting the contents, the Jeep popped into gear and drove itself through a K-Mart window. The regional security manager — that's Nat — was ordered immediately to the scene. While everyone looted the K-Mart, she loaded the Jeep's mail, which happened to include the deliveries for Lane's route, into her company car. For security reasons, of course.

The piece I saw first *was* a Laura Ashley catalog, and there was another one, from Sharper Image. There was also a bank checking account statement showing a six-figure balance, and a bond interest statement from a place called Alphatron Inc. For an antiestablishment pothead, Lane sure owned a lot of federal Treasury instruments. There was a new American Express card, too. Platinum. Lane McCarthy — boogieman of the people.

I went straight to the restaurant's pay phone, called Sharper Image, and ordered a $3,000 bracelet with the Amex card. I had Lane send it to Tipper Gore with a romantic gift card.

I could've kissed Nat right there. I could've married her, right in front of Andre. I probably should've, too, considering I'd be needing immunity from prosecution. Forget about Japan. The last half-hour's worth of federal offenses was good for a lifetime right here at Leavenworth.

In the meantime, we'd have to remember to thank Lane for the Dom Perignon.

Chapter 16

Traffic was heavy on I-95. The Beemer and I overheated together as we steamed slowly toward Brooklyn. I came home to fifty messages on my answering machine, all of them from Darryl. He was all fired up about some major guitar deal he didn't want to talk about over the phone. Fifty times.

So Darryl came to my house for dinner Saturday night. When I answered the door, I saw two very unusual things: Darryl, and a big red pickup truck tearing away from my curb. It burned rubber down the street with so much crap hanging out the back, it covered the license plate.

No one on my block would be caught dead owning a pickup, or stealing one either. It was a hot Caddy or nothing, so I couldn't imagine what that was all about. Darryl and I exchanged quizzical looks and shrugged our shoulders. Just another day in the blowhole of the universe.

We started to go inside, but stopped short when we saw two kids dive into my garbage, half of which seemed to be gone. "Get away from my trash, you little dipwads!" I yelled.

Oh, joy. The block association president would be on my doorstep directly, interrupting my dinner, demanding an explanation for my confrontational attitude toward the spawn of Satan. Last time this happened she showed up after midnight, with three cops.

"Look out! She's got a gun!" she screamed melodramatically when I answered her pounding in my robe and fuzzy slippers.

"That's right," I said, rubbing my eyes. "A big one."

When I moved in here, I made sure everyone in the neighborhood knew I kept a loaded Mossberg 20-gauge under my bed. Mine is the only house on the block that hasn't been robbed.

"You got a gun license?" the block association president shrieked at me.

"You bet your fat hairy ass I got a license."

I looked at the cops. "You got a warrant?"

There was a lot of shuffling and shrugging. I shut the door in their faces and went to bed.

* * * *

Whenever Darryl visits me, the UN calls an assembly. He doesn't come over often. He doesn't like spring-loaded children. He hates bringing his car here, because of the traffic and my neighbors' unpolished parking skills and the disproportionate number of car thieves per capita in Brooklyn. He doesn't dig boom boom music, either. Also, the disarray in my house drives him nuts. But tonight was special. Tonight we were celebrating selling John Entwistle a 1958 Explorer.

Explorers are goofy-looking things, straight out of *The Jetsons*. Gibson made fewer than a hundred, so you don't see Explorers too often, much less casually leaned against a pile of tractor retreads at a flea market upstate. Darryl and I stared at it, looked at each other, looked at the guitar again without saying a single word, and then bargained it down from $50 to $25. It was pretty ragged, so Entwistle only gave Darryl $50,000 for it.

What this meant, besides that Entwistle had more money than some developing nations, was that I could eat animal protein again and drink $75 Barolo. Darryl and I talked and tippled while I burned an expensive cut of dead flesh for him.

"After dinner, I'm cutting your hair," he said, flipping through a *Glamour*.

"Yeah, sure. By the way, that pickup pulling away when you got here — did you see who was in it?"

"Some guy. He jumped into that thing in a big stinking hurry when I drove up. Looked like he was going through trash bags. That's all I saw.

Well, that, and he had some kinda seriously blond hair. Lots of it, no roots. Tourists — gotta love 'em."

The thing is, there are plenty of trash pilferers here. We've got those stupid neighbor kids, for starters, and the bums from all the drug shelters and halfway houses the mayor so thoughtfully saddled us with. They're always stealing everyone's deposit cans and bottles. Nobody stops them because they provide the recycling service the city discontinued. But none of them be blond, much less drive brand new trucks.

Darryl certainly didn't seem concerned about a white trash guy in a hurry. After all, Darryl's from Queens.

"Too bad he didn't take *all* your garbage," he said. "Now you're stuck with it 'til the city picks it up next year."

We drained the first bottle of $75 vino. "Salute Gibson!" Darryl toasted in his best guido accent as he uncorked another.

"Lemme tell you about my new band!" he said, as if anyone could stop him. I heard in florid detail about the new lineup, and how none of them ever listened to him.

"We're only gonna play blues. And R&B. And a little roots rock'n'roll. Maybe some jump. I already got us three gigs!" He was all proud and puffed up. I quickly forgot about the stranger getting intimate with my garbage.

Darryl glommed onto my Rolodex, trawling through it as he talked about his upcoming dates and favorite guitars with his mouth full of smoked salmon. My cat Stinky battled him for the hors d'oeuvres.

Darryl chewed and oohed as he flipped address cards and pushed Stinky away. "Wow! Brent Muffberger!" he enthused, spraying fish and toast bits everywhere.

Go figure. A guy who drinks beer with Paul Simon acting impressed over a has-been sportscaster's home phone number. Must've been the

Barolo. It certainly made Darryl forget about my haircut. He didn't even seem to mind sitting in my half-renovated kitchen that would never be finished, with its ancient cracked sink parked on sticks and the naked stud wall I exposed to install all the new appliances I never got. That wine was so good, I was even able to convince him to go to a Ramones show after dinner.

Just before we left, the phone rang. Darryl answered it. "Yo! Nona's crib." Whoever it was hung up.

I last saw the Ramones ten years earlier, back when I mistakenly thought it'd be great to live at the beach and moved to Long Island. Or The Guyland, as we say — capital of electrical blackouts, fashion abortions, and witless motorists who constantly ran me off the expressway. I was finally driven away forever by the 300-pound insomniac who lived upstairs. Bigfoot, I called him. He was enamored of *Odd Couple* reruns and Frank Sinatra 45s, and the walls were thin. His notion of walking his dog was letting it piss over the side of his second-floor terrace, into my hibachi.

The Ramones didn't have fog machines and fans on autodestruct then, back before I mistakenly thought it'd be great to move to Brooklyn.

The show I hauled Darryl to see was at My Father's Place, a sleazy club in the otherwise upscale town of Roslyn. The capacity crowd was a bizarre mix of bohemians, bald people, teens with fake IDs, Island Park bohunks, and wannabe leatherboys. "Vinylboys," Darryl called them. We only stayed because he wanted to critique the hairstyles.

There was exactly one waitress in the place the whole night. She was wearing cut-out tights and making lots of money, especially from us. "Just keep 'em coming," we told her.

By the time the Ramones finally belched forth from a noxious green gas cloud, Darryl's voyeuristic enthusiasm had waned and he was busily going through my fanny pack, looking for gum. I made him put it down and dance with me. I was so drunk, I totally forgot about my fanny pack and left it on the table.

We were in the zone as my boys played at machine gun-like speed. "Psycho Therapy." "Do You Wanna Dance?" "Rock'N'Roll High School." Ratta tatta tat. And my all-time fave, "I Wanna Be Sedated." Because usually I do.

"This is pretty tame," Darryl yelled to me over the Ramones' Marshall amps. "I thought you said there was all kinds of violence at these things?" He seemed disappointed.

A grinning fan in a "Hands Across Your Face" shirt pogoed neatly behind us. Periodically he'd yell profoundly nonconfrontational things like "They're the best!" at the backs of our heads.

Darryl was right for once, I was thinking; this *was* pretty tame. And naturally, that's exactly when the punks and skinheads started slamming.

First there were two, then ten, then twenty. The civilized dancers with hairdos and manners found themselves on the floor or in strangers' laps. My fanny pack whizzed past our heads. Just your typical Ramones evening. But what happened next wasn't typical at all.

The nerds rebelled.

Half the house commenced belting the other half. The slammers' expressions changed completely as they reeled from unexpected right hooks and kidney punches.

Darryl and I sprang into middle-aged action. He dived headlong into a crush of tattooed nosering wearers. I chased the guy who was making off with my fanny pack. He was big and fast. We were both surprised when I dropped him.

The wienie uprising was brutal. The slammers were accustomed to oligarchic rule, and this was something new for them.

New for me, too. I'd never seen Darryl's social side before. Who knew he had one? He's a classic anal retentive. All the bills in his wallet are in numerical order, facing the same way. His toilet's so clean you can drink from it. He claimed to have other friends besides me, but I'd never seen him interact with them. Now here he was on the beer-flooded floor, in his pressed chinos and Lacoste shirt, spontaneously forging a meaningful personal relationship into someone's face.

Things went pretty well until he was forcibly removed from his new friend by a pack of do-gooders. While Darryl was detained, his new pal got up off the floor and charged me. Luckily my pogoing buddy was nearby. Together we grabbed Dar's attacker. Grinning maniacally at each other, we shook the living crap out of him, then hurled him face-first into the midst of an eye-poking fest.

It was a magical moment that was interrupted, unfortunately, by a fake biker with a perm who hurtled into me. Darryl and I decked him. I was just straightening his hair when the Ramones finished their encore and it was time to go. I was pretty pissed off. They never played "Needles and Pins."

Darryl and I punched our way out of the club and ran to his car, giggling all the way. We weren't ready to call it a night, so we went to Georgia Diner to relive our victories and compare hematomas. Feeling invincible, we ordered everything fried on the menu.

"I haven't had an adrenaline rush like this since I perjured myself in federal court," he said.

"Federal court? Dar, I never knew this about you. How come you never told me before?"

He shrugged. "It never came up before."

"*You* were up on federal charges?"

"No, no, not me. I was just a defense witness."

"And you made this magnanimous gesture to whom?"

"A mucky-muck bond trader with Drexel Burnham Lambert." That Darryl — he knows everyone.

"Are you serious?"

"Would I lie to you?"

The lucky defendant Darryl rescued was Carl Dixon, a Wall Streeter with killer instinct and lousy timing. Darryl had generously given Carl a bulletproof alibi for a critical moment in the history of fiat banking.

"They were trying to prove he pulled off some bogus trades that bankrupted the company. I swore he was dead drunk on my bathroom floor at the time and wouldn't get out," said Darryl.

And so Carl beat the federal rap, thanks to Darryl, with a timely assist from Drexel's night porter. He was in hock to his bookie and eager for side work. Carl and Darryl catered to his financial needs by commissioning a small task.

"Bond transactions," Darryl said, "aren't traceable if the paperwork disappears."

Drexel collapsed shortly thereafter, but Carl did not.

"He's at a place called Alphatron now," said Darryl. "It's one of those humongous bond trading factories that bilk old ladies out of their retirement savings."

I recognized the name. "They handle Lane's account," I said through a mouthful of fried onion rings.

"Did you just say *Lane's account?* No way! That boho fudgepacker owns *bonds*?"

"Yeah. Mostly treasuries, tax-free municipals, totally conservative stuff like that."

"Really? You know, if he owned stock in Commodore or Pioneer, *that* would be smart. GEOS and LaserDiscs are gonna change everything! But bonds — that's just ... bourgeois. Ugh!"

"Hey, everybody's gotta make a living. You steal guitars. Lane expropriates quarterly compounded profit distributions."

"Girl, you're scary. How do you know all this stuff about him?"

"A little birdie pooped Lane's bond statement right into my lap."

"Get outta here! If he's so rich, how come he plays dumps? And what's up with those holes in his pants? Can't he buy new ones? Don't tell me he thinks all those poor drunken club puppies will buy that shit about how he's one of them — on account of he's got holes!"

"Got me. I'd rather see the holes in his tax return."

"Haven't seen *that* yet, have we now? Nona, you are truly slipping. I bet Lane doesn't give a dime to needy animals *or* the Feds."

"Well, I *did* see his bank balance. Get this: His *checking account* balance is six figures. I mean, I'm lucky when mine's not overdrawn."

"So you're saying he doesn't live in that rustbucket van?"

"Nah. He just uses that to carry his wallet around. He lives in a house. I saw it."

"Did Robin Leach race you to the door?"

"Not hardly. Get this — Lane's the neighborhood trash. His yard is wicked nasty, and his roof has holes in it. Wouldn't wanna be inside that thing when it rains. Helluva view, though."

"So he spends all his money on — what? Drugs? Phone sex? Stilts?"

"Well, he has a satellite dish the size of Alaska. And he's got a $40,000 car nobody uses — a forest ranger's limo. Like anyone needs four-wheel drive in suburban Connecticut. It's a piece of foreign junk. I drove it six feet before it crapped out."

"Damn, Nona — you are the queen of spook!" Darryl said admiringly. Almost nothing impresses him, so I felt honored. "That tears it. Tomorrow I'm gonna call Carl. He owes me a favor."

When Lane awoke Monday afternoon, all his no-risk investments had been neatly converted for him into MGM paper. MGM was on the verge of filing for bankruptcy after Credit Lyonnais had poured $888 million down it, pretty much for nothing, in an attempt to save it from itself. Overnight Lane became the proud new owner of a shitload of MGM junk bonds.

While I've always believed every ham should own a little bit of showbiz stock — contribute to the cause, as it were — it was unlikely Lane's $450,000 infusion would make a difference in MGM's vastly deflated fortunes.

I hoped the call from his broker woke him from a peaceful sleep.

Chapter 17

"C'mon, Nona. It'll be fun!"

"No freakin' way."

"I'll pay."

"Yeah, right. Who needs a free one-way trip to Uranus?"

"Is that a 'yes'?"

One night not long after Lane's unfortunate investment setback, Darryl and I went to a blues club in Harlem. No, not the Apollo, not even close, but rather the kind of place patronized only by hardcore blues junkies. Darryl got a tip that Clapton was going to be there, so of course we had to go.

We didn't drive our own vehicles because we didn't dare leave them unattended on 125th Street. We didn't want to be walking around the neighborhood, either, so we flagged a cab that didn't want to go there, too. You could barely get a cab to take you to Harlem, much less find one to take you out.

"No no! No go to Harlem!" screamed the little foreign man driving the hack we jumped into and slammed the door before telling him our destination. If we hadn't threatened to report him, we'd still be trying to go to Harlem. You *really* had to like the blues to come to this place.

We hadn't a clue how we were going to get home, not that we were in any hurry. Since neither of us had to drive, Darryl and I mounted a full frontal assault on a defenseless keg of Bass. We sat in the back, at a small wobbly table covered with cigarette burns and graffiti, vanquishing a long succession of draughts.

The place was packed. Everyone but us was A-list. Buddy Guy and BB King stood by the women's room. At the too-close table next to us sat John Hammond, telling someone bawdy stories about Miles Davis. Apparently everyone else heard about Clapton being here, too, except for Clapton.

The atmosphere was intoxicating. Or maybe it was just the beers. At first we eavesdropped on the conversations around us, all of them about the making of music, the business of music, or the dirty laundry of music. Eventually Darryl and I became absorbed in our own ultra-fascinating conversation about UPS rates and lost interest in the room. We couldn't see more than two feet away anyway, the place was so crowded and smoky.

Some band was making noises. We had no idea who it was. But as long as someone kept playing and beer kept coming, we were happy.

The stage in this place was lit as flamboyantly as a back alley. We could barely see the players. We made a game of identifying them by their styles, which fought each other vigorously. Turns out we risked our lives to hear a moonlighting pick-up band.

Darryl and I guessed the bass player was Danny Gatton, except that Gatton's a guitar player, but then we figured Danny Gatton could probably play anything he wanted. The keyboardist was that woman from the *Saturday Night Live* band. We couldn't remember her name. Nobody can. She kept doing a barrelhouse thing that made everyone cringe. The drummer hitting the skins too hard could've been Peter Criss. Or not. Who could tell without the eyeliner?

We never pegged the guitar player. He was coaxing all these haunting, lyrical strains out of a weathered pre-CBS Tele and a ratty tube amp. He was a little guy who barely moved, except for his hands. They were flying. He played intensely and never looked up, never once smiled, didn't care whether he was the object of undivided audience attention like the others. They jockeyed like politicians, mugging at the unimpressed crowd and signaling the sound guy to turn each other down. They wore inappropriately shiny clothes. The guitar player was all business. He wore a baggy Fair Isle sweater, army surplus cargo pants, black Converse high-tops, and a tweed newsboy cap. He had longish, shaggy dark hair that clung to his nape, and prescription glasses with gold aviator frames.

From where Darryl and I sat, he could've been anyone. Or no one. Probably one of the others' grandkids. Some precocious little booger who wants to be Stevie Ray Vaughan when he grows up. For a couple of years, anyway, until he's playing "Jump" at bar mitzvahs.

Burning with curiosity, we finally had to go closer and see who he was. That's when the guitar player looked up, stepped toward a mic, and started singing a low-slung, sandpapery libretto. His voice started out like fois gras and ground glass. Then he let that thing rip, without ever going over the top or breaking a sweat. He must've had an eight-octave range. He hit notes only dogs could hear.

Darryl and I stood there, stunned. Damned if it wasn't Lane McCarthy.

Chapter 18

I ride my motorcycle all year, even when the weather sucks. I don't store my bike in winter like conscientious bike owners do, partly because nobody in New York has ever seen a garage. But mainly, I need for it to be where I can get to it fast. Sometimes you gotta go somewhere in a hurry. Sometimes you just gotta not be in Brooklyn.

The bike-in-winter thing is perfectly doable if you wear a million layers of clothes, and avoid driving after a snowstorm or in temperatures below 32 degrees. There's a traffic light on every corner, and their switches stick when they freeze. You're left with two choices: running lights at intersections where nobody can stop, or stopping at stuck lights until spring. Sometimes the city sands the streets, the ones in rich people's neighborhoods, if it's an election year. The city retired its snowplows and maintenance crews after the market correction of '87, when all the people who pay taxes moved to Seattle. In winter it's also smart to avoid trips on dark interstates and icy steel deck bridges.

The winter had been a dreary exercise in isolation for me. Luckily the Dinghies played the Lone Star, when the club couldn't convince any confederate bands that ice dams are cool. I was so glad to see *any* friends — even the Dinghies — that I couldn't complain about being clipped for the fifteen-dollar cover, and another twenty dollars for food I could've thawed myself, or even the Nelda sets the Dinghies were obliged to perform at clubs that took credit cards. Like them, I survived a delightful evening of song about garter belts and ritual murders by tuning it all out.

The Lone Star was a grease trap for displaced Texans on 13th Street and Fifth Avenue, with a forty-foot iguana on the roof. I am not making this up. It was an adequate live music venue, and a great place to spy on yahoos interacting with stock swindlers.

The main floor had a stage and a big dance area, with a very grand mezzanine that wrapped all the way around. That's where I always sat, upstairs. You could watch the stage, the bathroom, and the cigarette machine all at once, without ever getting up. But if you did, you could leave your purse and coat at your table, secure in the knowledge they'd still be there when you returned. Texans may batter their women and hoard gas in a fuel crisis, but they don't steal everything that's not bolted down the way New Yorkers do.

I quietly sipped a tequila and watched the pre-show action on the dance floor: Stetson-wearers gaping at apron-wearers scaring beeper-wearers with rubber knives. The Dinghies were down there, too, shmoozing music industry types for help with what was left of their careers. Alvin the bass player and Larry the drummer double-teamed some geek in a leisure suit, while Charlie the board man chatted up Neldaheads who'd swum over from Jersey. Only Lane was missing from this Mort Drucker-like scene.

The opening act paired with Love Dinghy was The Suits, the hobby band of a local businessman named Jay Weiss. Weiss' day job was co-owning the Happy Land Social Club, a firetrap that incinerated eighty-seven no-longer-happy patrons. He was as good a musician as he was a landlord.

While The Suits played, I had plenty of time to visit the head. On my way I saw Lane taking advantage of the same dead time to buy cigarettes.

He was wearing a Monster Truck Showdown T-shirt, with a gigantic Bert and Ernie bandage on his neck. He must've been pretty desperate for a smoke to be out without an escort. With his back to me. Alone. I wondered if he was high.

There were other things I wondered about him, too, things I'd never find on microfiche at the library. For one thing, I wondered what it would take to make him crap his pants.

He was looking down, counting change for the cigarette machine. I sneaked up behind him. Swifter than a pickpocket I threw my arm over his shoulder and around his ribcage, pinning him to me in a rescue lock I learned in a lifeguard class that had never been much use until now. Coins went flying.

If the cuts in his biceps weren't lying too, he probably could've thrown me. Pity he was crushed against the vending machine like that.

I pulled him to my chest so hard, I wondered if I'd cut off his circulation. But I could feel his scale-model heart thudding hard under my arm. His skunk-striped hair was in my face. I'd expected it to be polyurethaned into place because it never moved, but it was soft. It smelled like coconuts and smoke.

I wondered if his Levis were wet yet. Nope. Confident of his utter helplessness, I unbuttoned his jeans with my free hand and slid it down the front. "If I can get it up," I whispered into his cowlick, "can I have it?"

It all happened too fast for him to struggle, much less summon a pithy riposte other than the one from his pants. But if I were in his high-heeled boots, I would've at least said "Hey!" or something. I started to wonder if he was congenitally inarticulate.

Before I could find out, I heard someone coming toward us, calling his name. I let go of Lane and ran to the restroom.

Outside in the frozen slush and bitter wind, my bike no doubt was being stripped to the frame. Inside where it was warm, where people danced and laughed and chased each other around with toy buzz saws, my keys and unfinished Mezcal remained undisturbed on the table where I'd left them. Nat was there, too.

She'd come all the way from Rhode Island on a train, then commandeered a Midtown cab on a sleety Friday night, and found my camp on the mezzanine where she'd settled in with a toddy. Pretty good for a tourist. I was relieved that Bob had stayed home with a headache. Maybe he'd been refinishing yard sale antiques with the windows closed again.

Since Bob wasn't there to ruin our holiday fun, we indulged in squealsome girl talk. There was shoe shopping to compare, and spurned suitors to denigrate. Then I regaled Nat with the gripping saga of Lane's childhood.

Before I got snowed in for the winter, I'd visited his high school in North Smithfield. There I rummaged leisurely through old yearbooks bursting with McCarthys, from which I learned three critical facts: Lane was a distinguished member of the class of '69; he's worn his hair the same way for at least twenty-three years; and he's related to half the population of Rhode Island.

Apparently the McCarthys are one unapologetically prolific clan of Scotties. All the boys therein are nicknamed after predatory animals. Gator. Hawk. Hammerhead. Rex. Griz. I found many of them in phone books and called them. You'd think that Lane, with his insane mistrust of the press, would have them all in line by now. But they were thrilled to be grilled, unloading family secrets like loam at a sod farm.

They told me colorful stories, too, about the fun times driving their fathers' cars through farmers' fields and ruining them, and crippling guys who looked at their sisters for too long. That's how Lane's nose got that way. They told me the first car he ever owned was a tricked-out secondhand Olds 442, a monument to his prowess with everything but auto mechanics. He won it in a card game, lost his cherry in the back seat, then kissed the pink goodbye after a drag race in which he threw a rod clean through the hood.

The cousin called Griz told me Lane could drink any sailor under the table, and often did. He said Lane was arrested for disorderly conduct once, in a New Haven bar for clocking a Yalie who called him a homunculus, after Griz told him what a homunculus was.

Nowadays all the McCarthys have pretty much traded thugism for mortgages and hedonistic family gatherings. Being the official family VIP, Lane is a sought-after dinner guest. Especially this season, from the looks of things.

I see worse spare tires every day, on old winos and bus drivers and A&S shoppers. I guess our senses of scale differ. Lane apparently considered his tiny Yuletide paunch a runaway blob that could escape at any second from the three-pack undershirts he loved. Ergo, his chick-magnet costume tonight was a half-buttoned lumberjack shirt.

Up on the mezzanine, Nat and I enjoyed a gloriously unobstructed view down the front of Lane's outfit. That's when I realized his hair wasn't dyed.

We were soundly plastered and dangling over the guardrail, whooping it up. Lane buttoned his shirt up in a big hurry. For fifteen bucks, he should've taken it off.

After the concert Charlie the keyboardist and Larry the drummer stopped by our table to chat. Charlie must've been on a short leash because he hardly hit on us. Larry never hits on us, not that it never crossed his mind. But he has standards to uphold as the group's designated grown-up — something you'd never guess from all the Lycra he wears, and despite the industry rule that the drummer is usually the head Neanderthal. I know all about cavemen. I used to go with a drummer, a real guy's guy. I guess that's why he left me for one.

But Larry was okay. I knew he read books because he used big words casually. He never asked if we were models. Mostly we talked about motorcycles and the entertainment business and where to get unitards. He used to be into flat-tracking something fierce, before he became a responsible adult and started doing this.

"So glad you came to see us tonight!" he said. "We've missed you."

"Great outfits!" said Charlie. We were dressed like miners. "I mean, right, thanks for dropping by."

"Someone from Warner was here before the show," said Larry. "Said they wanna lay a new contract on us. I mean, how long has Lane been waiting to hear *that*? So of course, we can't find him anywhere. Then finally I see him and he's, like, catatonic."

I hadn't told Nat about the vending machine attack. We looked at each other and shrugged.

"Typical," I said. "So then what happened?"

"So then we sort of slapped him around 'til he could at least do the show. But the Warner dude left. And now we're going home, without a contract."

After that I didn't see Love Dinghy again for months. Bad timing, really. I was positive that little weasel winked at me from the stage that night. And that turned out to be the best thing that happened to me all winter.

Chapter 19

I turned on the TV. "The National Weather Service forecasts rain, sleet, freezing rain, snow, and hail, with a possibility of ice storms. And that's your local Action Weather outlook. Back to you, Jack Cafferty."

I turned off the TV and went back to staring at my computer. The work situation was a lot drier than the weather was. The last job I'd been paid for was the Marathon.

Every November the New York Roadrunners call and ask me to "provide support" in the New York Marathon. Every year I think no but say yes, because I need the money. Every year I kick myself afterward.

First of all, I get stuck shlepping for hours in first gear, trying not to hit thousands of "runners," some of whom take ten hours to finish the twenty-six-mile course. Seriously, you could walk faster. *Really, how is this worth anyone's time?* I'm always dying to ask someone, but don't. The whole time I'm fighting to stay upright at five mph, with orange peels stuck all over my tires and some reporter's cameras banging into my ribs, and spectators throwing water and other stuff too disgusting or indefinable to describe. Meanwhile, no-hopers are dropping all around me in piles, and I have to somehow not flatten them.

In December I wrote a feature about this noble sport for *New York* Magazine. At the last second it was whittled down to a sidebar for another feature about sweatsocks by an obese style writer who never ran for anything but a hotdog cart.

Altogether it spelled a historic season in publishing, a business that always seemed to be changing dynamically, and always in bad ways. Increasingly, my competition was the Jimmy Olsens of Generation X. Their idea of a feature involved hyperbolic scrutiny of BMX trials and Shannen Doherty. They couldn't construct sentences, or spell, or punctuate. No J-school for them! Why bother? They'd do anything to be published, including work for free. After all, they grew up in a jobless economy, unburdened by outmoded concepts like work for pay. They therefore appealed enormously to cash-strapped magazines that barely survived the market correction of '87. They also appealed to new magazines founded by ignorant cheapskates like Jean Poule. Unfortunately, that about covers all the magazines there are.

It didn't matter that my writing was better than theirs; expecting to be paid for it was automatic grounds for rejection. When I complained to Jean about my *Motorhead* pay being late, he just pointed to the toppling stack of unsolicited spec manuscripts holding open his door.

Undaunted, I pitched a hot idea about celebrity bikers to a West Coast magazine editor. She kept me on the horn, at my expense, for twenty minutes. She asked a lot of questions. I heard her pencil scratching furiously in the background. I mentally packed for a trip someplace warm. I wrapped my spiel. And then she said, "Well it's been nice talking to you, but we don't take pitches from freelancers."

I biked through frozen slush to lunch in a damned fern bar with a New York editor. She didn't give me an assignment, either. She did say I had to give her twelve bucks for my burger. She put it in her $130 Coach wallet and paid the tab with a company credit card.

Finally the *Voice* asked me to write a 2,500-word feature on motorcycle culture. Every time I talked to the editor, he changed his mind about what he wanted until it became a 1,300-word filler about sex, with a photo of a motorcycle. The day I turned it in, he quit. His replacement was a football buff who stripped the word "wops" from the part about Ducati. "It would offend people," he explained. I guess he meant the nice people who buy his paper for the classifieds seeking expert oralists and jocks with big tools.

My new editor reduced two whole columns of the piece to this:

Appropriate motorcycling attire is essential for two reasons: 1) getting dates, and 2) an excuse to get a bike. Hardcore bikers will numb you with technical jargon about aerodynamics and braking horsepower, but biking is really all about the leather. And anyone who tells you leather isn't about sex is lying.

The final 1,085-word version was hidden inside the back cover, behind hundreds of the vilest personal ads in recorded history, with a gigantic football score box smack in the middle. It appeared in the same issue that likened arms dealer Adnan Khashoggi to a Lower East Side Jew, suggested homosexuals' foreheads be branded, and called Harley owners "balls-out, knuckle-dragging, Bud-guzzling, loud-farting men."

* * * *

That January the beleaguered premiere issue of *Motorhead* was still "at the printer's." There wasn't much point in me going to Newport. I didn't even know why Jean Poule kept the office open, much less how he paid the rent. Jean owed Don DeRosa a *lot* of money.

"He keeps saying he'll get it," said Don morosely. He wanted to believe. More than that, he wanted *Motorhead* to live. It was his masterwork, his baby, his Dulcinea. The money was secondary to Don, although his wife placed it higher.

Every day Jean would tell Don the money for the printer was practically in his hand. After four months of that, Don was convinced that what Jean had in his hand wasn't something you took to the bank.

"I heard Jean on the phone with someone," said Don, who never used to eavesdrop before he met me. "Get this — he was negotiating to buy a *second* magazine for his friggin' empire! I sure hope he can work a computer."

Back at home, Darryl was too busy with his new band to broker guitars with me. I was so broke, I actually offered to write a piece for *Self* about how much fun sport biking is for women. Like I would know. "Our readers don't get humor," *Self* wrote back, "but call us if you have any story ideas on bulimia."

I hustled every connection I ever had. Finally I got commissioned to produce a pro bike racing team's press kit. It was a lot like what I used to do in advertising, except they didn't want anything too creative — "Racing Like You've Never Seen It Before!" — zzzzz. But it paid the rent, and the young racing studs were adorable. I even dated one of them until I found out he was married. At least he wasn't a musician.

We shot a bunch of totally cool action rolls at the Bridgehampton race track, with everyone throwing snowballs and crashing into stuff. I enjoyed many five-dollar expense account beers with cute guys in snug leathers competing for my attention with crash-and-burn stories. "Did I tell you about the time I did a hundred-sixty feet of San Diego Freeway on my ass?" "Oh, yeah? That's nothing! Listen to *this*..."

Being the out-of-towners, they'd say "Where to, Nona?" Then we'd noisily descend upon Harry's Bar in the Woolworth Building downtown, much to the dismay of the newspaper curmudgeons who piss that hydrant. Sometimes I'd take them uptown to the Rainbow Room, where NBC execs could eavesdrop on us. The bike dudes loved every second of it. It certainly kept me in good spirits and out of lowlife bars.

When the media kit was done, the motorguys went back West and I was at a loss for something to do. Nat wouldn't come to New York anymore, and it was too fucking cold to drive a motorcycle to Rhode Island. Darryl was getting more music work, which made him more cheerful and less available. His new band, the Mash Notes, was actually getting decent bookings.

Darryl and I went out occasionally for fun, but only on shopping trips if we had a line on something special. He didn't have time anymore to spend all day on the phone, shaking the trees for cheap guitars and rich suckers.

So I started writing a novel about a bunch of cutthroats and backstabbers in the publishing business. It was exceedingly black and not all that fictitious. "This is not a novel to be tossed aside lightly," Dorothy Parker once wrote. "It should be thrown with great force."

The working title was *Quest for Crap*. Everyone pressed for details. I told them it was a tender love story. Just as surely as taxes rise, everyone would ask, "Am I in it?" I always told them, "You could be, if you do me." Most people laughed it off.

I didn't have a real excuse to visit Rhode Island again until spring, when Nat invited me over. I learned my career wasn't the only thing that was mutating.

Chapter 20

When I wasn't looking, Nat's relationship with Bob had metastasized into a giant pile of ick. Being Bob's dreamgirl now took up all her time. That, and retirement planning.

The US Postal Service had announced sweeping layoffs of middle management, and Nat wanted to line up some options in case they showed her the door. And fine options they were. More half-assed concepts didn't exist in a JC Whitney catalog.

If she was canned, Nat got a $35,000 severance. "Securing her future" was what she called investing it in loser franchises like janitorial services and butt reduction clinics. Bob had plans for Nat's severance, too. If they paid off the note on his house, and his boat and his truck, then they'd *really* be happy. She honestly thought these schemes splendid. His dick must've been huge.

Picturing Nat deliberately pissing away her nest egg was a major barf fest, but I honestly didn't resent the time she spent with Bob. Usually I was two states away, writing. What I couldn't see couldn't gag me.

What I *did* resent was being invited to visit, and then driving 150 miles only to be told, "We'll chat later. I've gotta go get highlights." Or stopping by various boat people's houses with Nat to run errands for them before stopping by Bob's to grope and drink as if I weren't there. I started to leave when she and Bob went at it, only to remember I came in her car.

I tried to make Nat see that picking up dry cleaning and making canape trays for people with household staff isn't a shortcut up the social ladder. "You're just jealous," she said. Things weren't the same after that.

On my next and last visit, Nat and I were supposed to go to a Van Damme/Lundgren double feature but she beelined it to the Wickford marina instead. I felt like a hostage as she parked her company car in the marina lot.

In the parking spot next to ours, a boatster was climbing out of an old Mustang coupe. I had a Mustang once, a '66 289 V-8. I got it when I moved to Long Island. It was perfect. Then I moved to Brooklyn.

I learned a lot about vintage Mustangs before mine vanished. Like, what hardware was interchangeable from year to year, and what to do when you couldn't get what you needed. Pattern replacements didn't exist then. My throttle control linkage was plumbing parts and a coat hanger. You wanted parts, you improvised, or called a junkyard. Or stopped by Nona's.

"That a '66?" I asked the boat dude.

"'64 and a half." End of reply. *How odd*, I thought. Mustang owners usually can't shut up.

"All original?"

"Yep."

Right. The color looked like he was going for Candyapple Red, but it came out more like Benadryl. The ten-spoke wheels were off a '66 Shelby GT350, a car so different from this one, it never should've been called a Mustang. Sighting down one side of it made me want to buy stock in Bondo.

"Six-cylinder, huh?"

"Nope. A 302 V-8."

Whoa, pal! Not so many words at once. I'm just a chick. "Automatic, huh?" I asked.

"Yep."

I knew it! Real men drive stick. He stepped on my toes as he walked away and didn't apologize.

"Quel bozo. No way is that thing a '64 and a half," I said to Nat, who couldn't have cared less. "And 302s weren't even available until '68. They only came with manual transmissions. That rear panel's from a '67, and God knows what the rest of it was before all that body work."

Nat groaned. "Is there some point to this, besides showing off your great useless knowledge of obsolete vehicles?"

I tried to calm down. It wasn't easy. What I really wanted to do was pound her into a moist, unrecognizable mass.

"As you know, I have a great useless knowledge of many topics. I was merely trying to illustrate that your good friend over there —" I shot him the bird "— bought a bill of goods, because he's a stupid arriviste someone saw coming. Or he thinks we're a couple of airheaded broads. Or both. Anyway, my point is that he ruined a perfectly good car and he doesn't deserve to live. Nat, why do you *bother* with these assholes?"

She didn't reply. She was mesmerized by something in the near distance. It was Bob, waving from his dumb boat.

We reached the dock after a walk that took centuries. There was a lot of embarrassing groping. When they came up for air, Bob remembered to say hello to me.

He was dressed all in dung-colored Polo that I recalled Nat telling me came from a seconds outlet in Fall River. As this was an unannounced stop — unannounced to me, anyway — I was wearing Tony Lama cow-cutting boots with leather soles and heels. Bob eyed them and scowled but said nothing, just watched to see how many howling black skidmarks I'd leave on his immaculate white fiberglass deck. I knew it was killing him to shut up about it. It was the high point of my day.

This was the first time I'd been allowed so close to the fabled boat. I was surprised it was only twenty-five feet long; Nat kept calling it a yacht.

On Bob's suggestion, the three of us crammed into his tuna can of a hull. With every move I felt a sharp pain administered by his fine teak laminate cabinetry. "It's nice, huh?" Nat said to me.

Bob poured scotch over ice in giant tumblers for himself and Nat. "What can I get you, Nona? Scotch? I have bourbon." It was noon.

"Got a Coke?"

"Diet. Is that okay?"

I hate diet anything. Gad, the chemicals! "Sure," I said. I like that — guy packs away 999 calories per snort all day and hedges his bets with low-cal mixers. Too bad he didn't get cirrhosis and die already.

Bob sat down on a little wooden box. I thought it was a trash bin, but it turned out to be the engine. I watched him polish off a package of Mallomars by himself. Then he regaled us with a stultifying discourse on fuel injection. There was a fly buzzing in circles that couldn't find its way out. I felt a spiritual kinship.

"You two come back tonight. We'll take a cruise!" Bob said too enthusiastically. Just what I had in mind — slaloming through heavy marine traffic in the dark in a plastic tub steered by a drunk. "In fact," he said, "Nona can bring a date. That'll be fun!"

About as much fun as a seized piston. But the operative term here is "date." Bob obviously preferred me paired with someone who wasn't Nat. Like any card-carrying American homophobe, he was having problems with the two-babes-on-a-bike thing. By his retarded logic, I was competition. What an ass. I don't even like blonds.

I told them boats make me seasick, so Nat invited Bob and me to her house instead for dinner. I brought the biggest fruit basket I could strap to my bike. Bob arrived empty-handed. "I couldn't think of anything to bring," he actually said. How about flowers, wine, ice cream, Bob? You cheap turd.

Afterward we took Croesus to a Throwing Muses show. We all went in Nat's company car, with her driver side mirror sheared off. She wouldn't go anywhere on my bike anymore. Her boyfriend who totaled a Bobcat after a three-scotch lunch told her bikes were dangerous. I tried not to clutch her dashboard too much, and prayed she wouldn't parallel park. She parked head-in in a nearly empty lot.

I tried hard to make Bob feel he wasn't being cut out, for all the good it did. I didn't want to be in a contest, but Bob insisted. At the club there was a big three-dollar cover. In a classic fuck-you move, Moneybags paid Nat's and his entries and just kept walking.

Now, I may be a plane crash on wheels and an unrepentant blasphemer, but I still have more class in my little finger than Bob will accrue over ten lifetimes. I blew the month's Visa payment buying rounds, because Nat was under some kind of voodoo spell and Bob wasn't reaching for his wallet, either. He thanked me by pawing Nat in a corner.

Nat didn't see anything wrong with me having to talk to polluted grocery store baggers all night. Then she wanted to leave before the show was over so we could "beat the rush" out of the parking lot, the one with one other car in it. She was serious; I busted up laughing, and so did she, eventually. But she'd stopped being fun.

I called her after she moved in with Bob. He answered the phone. He said he hadn't seen her for a whole three hours, then ultra-subtly broadcast his suspicions regarding her whereabouts. "Where are you?" He was actually yelling at me.

"What do you mean, *where am I*? Like, geographically? In Brooklyn. In my kitchen. At the table. Alone. Why?" Good. Maybe Nat had a life after all. *Duh, Bob. If you can't handle it, maybe you're the one with the problem.*

"Uh, no reason. Just wondering. Well, I'll tell her to call you." She never did.

Chapter 21

"Woo woo, honey! Bet that feels good!"

"Yo, Mama — can I have a ride?"

"Ay yi yi! Lemme go wichoo!"

In New York, every street corner's a stage, and every ride is theater. Not theater for me, usually, but definitely for someone.

People who don't ride motorcycles have ludicrous notions of what the attraction is all about. It would break their hearts to know that modern motorcycles don't vibrate. Well, they don't except for Harleys, but those are soulless, leaky throwbacks to a time of war shortages and a lot of money for nothing, if you ask me. Anyway, I never experience orgasms from splitting lanes or outrunning cops or buzzing Hasids on Williamsburg street corners. However, I do get a lot of quality thinking done on my bike, especially at eighty when I can't write anything down.

Another thing that's hard to explain is how you steer a bike from the solar plexus, not the handlebar. You mesh with it, becoming an integral component of something larger than the sum of the parts. There's nothing more exhilarating than exploding through a headwind, or throwing down in a flat corner at speed without the safety net of automotive sheet metal. It's a miracle it's legal.

I just flat like to ride. My bike is sublime, tight, humming, light. At 3,500 rpm the engine starts singing. At 100 mph, a kind of sensuality overtakes you; you lie across the tank, checking under your arm for flashing lights while the air pushes at you like a wall, and you push right back to stay on. The world is reduced to gloriously colored ribbons, the rush of wind, the exhaust note.

That's why I was furious the day in March when Don DeRosa told me *Motorhead* would no longer be providing excuses for interstate road trips, the only thing it had ever been good for.

"Jean couldn't get the rabbit out of the hat," Don said, "until after it was dead."

Not that anyone was surprised. But we'd all prayed *Motorhead* would shlog along desultorily forever. Jean Poule was so immersed in his glamorous new identity as a publishing magnate, everyone assumed he'd find a backer eventually. *Motorhead* was all he had. But all Jean found was a zillion creditors eager to garnish his desktop publishing system.

When I stopped by the office for the last time, Ralph was extra busy on the phone, selling ads Jean would cash the checks from and never print. The accountant's office was empty, which meant no paychecks. There was only a pile of mail. No one was looking, so I checked it out. All bills.

Motorhead's kitchen was stripped bare. I didn't hear the familiar background noises of faxes and printers. Gone were the impassioned debates over the whereabouts of shop tools. All the tools were gone, too.

I was comforted to see Joe the art director in his office, fooling around with his Mac as usual, but then I saw the room was otherwise empty.

"Freelance work," he said when I poked my head in his door. "Already took my personal stuff home."

I asked him for a laser print of my one and only *Motorhead* column, so I could use it for a clip. Joe had set it up real nice, too, with a sexy photo of me and cool graphics. It was the best piece I never had on a newsstand.

Five minutes later Joe was disconnecting the printer it came out of, unplugging the computer it was stored in, and loading them into his car.

"Jean said I could borrow this stuff to do freelance work at home," he said, "because he owes me five months' salary."

If it was true, it was the only moneymaking idea Jean ever had. And even if it wasn't, Joe certainly deserved *Motorhead*'s Mac more than Chase Manhattan did. I helped him carry Jean's hardware to his Nissan.

As we sneaked past Jean's office, I overheard him on the phone, telling someone *Motorhead* was "at the printer's."

Chapter 22

For once it wasn't raining in Newport. I was too bummed to be excited about it, and too angry to deal with Brooklyn, so I drove to a dive Love Dinghy was playing in Westerly. A drink always smooths out life's ruts, especially when someone else pays for it.

The street in front of the club was dug up for road work, so no one could park. The club knew better than to box with City Hall and waived my cover. I waved to the Dinghies on the stage. They all nodded and smiled at me, except for Lane. Creep.

Between songs I asked Larry if the band could play "I Wanna Be Your Dog," a one-chord Iggy Pop S&M tune. Joan Jett and the Clash covered it. It wasn't really Love Dinghy's style. I just felt like hearing Lane beg to be slapped around.

"I'll check," said Larry.

They played "Under My Thumb" instead. A barrel of laughs, these guys.

I looked around at the dozen other patrons, each one more depressed than the last. You know how, during lean times, sensible people rein in their behavior — cut their losses, postpone discretionary purchases? Well, none of them was in this bar tonight. Clearly I wasn't alone in my fiery, don't-worry-be-happy downward spiral.

I ordered a tequila and paid for it with a ten-dollar bill I swiped off Jean's desk. I told the bartender to keep the change.

Microseconds too late to pay for my drink, some jerk sat down next to me and commenced shrieking the Ocean State's most overworked pick-up line into my ear.

"That's my cousin up there!" Didn't Lane's family know about birth control? "Loudest band in Rhode Island!" he yelled over Love Dinghy, bouncing in time to "Summertime Blues."

"Loud, yeah." I yelled back. "Sense of humor, no."

"What happened? They back a van inta your car?"

"If they did, they'd be the deadest band in Rhode Island."

"What, then? They stood you up? Stole your lawn furniture?"

"Assholes won't play a request."

"Oh, that. Lane's kinda uptight that way. He gets mad, anybody requests something he didn't write. Don't mean he won't *play* stuff he didn't write. He just don't want nobody askin' for it."

"Seriously, that's twisted. What does he think drunks want — art? Is he psychotic? Having Agent Orange flashbacks or something?"

"Nah. That's war stuff, right? He didn't go to no war."

"So Twinkletoes dodged the draft, huh?" Obviously. Going to war would've made a man out of him. Or a vegetable. Lane was comfortably neither.

The fact was, every guy his age had to register for selective service when he turned eighteen. Of course, everyone didn't have to *go* to Vietnam, only boys without rich daddies or serious deformities.

"Yeah, he got a college deferment or some shit. Good thing, too. He never woulda made it in Canada. Real all-American dude. Always hittin' on chicks. Beatin' on guys. Surfin'. He went off to study at UT, Austin, instead of shoot commies."

"So he wasn't a cyclops once?"

"Not before he left. But when he came back, he'd changed. He was real different."

"Meaning what?"

"Meaning he didn't wanna have fun no more. Stopped pickin' fights. Wouldn't drink. Didn't date. We didn't see him much after that."

"Life of the party, huh? Maybe he just grew up."

"You talkin' about *that* guy?"

We turned in unison to see Lane singing "You Really Got Me" and attempting a split, only his pants were too tight and it wasn't going so well.

Lane's cousin grimaced. "They got a big music department down at UT," he said, "a pretty good one, from what I hear. But Lane mostly went there to smoke dope and hang out in clubs. That's the only reason *anyone* went there then. It was hippie kamaloka."

"Well, they sure failed to make a proper flower child out of him. All those stevedore outfits are a laugh. And his house is a movie star palace."

"I know! The family calls it The Mausoleum. Thank god he's sellin' that thing!"

* * * *

I contacted a real estate agency in Groton and ended up joined at the hip to a two-hundred-pound runaway train named Agneta Franklin. I told her I was looking for a handyman special overlooking the Sound.

"I have just the thing!" Agneta said and gave me directions I didn't need.

You probably guessed this already, but a fixer-upper on Long Island Sound is not the same as a fixer-upper in Bed-Stuy. When Agneta started prying to discover how I could afford such a fine property, I told her I was a famous novelist. "Just got a monster publishing advance," I said.

"Oh, you're writing a book!" she squealed. "Can I be in it?" You betcha.

Darryl reluctantly lent me his car, which was as immaculate and unblemished as the day it was new and he wanted it to stay that way. He wouldn't even let me get into it until he'd fluffed up my hair properly. I put on my Armani suit and drove to Groton.

After the Nelda album laid its golden egg, Lane had incorporated himself in Connecticut to keep leeches from sucking on his assets. That's how I was able to get a Dun & Bradstreet report on him, and found out John Mellencamp had sued him for stealing a riff. It wasn't even a good one.

The thing was, Lane stole something from every song he ever heard. All musicians did. Especially Mellencamp. Anyway, they'd settled out of court. The best I could imagine, what with all his other recent financial setbacks, Lane was selling his house before a judge could seize it.

When Agneta and I arrived, Lane wasn't home. We probably would've gone at each other like pumas if he was, leaving Agneta very confused.

She and I passed the Range Rover, still blocking the driveway. Agneta unlocked the garage door and we went inside. On one wall hung expensive mechanic's tools, safe under a thick blanket of dust. Also in the garage were a white Shelby Cobra, a gold XKE Jag, and the world's biggest oil stain. The cars looked more like investments than rides. I could just hear Lane's accountant: "Go forth my son, and appreciate."

We went inside the house. I caught my breath. Agneta thought this was a good thing.

The exterior left a lot to be desired, for sure. But it was positively alluring compared with the interior.

First of all, it looked like a decorator had attempted an intervention, long ago, without bothering to ask Lane what he liked. Granted, I knew next to nothing about what he *did* like, but I knew more about Lane than Lane's proctologist, and I was sure poisonous foliage wasn't on the list. The living room was a riot of hibiscusy drapes, gardenia-covered upholstery, and wall-to-wall orchid carpeting that gave me a shock every time I touched a doorknob.

131

A classy nonbotanical counterpoint was the bucket of empty beer bottles. The glass tables were covered with fingerprints and condensation rings from dripping glasses. Ugly 1950s French provincial cabinets were loaded with by-the-pound books and lava lamps. I was positive the garbage was Lane's, but I couldn't picture him specifying Venus flytrap slipcovers any more than I could see him reading *Doctor Zhivago*.

Agneta and I hacked through the jungle to the kitchen. It was peculiarly antiseptic and uncluttered, for a slob's. I peeked into a cabinet. Alongside stolen barware were countless boxes of instant food. Mix with water, microwave, toast-n-go. Soup, oatmeal, pudding, Pop-Tarts, canned icing. Yech.

Oddly, or maybe not, the rest of the house resembled a Motel 6. No moldings, no baseboards, white-painted sheetrock walls, commercial fixtures swiped from city projects. There were water stains on the ceiling where the roof leaked.

There was one thing you could never accuse Lane of, and that was having any style.

Agneta and I pushed on. There were four bedrooms in this house once, before Lane cobbled two together into a ramshackle studio — always a desirable feature in a family home.

So far, the studio was the only interesting room in the whole house. It was exactly what I imagined the inside of Lane's head looked like.

Covering one whole wall were shelves of vinyl albums and CDs strewn haphazardly, as if someone had ransacked them. Nearby was a beat-up couch with a thousand stains you could smell across the room. Other thoughtful touches included the makeshift soundproofing everywhere but the floor: egg cartons, fiberglass batting, quilt stuffing, styrofoam. "But you can fix that!" said Agneta brightly.

The studio was tastefully accessorized with amps, speakers, mics, recording equipment, miles of tangled cable, a wormy Spinet, piles of T-shirts and sneakers, a zillion guitars, leaking beanbag chairs, a dead dumbcane plant, empty beer cans, full ashtrays, and unwieldy stacks of motorcycle magazines and sheet music.

Agneta sighed. Lane was either damned cocky or real stupid to let her show his house like this. Its only redeeming value was one of the guitars in the studio. It was a Broadcaster. Darryl would come in his pants if he saw it.

The Broadcaster was the first production solid-body electric ever made. Fender built a few around 1950 before changing the name to Telecaster, after Gretsch made a big stink about owning the Broadcaster name. I'd only seen them in pictures. Darryl spoke of them reverently. The bodies weren't contoured like newer Teles, making them harder to play, but they make a deep thumping sound and are ultra-desirable. In good original condition, a Broadcaster was easily worth $12,000.

I wanted to look more closely, but Agneta steered me away. "Let me show you the bathrooms!"

I wondered if I'd gotten shooed from the studio because of the mess, or on orders from Lane to keep tire-kickers away from his precious crap. For a guy hard put to express anything personal, he sure didn't have any trouble ordering people around. First he had his teen gang, then his band, then roadies and toadies, and now he had Multiple Listings to harass. My guess was he's the type who doesn't share his toys. Doesn't even want you to look at them. But I guarantee you this: Lane McCarthy uses yellow toilet paper with little green smiley faces.

Sitting on his bathroom counter was a twelve-ounce jar of Elizabeth Arden 8-Hour Cream. His medicine cabinet hovered just beyond my reach, like unattainable treasure. I wanted to check out his brands of expectorants and meth, his big stash of gelatin pills, but Agneta was in the way. I imagined Lane with 8-Hour Cream glopped all over his face and laughed.

Agneta was unphased. She finished her monologue on the tile layer's art and preceded me out of the bathroom; I took the opportunity to dip Lane's toothbrush in the toilet.

So far the only thing special about this house was its affirmation of the many Lanes: corn pone Lane owned the jungle room; bat radar Lane ruled the garage that time forgot and the kitchen; and Heartland Lane belonged to the studio and Motel 6.

Agneta didn't seem bothered that I was more interested in the decorations than the house. It was so relentlessly seedy, I figured this happened to her every time she showed it. Most people would at least paint their home before putting it on the market. But Lane wasn't most people.

There were no fancy plants around, no zany expensive toys, no signs of the undocumented household help I knew he could afford. The family room was empty except for a seven-foot stereo TV. He probably needed that to see himself on his music videos.

There were no family photos or sentimental keepsakes on display except for Lane's multi-platinum award, and framed posters hawking his appearances back when Radio City and the Hollywood Bowl still wanted him. He'd hung a few photos of the band at the RIAA ceremony. They had more hair then and less lard, otherwise they looked the same. There was also a framed, full-length publicity shot of Lane wearing a pouty expression, holes in his pants, and an outsized boner. Darryl would've accused him of showboating and airbrushed it out.

Instead of big-eyed urchin prints in keeping with the motor inn theme, there was an autographed Mellencamp poster signed "To E, Keep on trucking." I didn't know what to make of a bizarre doorstop that looked like a dehydrated fruitcake.

Agneta dragged me away to the bedrooms, both as clean and stripped down as the studio was disheveled. The trash cans were free of cigarette butts and bloody tissues and crumpled paper with handwritten lines of poetry ending in try/cry/pass me by. There were no slippers under the beds, no dogeared *Guitar Player*s on the nightstands. I didn't even see an alarm clock. I'd never have guessed which bedroom was Lane's, were it not for one tiny clue.

One of the bedrooms had a little drop-front desk that was open. On it was a phone, and next to that lay an antique silver cigarette case. It had a Victorian repousse design of partridges and hokey swirly things. In this vast wasteland of facelessness, it stuck out like an eyepatch.

I couldn't imagine Lane in some faggy antique store going, "Oh, I must have that!" It had to have been a gift. A gift that meant something to him, if he'd bothered to keep it.

Agneta turned away to natter about the view. I put the cigarette case in my pocket.

"Show me the closets," I said when she turned back around. There was a bank of them along one wall. She opened one section with a flourish. "Voila!" oinked Agneta.

It was full of women's clothing. So, Lane did have some long-suffering girlfriend after all. I was curious and disappointed at the same time, because I'd covered that ground in my research and turned up nothing — never saw her, never found marriage records, never heard any talk, not even from Lane's diarrhea-mouthed kin. Plus there was only the one toothbrush in the bathroom. Not that that was significant. A fundamental tenet of rock'n'roll life is that wives don't count. They're as welcome as snipers at gigs, narcs at afterparties, a barrel of snakes in the studio. The last one who got in was Yoko, and everyone knows how *that* ended up. They probably aren't even allowed to brush their teeth.

I wondered why musicians are allowed to breed in the first place. Whenever I went anywhere with Darryl's bands, they pretended I was the furniture. If I tried to help carry their equipment, they'd grab it away even though I was bigger than all of them. And I wasn't even technically a spouse. Poor Lane's girlfriend. He probably locked her in the basement. Agneta wouldn't show me that.

Well, it must be real romantic living with a smoking singer who hacks up phlegmballs all day and chains you to the boiler. As Agneta extolled the homey virtues of Lane's vampire love nest, I made a mental note for later to find a way into his cellar. At the moment I had a more pressing curiosity.

I ached to go through his drawers. Odds were they were full of briefs and wifebeater shirts, but you never knew. Darryl left his drawers open once and I saw freon and poppers. I loathed myself for not having planned some diversion to get Agneta out of there.

As if on cue, suddenly there were vehicular noises from the driveway.

"Oh, good!" Agneta said. "You'll get to meet the seller! I'll be right back."

For a long second I was numb. I could think of nothing I wanted to do less than meet the frigging seller. I glanced at Lane's dresser again and overcame an adrenalin rush that would've given any normal person a coronary.

Lane's top two drawers were full of BVDs, white crew socks, and tank shirts. White socks, Jesus! Also his girlfriend's underwear, playing cards, a Swatch that stopped running eons ago, twelve classic examples of leather jewelry from the '70s, a loaded Sig Sauer 9 mm automatic pistol, a bunch of terry wristbands, a wallet-size photo of Dion, a bunch of old *Sports Illustrated* swimsuit issues, a pair of hopelessly outre tortoiseshell eyeglasses, and a hair dryer warranty. The bottom drawer contained six pressed, carefully folded pairs of Levi 512s with twelve painstakingly clipped holes in the knees.

An entertaining notion struck me as I defiled Lane's sanctuary. While he was in no way effeminate or androgynous, it was somehow impossible for him to suppress his lunar side. There were wickedly distaff elements to him — the coyness, the slavish dedication to maintaining his body shape. The jewelry. The high heels. He wore contact lenses out of sheer vanity. His retro hairdo screamed unisex salon. *Here's your gown, Mr. McCarthy. Will you be having a facial with us today?*

He'd make some ballbuster a wonderful girlfriend.

Just then I heard a door slam. I shoved the drawers closed and whirled around as Agneta exploded back into the room.

"False alarm! Yard man!" Agneta announced cheerily.

"So — how much for the house?"

"A million two, but that's just the asking price. You can dicker."

I almost choked. *A million two? For THIS?*

"Throw in the cars and we'll talk."

Back in Darryl's Toyota, I pulled out Lane's cigarette case and opened it. In it was a Polaroid of the ugliest woman I ever saw. She was wearing a tie-dye dress and granny glasses. She had love beads and legs like a weimaraner.

I started laughing out loud. Why would anyone with that much dough *want* to play in rock'n'roll hellholes, live with a bunch of Methusalahs out of a trunk, and date skanks?

Either Lane was one taco short of a combination, or he had more balls than Wimbledon.

Chapter 23

July in New York is delightful: ninety degree heat, ninety percent humidity, ninety million rats. July is also when the human population doubles, as the snowturds emerge from the sewers to live on the sidewalks. And if you drive a motorcycle with an air-cooled engine, it overheats on your gridlocked trip out of the ghetto in search of air conditioning.

I was in a perfectly chilled Brooklyn Heights newsstand, contentedly reading magazines I had no intention of buying when the peace was disrupted by a dumb-off across the street. Black-and-whites were everywhere, wailing. Cops poured into the Gap to subdue robbers threatening pocket Ts at gunpoint.

On my way over to check it out, I was distracted by a frock in the Gap's window. I don't usually shop the Gap. I'm a little too jagged around the edges for them. Today, however, the cops had their situation, and I had mine. It was short, black, and sleeveless, and made out of rubber or something. When the police left to chase a woman with an Uzi who kept screaming "I didn't do nothin'!", I went inside. Huzzah — no line for the dressing room. The dress fit like a prophylactic. I stuffed it in my shirt and went home.

Later I was out on my hot sidewalk, roasting my way through a valve adjustment, when my phone rang. Normally I can't hear anything outside besides automatic weapon fire and bloodcurdling screams, but today I'd left my front door open, hoping an editor at *Rolling Stone* would call between spliffs. I was so desperate for work that I'd actually pitched a story to *Stone*, despite the Del Shannon debacle. Kurt Cobain already agreed to an interview. *Stone* would probably just steal my idea for Hunter Thompson, but if I didn't try at all I'd get nada.

I scooped up the tools and valve covers strewn about so they wouldn't become a neighborhood donation. Then I went hauling ass up the stoop with all of it to grab the phone before whoever it was could hang up.

It was Darryl. "You sound out of breath. You okay? What's going on?"

"I'm writing a treatment for a screenplay."

"Oh, great. Something you can *really* cash in on. What's it about?"

"A blind paraplegic orphan struggles against fate to become the first black CEO of a Fortune 100 company. Hey, you called just in time. I got a technical question. Is the opposite of frontal nudity *backal nudity*?"

Darryl sighed. "How's *Quest for Crap* going?"

"Not bad. I have fourteen chapters finished."

"Really! Am I in it yet?"

"Dunno. Have you done me yet?"

"Maybe later. Don't forget, I'm cutting your hair tonight, and then we're going bowling. Listen, tomorrow I'm playing blues in Rhode Island. Wanna go with?"

"Sure. Okay if I wear a dress?"

Several beats went by without him.

"Darryl? You still there?"

"Yeah. Dress. Sure. Why not?"

It was a new concept for him. He handled it pretty well.

"You'll keep goons away from me, right?" I asked him. This was a reversal of our usual arrangement. I was full of new concepts today. Poor Darryl.

"Yeah, yeah. You meet me there, okay? I rented a truck. Gotta pick it up, pack it up, and be in Providence at five to set it up." He gave me directions and hung up.

I was glad I didn't have to go in the truck with him. He's not a great driver, being a New Yorker. Besides, it was hot and I wanted to cool off. Always a good excuse to ride my bike.

The next day I chuffed over to Galo on Madison for Italian footgear to complement my trashy new dress. Before the cops could ticket my bike parked on the sidewalk, I scored some slim, black, calf-high boots with pointy toes and spike heels — just your basic go-go-fuck-me shoe. Perfect for interstate travel.

The only other time I rode my bike in a dress, some guinea chased me all the way across Bleecker, and my skirt wasn't even blowing up over my head. So that evening I smothered my new rubber dress under Army mechanic's coveralls.

Thus prepared, I threw the Beemer vigorously all the way to Darryl's gig. Lately I'd taken to tossing it around like the small, light bike I ought to have but never will.

People say Beemers don't flick, but mine does. Of course, this necessitates hanging way off the seat in situations where just throwing down any other bike would suffice. That's because of my saddle's classic German styling: high and straight and hard as a diving board. Flicking's a whole lot of work for not a lot of payoff, but it keeps me from getting fat. I'm not shaped like a guy below the collarbone, but the way I usually dress, who could know?

I arrived for Darryl's gig early, smashing the sound barrier all the way. Darryl had been keeping an eye out for me. He ran out to the street as I rolled up.

"Wait'll you see *this*!" he called out, panting. "I bring every piece of equipment we could possibly need. I rent a truck big enough to haul every space heater in Lefrak City. And the stage here — it's the size of a postage stamp! The whole club's the size of *two* postage stamps!"

"Think of it as an investment in your career. You're the feature act, right?"

"Yeah, right? We're the opening act. For the Spasmodics."

At that exact moment I dropped my coveralls, which didn't help his condition any. He unsuccessfully pretended not to gawk while I bent down to lock my helmet to the wheel. I put the coveralls in a saddlebag and pushed Darryl toward the club.

As we walked in, I heard someone gasp. Everyone was looking — at my guns, at my fuck-me shoes, at the sexpot bedhead haircut Darryl had given me.

Had we been in New York, I'd look like every other woman in the room, and half the men. Not here. Everyone was staring at me, following me — especially the ones who saw me pull up on a steaming Teutonic hulk of unladylike technology. It was hopeless. All I could do was sigh, and try to calm Darryl down.

Darryl kept zombies off me, like he promised, for about two minutes. He certainly had his work cut out for him. Half the men wanted a date. Some of the women asked where I got the dress. Most of them wanted to fight. Darryl was visibly relieved when he had to go and play.

He wasn't kidding about the size of the club. It was way too small and intimate for my liking, much less for Darryl's band's equipment to fit onto the stage along with the Spasmodic's equipment and Darryl's band. But they were hotter than tar in July.

Darryl is genuinely talented, unlike most guitarists who are quick to announce they're more fabulous than Jesus before doing their awful Jeff Beck imitations. For forty-five nerve-racking minutes his band tried not to elbow each other as Darryl played heartbreaking blues on a $10,000 Les Paul for nincompoops who'd paid to hear goth crap.

The manager told Darryl they were too loud, so they cranked everything up all the way, seeing as how they probably weren't coming back. The Spasmodic's fans eventually succeeded in booing Darryl's band off the stage.

The Spasmodics piled onto the stage to thundering applause. They were a predictably derivative metal act, all studs and spurs and bad haircuts. Darryl and I couldn't figure out why the Spasmodics weren't opening for Darryl. Their first song sucked so loud, I split halfway through.

Darryl didn't want to stay either, but his equipment was scattered and his band was drinking instead of packing. I hung around while he hustled his stuff out of the Spasmodic's royal way. I wanted to help him load out, but he said it would just cause a riot.

So Darryl had to load the rental truck by himself, and guard it until the Spasmodics got done using his amps for launch pads. And after that, he'd have to settle a slight misunderstanding with management regarding the misappropriation of door receipts.

"Arthur," he said to me between trips in and out of the club.

"What?"

"The state hair of Rhode Island. Arthur. Listen, I don't have time to babysit you, and I don't want your help. Go home." I think he just didn't want me to see him cry.

I went out to my bike and started removing the ten million locks I always clamp onto it when we're apart. I was bent over fetchingly with my butt in the air when a familiar voice spoke to it.

"Are we out slumming tonight, darling?"

I whipped around to see Larry Ochowitz, the drummer of Love Dinghy.

"Hello, Luv! What brings you to this little corner of hell?" he asked cheerily.

I kissed his cheek and told him how Darryl and I had just been dissed off the face of the earth.

"Cogito, ergo dim sum," he said. "You're way too marvelous for these cretins anyway."

"And you're here for, what? The salt air?"

"Well," he said with mock enthusiasm, "We came to see the mighty Spasmodics."

"They already started. Too bad. You missed the good show."

"Figures. I heard a really hot New York roots band was opening for the Spazzos. So I was glad the trip wouldn't be a total loss." He made a pffffft sound, the puff of air blowing up his thin bangs. "Metal's not exactly my favorite kind of music. But a couple of Spazzos are Lane's cousins. He wanted to see them. Kind of. Mainly, he wanted to be seen seeing them. And since he goes for that whole fucking entourage thing, we all hadda go."

I looked around and saw no one.

"They're all still in the van," he said, "arguing over who's gonna walk in front."

Larry had quickly volunteered to be the driver ("Carpe carp," he said), and as such was exempt from flower girl duty. "Driver's gotta park the van after everyone goes in," he said. "Hardship tour of duty."

He and I leaned against a graffiti-covered phone booth, settling into a discussion of the new Guzzis. I updated him on my ex-job at the late, lamented *Motorhead*. He mentioned he was a fan of my work, and complimented me on my most savage articles. I was thrilled.

"So what're you up to now?" he said. "Writing anything mean?"

"Yes! A whole book."

"About motorcycles?"

"It's a tender love story. With motorcycles. And cheeseburgers. And the righteous wreaking vengeance on the wicked. It's called *Quest for Crap*."

He gave me a sly grin. He was about to ask if he was in it when Charlie the keyboard king appeared out of thin air, like a falling brick. Charlie didn't want to see the Spasmodics even more than Larry didn't. His eyes were bugging out at my dress.

None of the Dinghies knew I could do the girl thing. Charlie shoved his hands into his pockets, then pulled them out again, then jammed them back in. He opened his mouth. Nothing came out.

"Charlie," Larry said just in time, "Some townie followed Lane into the men's room with a camcorder. Go throw up a smokescreen so he can pee and get outta there."

I never saw Lane get out of the van. Charlie left obediently, albeit reluctantly. I'd have to remember I owed Larry a big one.

He was smooth at pretending to not look where he shouldn't. Or at least, he wasn't looking when I was looking back. I wondered whether he was the coolest kid in school twenty years ago, or the one who got wedgied.

Larry was curious about the skillset required to ride a bike in a dress. "I've done plenty of crazy stunts on bikes, and I've worn lots of stupid costumes, but I can't say I've ever done *this*," he said. "Got any tips?"

I turned away to pull the ugly-ass coverall out of my saddlebag, so I could demonstrate the fine art of slummage. While I was fiddling with the luggage lock, I heard a third voice behind me.

"What's going on? C'mon. We gotta go in now!"

It was Lane's voice, talking more or less directly to my ass.

"Okay," said Larry, "in a second. I'm just saying goodbye to Nona."

I abandoned the lock and stood, all 5'12" of me in those damned boots, to face all 5'6" of Lane. He must've been wearing lifts. That wasn't the funny part. Wait for it.

Lane didn't run.

"Lane, Nona's writing a book," said Larry, gallantly trying to jumpstart a civil three-way conversation that was dead before it began.

"Great," mumbled Lane. "We're gonna miss the show."

Bat radar Lane just stood there, scowling. He didn't acknowledge me the whole time he was male bonding with Larry. He'd never talked to me at all after we met in Jersey. Why start now? I could get the wrong impression, think he was human or something.

I would've been angry if it didn't fascinate me to watch him give orders to everyone, especially Larry. Larry has a good four inches on Lane and a Flaming Maggots From Hell tattoo.

"Sorry, Nona," Larry said to his shoe boots. He was some kind of saint to put up with this shit for decades. That, or very deluded.

Anyway, I didn't budge. Over their shoulders I could see Alvin and Wizard on the other side of the street, arguing and hitting each other as they ducked into the club.

Lane sighed and ran his hand through his hair. He closed his eyes, then pressed his palms into his forehead. Little silvery whiskers were just starting to sprout on his chin.

"I had three hours of sleep last night. Just go in there and find me a seat," he said to Larry.

Larry said goodnight to me and departed. I presumed Lane would up and follow him, having spent the last year and change demonstrating he had less than no use for me. Instead, he turned to face me.

"So what's this book about?" he said. "Am I in it?"

Chapter 24

The list of men who've warmed my passenger seat is, like the men themselves, very short. There was the erstwhile Stacy. And Darryl. The pro racing team thought it was a hoot. So did the photojournalists I toted around the New York Marathon, but they don't technically count as men. A cute bass player I dated for a while was game, until his friends found out. The mere thought of it gives most men apoplexy. And then there's Lane.

"You ever done this before?" I asked him. No reply.

"Don't use the exhaust for a handgrip. Don't put your feet down before I do." *Like they'd reach.* "Don't help me hold the bike up. Do exactly what I do. If I lean, you lean."

He nodded at my zipper as I climbed into my coveralls. This required folding the hem of my rubber dress nearly up to my pubes. Lane observed wordlessly but with great interest.

I did a quick mod to my bike. I always adjust the suspension for a passenger. I was merely being considerate when I asked him how much he weighs.

"One fifty," he answered with a straight face. I mentally subtracted fifteen.

"You little squiff," I muttered.

"What?" he said.

"I said, 'I like the spring stiff'."

I finished adjusting the monoshock. We got some things from his van, smushed them into my saddlebags, and took off into the night.

Most of Rhode Island is sparsely populated quicksand bogs. Unlike what I was used to in New York, I'd never seen anything here, alive or otherwise, to collide with — no wildlife, or escaped farm animals, or abandoned cars. Nothing. They don't bother making people buy car insurance in Rhode Island. They don't even have a helmet law.

Lane thought it would be cool to blast unfettered through the blackness, salty wind whipping our grey streaks. And so we rode bareheaded, an activity I generally equate with suicide. I'm reckless, not stupid.

So this was my first time riding without a helmet. It was also the first time I could actually understand a passenger talking to me. Finally — I'd solve the mystery of whether Lane was polysyllabic! Anyway, that's what I hoped.

His story about a short-lived romance with British steamers shed no light whatsoever. He told me how he'd owned some pre-unit Triumphs, years ago. They were the only superbikes around then with seats low enough for his feet to reach the ground.

"I got tired of them crapping out at night in the middle of nowhere," he yelled into the wind, "so I sold them to Billy Joel."

Lane did use one trisyllable word, shitforbrains. Mostly he was preoccupied with maintaining a handhold and keeping my hair out of his face.

As we cruised along I-95, something flew out into the road in front of us. Assuming it was some of that outlaw poultry I thought didn't exist, Lane screamed "LOOK OUT!" in my ear.

I swerved. I recovered. I gave Lane my elbow. The thing in the road was a plastic bag.

He laughed into the wind and said something like "Mrff nud fucking tourists garf. Hahahahahaha!"

That was pretty much the extent of our convo. We took Route 4 and then headed south on Ten Rod Road, two lanes of paving perfection connecting us to Wickford like blacktop umbilical cord.

Nothing's better on a summer night than a motorcycle ride. Well, almost nothing. And 2 a.m. is the optimum time to visit the marina, when the boat people are home in bed with headaches.

The place certainly seemed deserted enough. We strode unchallenged to Bob's boat.

"You like this thing?" I said to Lane. "Belongs to my good buddy, Bob."

Lane made a face. "Why don't these swells lock up their stuff?" he said.

I gave him the tour. We started by strolling the length of the boat. Seconds later we were at the other end, checking out some massive hull scrapes.

"Here's where Bob ran aground at Block Island," I said.

I pointed to a crack in the fiberglass with strings coming out. "Here's where he creamed the dock."

We struggled up the side and into the molded white deck with our two-inch heels. I showed him a fondue-burner-shaped scar. "Bob's birthday."

"Wasn't this a boat once?" said Lane.

"Bob's renovating it. He's on a liquid diet."

I explained about the scotch and the boat people, about how Bob had convinced my oldest friend that I was a foaming-at-the-mouth lesbian so she'd spend more time with him and not me.

"If his plan worked," Lane groused, "then maybe he's right."

"Very funny. See, you'd *never* say that about Bob if you actually knew him. He wouldn't recognize a dyke if she drove a Fat Boy over him. He's too drunk and stupid. And full of shit. Let's just say Bob has culture issues."

"Well, he can't be all bad. He's letting us use his boat."

Lane inspected a fist-sized hole in the cabin wall, then jiggled the door handle. It was locked. Just as well; the liquor cabinet was probably hoovered dry anyway.

We collapsed in the sunken floor of Bob's monocoque deck. We found the collection of vintage compasses he was drunk or stupid enough to leave in a storage bench, and proceeded to take them apart.

Lane wasn't saying much as he made little piles of prisms and magnets, so I attempted small talk. Not my forte, I'm afraid.

"Do you read?"

"Do I have to?"

"Not books. Magazines. The pablum of the masses. *Rolling Stone. Premiere. The Star.*"

"I drink. A lot. I listen to music. Sometimes someone drives me somewhere. I play my guitar. Someone drives me home. I go to bed. I don't have time to read."

"That's too bad. I read everything. I have to. The world of magazine publishing is my very special personal hell."

"You're a lucky woman. Got any beer?"

"No. But *you've* got lots of friends in publishing. I wrote this really great article about you, and no editor would touch it because you wouldn't give me an interview..."

At that, his eyes suddenly narrowed; his hands clenched. "You brought me here to talk about *that*?"

Oops. Before my eyes he became someone else, someone angry and trapped. The other, relatively charming Lane was gone.

"Is that all you want — an *interview*? I'll give you a fucking interview!" He slapped both palms on the deck and drew up his knees, as if to lunge.

"No! Wait a minute," I said, scrambling backward. On the laundry list of everything I wanted from him, an interview was lower than last.

He paused, waiting to see how I'd screw this up even more.

I decided to feed his overweening ego.

"I was just going to say, I had to do more research than usual to sell the piece, because I didn't get the interview." He squinted at me, waiting for any reason to pounce. "And I heard a lot of interesting things about you. During my research. For the article."

"Like what?" He was still pissed, but he sat back down. Arrogant little shit.

"Like, you got out of the draft by wearing lace panties to the physical."

Abruptly, Lane started laughing.

"I also heard you don't have a sense of humor," I said.

"*Me*? Who told you *that*? Bob?"

"No. Bob said you're a great kisser."

He totally cracked up.

I'd never seen Lane laugh before. He had an obscenely big and sensual mouth, now making the most beautiful smile I'd ever seen on a man.

He relaxed again, stretching out his legs with his feet next to me. I pulled off his boots and was surprised that he didn't fight me. He thought I was being friendly. I was actually trying to slow him down in case he came after me again, the next time things went horribly wrong. *Just* try *running on molded fiberglass in your socks, Lane. Your* stupid white *crew socks.* Christ.

I glanced at his boots then, just to make sure I hadn't tossed them someplace that would make him mad. They were far enough away to give me a head start, but close enough to see inside. One had a big wad of currency crushed up in it. What kind of freak deliberately ruins something you can exchange for beer?

We sat there for a while, me rubbing his feet, he telling me the spellbinding history of transistors. Had transistor not been a three-syllable word, I still couldn't have stopped looking at him. In the dark his face was like a little boy's, so open it made him seem innocent despite jeans so tight and weft-free, he had to carry his keys in a fanny pack.

So there I was, finally getting accustomed to Lane talking in complete sentences and laughing, adjusting to the smell of his feet and him appreciating a punchline, when of course he went and ruined everything.

"I gotta ask you something," he said.

"Sure. Anything. What?"

And then he said something no sane man would *ever* say to a prone woman in a rubber dress who was checking out his pants.

"Don't take this the wrong way. But, are you gay?" Way to go, Buzzkill.

"Just a minute, let me check. Nope."

"What about Nat?"

"Nat?! Are you *kidding* me? Jesus Christ, no! Not gay!"

Ugh. Could tonight possibly get any worse? Yes! How about this: Lane suggests threesome; Nona is arrested for murder.

"How about you?" I asked him, disgusted. "Nailed any guys?"

"No." He looked hurt. *Fuck you, Lane.*

"Hey, I gotta ask *you* something. Do you need a ladder to shave? A phone book to see over the dashboard?" He just stared at me, stunned. "You're truly the world's biggest turd! I thought this was a date. Gad, don't you even know any pick-up lines?" Too bad he couldn't say he was Lane McCarthy's cousin.

His face hardened then, and he clammed up. His silence was so complete I could hear marine life swimming around us. I heard a tiny bell on a buoy a mile away.

Finally he drew a breath. "You're the scariest woman I ever saw," he said, reaching for his boots.

"*That's* a line?"

"It's the truth. All those skinned animals you wear. And you're always fighting with someone. You got a mouth like a Veg-o-Matic."

"And that makes you, what? The national treasure?"

"Christ — you're seven feet tall!"

"I'm only six-six in flats."

"And that friggin' bike! How'm I supposed to compete with a hundred-mile-an-hour vibrator with five speeds?"

"That's a hundred and ten miles per hour. And it doesn't vibrate. And if I'm so bloody awful, what're you doing here?" I expected him to blame it on Dos Equis, but he surprised me again.

"You jumped me — in public, in broad daylight. I thought it meant something."

"It was at night, in the back hallway of a hellhole. It meant something, alright — you, wrong place, wrong time." He looked genuinely crushed. "Okay, I apologize. I'm sorry for calling the Lone Star a hellhole. It's more like an armpit..."

He jumped up before I could finish. I pushed him back down.

"Yo, Einstein — lemme explain things so that even *you* can understand them." I grabbed the boots from his hands. "One: I like my bikes fast, and my men slow." I threw the boots aside. "Two: I've got a crush on you like ten tons of prime backfill."

Turns out his cousin was wrong about the pole up Lane's ass. It didn't take much to loosen it up. Nat was wrong about Lane, too. His butt was smooth as a Testarosa bucket. And he didn't have on lace panties, either. He didn't have on any panties at all.

Seconds later Bob's boat was thumping the dock like a Dee Dee Ramone bass line.

"It's got a good beat," announced Lane, without missing one. "I give it a nine."

Bob was unlikely to notice a couple hundred more dents, but a voice from another boat yelled at us to shut up. There probably was someone on every tub parked there, watching us in abject horror. We were laughing so hard at the thought, we didn't know how long the security geezer had been standing there.

"What're you doing?" he said, like it wasn't obvious.

"Collecting bacteria samples," I said. We broke into new fits of laughter.

The guard just stared stonily at us, unamused by two buck-naked Boomers desecrating an exclusive recreational facility. He waited for a better explanation.

Lane located his ATM boot without disengaging and pulled a sweaty fifty from it. He threw the wadded-up bill at the rent-a-cop. "Bob sent us," Lane said to him.

We buried our faces in each others' necks and started laughing again, kicking the hollow deck with our feet. The booming sound echoed over the marina. The guard bent down to retrieve the fifty, muttered something about damned kids today, and disappeared.

The night air was damp and briny-smelling as we lay in a traction-defying slime of bodily fluids and dew. I was exhausted and limp. Lane wasn't.

"Okay," I said, "but this time, slow down."

"You're the boss," he said, and hammered me until I screamed. The dock was a shambles. Ship radios crackled all around us.

"It's so noisy here," Lane said distractedly, playing with my hair. "Music would be nice. Where'd you put the boom box?"

I couldn't remember one. "I thought you had it."

"No problemo. I got this covered. Tell me what you wanna hear."

"'I Wanna Be Your Dog'."

"*Why*? It's a one-note punk song about doggy sex."

"So what? Jesus — what do I have to *do* with you to get a request played?"

And with that, Lane sang it for me. I didn't even think he knew it. He wrung it into a country arrangement, making his voice break over poignant sentiments about canine disobedience. During the bridge he made kennel sounds where pedal steel guitar would've been. Out of the night a dog howled back.

Nobody bothered us again. I think they were afraid.

But if Lane was nuts, at least he wasn't dangerous. Chronically indefatigable, maybe. If he really got only three hours of sleep the night before, you'd never know it. The whole time he had his head between my legs I was thinking what a waste that I never made more sapphic friends. That was before I totally lost control and knocked Bob's anchor into Narragansett Bay.

Funny, but Lane never did make that orgasm face like he does onstage, even though he had countless opportunities. He was more subtle with a small audience, and a lot messier.

"Put your boots on," he finally said.

"Huh?"

"Boots. Now. Just do it."

We stood on Bob's deck in the moonlight, wearing nothing but glistening slime and leather-soled roach-chasers. Then Lane taught me every Dion move he knew.

* * * *

Rhode Island is really more like a big town than a small state. The next day's *Providence Journal* contained the following item:

> NORTH KINGSTOWN: A Cranston couple arrived at the Wickford Harbor Yacht Club yesterday to find their cabin cruiser vandalized by trespassers, who reportedly left behind more than they took. The white deck was covered with indelible black marks of unknown origin, several Beacon packing blankets, and a stuffed armadillo. Marina security claimed to have thwarted a robbery, but offered no further details pending an investigation. The boat's owner requested anonymity. No suspects have been charged. The boat's anchor is still missing. Anyone with information is asked to call the Wickford police.

Chapter 25

My coach turned back into a pumpkin, like it always does, after which Lane didn't show up on my stoop with azaleas or Dos Equis or anything. I knew better than to expect grand gestures of affection from him. What I didn't expect was him not showing up at all. He didn't even call.

Not that I'm so great at relationships myself. I'm aloof and solitary, basically because I believe everyone else is an asshole. I don't need a better half to validate me, or any other kind. But I'm not a total philistine, either. I send thank-you notes. I buy rounds. I go on second dates. I apologize when I'm wrong, which is just about never.

Lane, on the other hand, was antisocial for reasons I didn't understand. I could cast nets forever and never figure him out. All I know is, you can't change people. You can x-ray them, but you can't rearrange their organs.

Anyway, I had better things to do. "It serves me right," said Dorothy Parker much better, "for putting all my eggs in one bastard." Lane could go fuck himself.

Naturally, the instant I wrote him off, information about him started hurling itself at me. Great, steaming, cacophonous gobs of information. And the more I found out, the less I wished I knew.

The first payload came as I comawalked through a press party for a big-budget dud film I agreed to review. I wore my navy Anne Klein blazer and grey slacks. Yes, I have stuff like that. I combed my hair. Gotta look nice for the Plaza, right? Mistake number one.

All the media toadies at this thing wore name tags, including me. Mistake number two. A doughy *Greenwich Times* hack I didn't want to meet introduced himself.

"Hi. I'm Howard. Big fan. Genius piece in the *Voice*!" It was about decorating your house with junk. Writing for the *Voice* — mistake number three.

Howard and I started out lying to each other about our success in publishing; five minutes later we were both confessing we were just there for free seafood and mimosas and to see if Mel Gibson was going bald. He said the *Greenwich Times* had busted him down to nightlife reporter. To someone with zero job, this didn't sound so bad.

I congratulated Howard on still having a gig, mentioning my unpaid stint at *Motorhead* and my failed investigative feature about a certain luckless Rhode Island band. That got him going, alright. Turns out he's Lane's sister's ex-husband.

I felt trapped in the special all-time loser edition of *Jeopardy*. Answer the statement with a question for a prize. Buzzers ready?

He went to Vietnam, where he disgraced himself literally within minutes. Would that be ... Lane?

Howard said Lane did go to the war, where he immediately contracted chicken pox. While he was in quarantine picking at scabs, the rest of his squad was annihilated. "His father called in twenty years' worth of favors," said Howard, "and the government just sort of forgot to call Lane back to duty."

An aging has-been with a convulsive stage style who is comically cataleptic in real life. Lane again?

Howard said Lane was a social vacuum. Never partied, wasn't fun. "Except when he's mad," Howard said, laughing. "We called him Saint Helens behind his back."

I could easily picture Lane at his in-laws, them fawning all over him because he was the most famous person they knew. *"Where do you get the inspiration for your songs?"* they'd gush, and he'd have to make nice when all he wanted was to eat baloney sandwiches and light farts like everyone else.

I suppose almost being napalmed to death can put you on intimate terms with your own mortality. At the very least, it could certainly warp your personality forever. But I've been almost dead way more times than Lane, and I don't keep automatic weapons or petrified cakes in my house.

Howard didn't know what happened to the guy who'd christened Bob's boat with me. Neither did I. The difference between me and Howard was that I wanted to find out.

First I left messages Lane wouldn't return at the phone number he didn't know I had. Maybe I left too many messages, because he disconnected his phone. I faked a Selective Service notice informing him he was required to complete his unfinished tour of duty and must report immediately for a physical. I left it on his porch personally so I could watch him read it, and then tell him it was a joke. I spent all day ringing his bell and waiting in his bushes; when it got dark, I bagged it and went home.

Having run out of other bad ideas, I gave up and paid four dollars to see Love Dinghy at a gig. Lane tried to dodge me. The most conversation I got out of him was that he'd sold his house and moved. "Unplugged the phone 'cause I don't live there no more. Joe, bring me a Dos Equis, will ya?" he yelled with his Walkman cranked up all the way.

When his band started playing, I bellied up to the stage and flashed my bra. Lane's eyebrows shot up, but it turned out he was reacting to that creep Roger, who was standing behind me. Lane knocked over a mic stand, banged the wind out of Charlie, and tore out the back door right in the middle of "Born to Run." Alvin and Larry had to go out looking for him, after they winched Charlie off the floor.

Roger eventually caught up with Lane. I watched them from a distance, Roger waving his hands like a distraught bubbie, Lane looking unhappy, both of them smoking and talking at the same time. The scene was oddly familiar. And then it hit me. Roger was the guy Lane had been talking to at McDonald's, the one I'd guessed was his agent, that night I fixed Lane's van.

If this guy was Lane's agent, he certainly was dedicated to follow Lane all over the club circuit this way. He could've scored a more appreciative client, that's for sure.

From the looks of things now, Roger probably wasn't Lane's agent at all. Maybe Roger and Lane took a boat ride together. Maybe Roger was hanging around Lane for the same reason I was.

Lane had clearly demonstrated he wasn't the type to call the next day, and Roger had all the earmarks of a sore loser who didn't know when to move on. I remembered all the Mrs. Him clothes in Lane's Groton closet. Another relationship — or an aversion to them — was the most reasonable explanation for Lane treating all of us like crap.

I took out my frustration on a mouthbreather who wouldn't stop pestering me. He went through a plate glass window. I went home alone.

After that happened, I started getting weird hang-up calls with annoying frequency, even on my answering machine. Darryl always leaves a long message, especially when he has nothing to say. Editors delight in informing me they're not buying my pencils. Telemarketers only hang up after I say, "I'm having dinner now. Give me your home phone number and I'll call you back later."

I suspected the hang-ups were Lane, checking to see if I was waiting around for him to call, which I wasn't, most of the time. The calls usually came at night. There was often canned music in the background, as if they were being made from a bar pay phone. He never said boo.

He was worse than the editors at the *New Yorker*. "Dear Ms. Gold: Thank you for considering us, but your proposal does not meet our needs for all eternity."

Chapter 26

A couple of weeks after I wore out my welcome at Lane's office, Darryl and I sat on the roof of his apartment building in aluminum lawn chairs, working our way through a cooler of Molsons, alternately picking roof tar off our soles and watching a lunar eclipse. A *Greatest Hits of the Sixties* ten-tape set, not available in any store, was playing and playing on his beach stereo.

Back in the bad old days, peasants believed an eclipse signaled the end of the world. Now it's just an anthropological footnote as they shoot each other over drugs and sheepskin coats. Darryl and I moongazed and listened to not-so-distant machine gun fire.

The moon was the only heavenly body visible in the orangish night sky. The stars couldn't compete with the smoggy haze and city lights. I used to look at the night sky often, when I lived in places where there was one, when I still had a conscience. I stopped stargazing after I moved to New York.

Frankly, I'd rather have been out riding than sitting on Darryl's roof. It was more important to him than to me that a total lunar eclipse occurs only once every six years in Jackson Heights. What with all the bullets flying around, who knew if he'd be around for the next one?

I was only there because he'd requested my company. And stupid as it sounds, I was also there to share something with Lane. I knew he was somewhere, using his rhyming dictionary for a coaster, watching this eclipse with hooded eyes and wondering why his ship sank.

I didn't have many chances to see what he saw. And I don't mean those cross-eyed drunks draped over his foldback monitors, mooning up at him. I mean his perspective on life.

"Darryl," I said, ruining the meditation-like solitude on his roof, "don't guys have anything to do besides think up weird behavior?"

"What're you talking about?"

"For starters, why do they defile your sanctuary, and say they'll call, and then they don't?"

"Not this again. Nona, I know you've got his top secret unlisted phone number. Why don't you just call him?"

"I did. Had a serious talk with his answering machine."

"What part of 'no' don't you understand?"

"Just tell me what I did wrong."

"Probably nothing. Guys just suck."

"Not as well or as often as they should. Why won't he return my calls? Do I have three heads or something?"

"Maybe he's married."

"Maybe. Dunno. Nobody talks about it, and I couldn't find a marriage record anywhere in the Northeast."

"Remind me never to make you mad!" He laughed and fished a beer from the cooler. "Could just be that *I'm* not his type. Lane's seen us together so many times, maybe he assumed the obvious and doesn't want a three-way. Or maybe you just pissed him off. It's not like *that's* never happened before."

"Darryl, I let the guy plunder every orifice I've got. How can he *possibly* be pissed?"

"For starters, you violated protocol. Fun *never* overrides protocol," he said. "It's all kiss kiss, bang bang, 'Love me 'cause I'm fab, yeah yeah yeah.' It's part of the act. Maybe he calls after. Maybe he doesn't. But you don't call him. You crossed a line. And you blew it. *Capisce*?"

"No, no *capisce*. You just said yourself I should call him. Besides, I *always* go where I'm not invited. I'm press."

"Some people can't handle it. They expect you to know your place."

"My *place*? If there were a big neon sign over it flashing 'HERE IT IS!', I wouldn't know my fucking place."

"You're not supposed to be the one in control. You keep forgetting — he's a musician."

Darryl was wrong. I could never forget that Lane's a musician. No one could. He wore it like a mink stole.

"So what? He can't be a musician and a mensch at the same time?"

"Nope. Nona, he needs someone like you around like he needs a stroke. Getting his pants off probably was an accident. He probably never meant for things to go that far. Look, men are wired different from women. You of all people should know we think with our dicks. And musicians are worse than men, with all that Harlequin romance bullshit they foist on their audience. Sometimes there's collateral damage. I'm sorry it had to be you."

It irked me that Darryl would side with Lane, like they were brothers in some screwball fraternity.

"So you're calling this an accidental depantsing?"

"Not for nothing, Nona, but you had on that... *dress*! Jesus! And your hair — you looked like you'd been at an orgy!"

"Well, whose fault is *that*?"

The bottom line is, I know an accident when I see one. Hell, I *invented* accidents. *This* was no accident: A nylon line had lain coiled on Bob's deck. I'd asked Lane — asked him, mind you — if I could tie his hands with it. First he looked at me like I'd asked him to defuse a bomb, and blushed so deeply I could see it in the dark. Then he said okay. It sure didn't feel like an accident *then*.

By now Darryl surely regretted inviting me over. I was personally casting a full-blown pall over Earth's lone satellite, complaining about the soap opera he was happy to have missed while we were too busy for each other.

"Nona, just forget about it. *He* has. Anyway, I'm telling you, he's not good enough for you. He's an insufferable phony who bought into all that rock'n'roll royalty crap and he expects everyone — you included — to tag along. Don't you have enough problems without his stupid midlife crisis? Where's your dignity? Stop acting like a girl! You're losing it, and I can't watch anymore. Here's a nice eclipse. Look at it. Have another beer." He reached into the cooler and rummaged around.

I must say, that was certainly the longest lecture Darryl had ever given me about anything, including guitars, even though it wasn't what I wanted to hear. He has no romantic streak unless a choke-chain figures in the equation. I thought about calling Nat for a second opinion about Lane, but I already knew what she'd say if Bob let her: *Quel jerk.*

"Okay, you're right." I hate it when Darryl's right. "I am in hell." I said it so quietly he barely heard me.

"What did you say?"

"I said, please explain one more thing and I'll shut up. Before I realized I was just a fatuous protocol violator, I might've changed. I stopped yelling at everyone. I stopped having nightmares. I stopped dreaming about hitting people. How is that the upshot of collateral damage?"

Darryl started laughing.

"Don't laugh at me. I'm serious!"

"I know," he said. "That's why I'm laughing." I missed Darryl desperately.

"Fuck you. Listen, I even stopped avoiding eye contact with New Yorkers. I actually looked total strangers in the face. I smiled at them. People kept checking to see if their flies were open. I told an editor 'Have a nice day.' I heard music, all the time. I bought a frigging underwire bra..." I stopped, having thought better of divulging the last item. "I didn't change so much that I won't rip your lungs out through your nose if you tell anyone."

"Your secret dies with me!" He was loving this part. "So, you say you hear music? There you go — it's only a brain tumor. That's operable! They'll just cut off your head and everything'll be fine."

"Thanks. Brain tumor, my ass. It should be so easy."

"Stew away, babe. Anger is your brain's way of keeping your heart from giving up." Pretty philosophical, for someone with a tub of Crisco in his glove compartment.

We went back to moongazing, but I kept seeing Lane's face blushing even after I didn't want to anymore, until the last iridescent sliver of moon was finally swallowed by the big black shadow, and there was nothing left but red mist.

Chapter 27

Maybe I needed a time out. Some physical distance between me and my problems couldn't hurt, right? I would take a vacation! Something I hadn't experienced since the crash of '87. Anyway, that's what I believed in my fevered state.

I couldn't afford a $200-a-night hotel anyplace I really wanted to go, and I'd been avoiding my mother since I fled to Cooper Union, so the choice kind of made itself. The good news was, Mom had a place where I could stay for free. The bad news was, I'd have to stay in it with Mom.

Her lovely suburban ranch home in Texas is where she still cooks food until it's black and stiff, or black and limp, depending on how it started out. It's the place where I started my first diary, wrote racy short stories about cowgirls, and asked her what a masthead was. She told me it was an ear boil. That was before all the art and language classes, and later all the pot, tough love, and screaming. Let's just say she gradually became unsupportive of my teenage artistic aspirations.

My last official activity as a Texan was getting arrested for grand theft auto at eighteen, by big redneck cops who watched too many action movies. I didn't actually steal a car, just borrowed one without permission, not that it mattered. I got a train ticket the same day I made bail. I fled the Lone Star State with my contusions and never gave it a backward glance.

So I can't say I looked forward to this visit. The best part of it, it turned out, was getting there.

Nowadays I pretty much have to be drunk and tied up to fly, because I refuse to go anywhere on twenty-year-old commercial airplanes. You wouldn't keep a car that long. All I can think about while mentally holding aloft geriatric aircraft is Reagan busting PATCO, and terrorist bombs, and notoriously malfunctioning Boeing autopilots. I'd gladly have taken a car on this trip if I had one, but Lane fixed that. So I took the Beemer.

Bikers call this "a ride with a destination." I slept in a train station the first night, a bus station the second. It wasn't so bad. Small children invariably found me fascinating. Everyone else left me alone. I visited every motorcycle museum near a highway exit. In Tennessee I went to see the King's Things at Graceland. In Arkansas I ate biscuits at Earl's Hot Biscuits.

It was a fun trip, really, until the last mile. First I inadvertently cut off a funeral motorcade. The police eyed me menacingly — they finally had a VIP to escort, and by god, if I messed this up for them, it was slammertime again.

Then I rolled up to my mother's house a few minutes later. My family didn't even know I had a bike. It was better that way. They couldn't handle the culture shock, and I couldn't handle the nagging.

That's a thing regular people don't understand about Texans: Their buildings are steel and glass, and everyone has cell phones and faxes, but they're still fighting the Civil War. They haven't gotten to suffrage yet. Girl on bike was a bit much for them.

Not surprisingly, Mom looked at my dirty bike in her driveway and asked when was I getting a car. "You oughta get rid of that thing," she said, "before someone gets hurt."

I felt more wistful than anything else. That's exactly what she told my father, too, the proud owner of an Indian before my mother ground him into a paste of his former self. Nobody remembers anymore what model it was, and now it's too late to ask him. There were lots of questions I never got to ask him, because I bailed so soon and he expired so young.

Family. You call them, you write. But eventually you have to actually go back, before you can't.

The memory of my father looms large in my family, who didn't give a shit about him when he was alive. He collected old construction equipment the way other people collect baseball cards. Ostensibly they were for use on his other collection, a bunch of useless properties that were all triangle shaped and unbuildable. A Coney Island fortune teller once told me, "Your father owns property with oil on it." She drew a picture of it. It was a triangle. I never got the chance to show it to him. It would've made him laugh.

When I was a kid, he and I spent our Saturdays on cherry pickers. He let me operate the forklift. He taught me to drive cars.

"Always do your speeding in the right lane, Noodle," he'd say. "Steer into a skid and west of a tornado."

I could've been the son he never had, were it not for my idiot brother. But I was the one he took on trips. When I was nine we went to Bonneville Salt Flats to watch Bill Johnson set the world record, 224.5 mph on some banana thing he swore was a Triumph. We did stuff we weren't allowed to do at home — left corndog crumbs all over the sheets and watched monster movies all night on the motel's black and white TV. The next day we screamed with laughter at the local go-kart track, our hair soaked with gasoline, as we ran everyone else into the rails. We never told Mom.

Anyway, I think his old Indian was a Scout. Mom made him sell it and wouldn't let him get another one. He never got over it. Every time I slobbered over Allstates in the Sears catalog, he'd just quietly say "No bikes, Noodle," and hide the catalog someplace where I'd find it immediately.

He would've liked the Beemer. "When you gone git ridda that thang?" I could hear him say. "It's dangerous! Hey, Noodle, what's that — an overhead valve? Look at them damned cylinders stickin' out sideways. Wait — where's the chain? That a *shaft drive*? Let me ride it!"

Just before I got it, he went and died. Mom unloaded all his precious triangles and cool machines on the first sucker who came along.

* * * *

"It's not the tragedies that kill us," said Dorothy Parker. "It's the messes."

My family, what's left of it, will never change. And I'd be lying if I called that a comfort. Mom was still teaching tenth-graders that babies come from faith and prayer. My moron brother was still telling me to shut up no matter what I said. Mom invited all my secondary relatives to stop by any time, over my strenuous objections.

The first multigenerational family gathering was a circus of drama queens and too many nieces and nephews needing introductions to editors. My blowhard brother was hitting everyone and telling them to shut up. My mother's mutt was howling along with "Buffalo Gals."

I escaped to the backyard with a bucket of beers and my cousin Ronnie. He was the only one I was glad to see. He and I are the only Golds without brain-eating parasites.

"Nice wheels!" he said. "Wow! Who'da thunk it?"

The air was impossibly hot and humid. I was suffocating. The yard was full of flies and mosquitoes, huge ones. Ronnie and I could hear our kin inside, laughing and applauding the stupid dog in air-conditioned comfort. Malaria was better than going back in there.

"So, I'm hanging out with famous authors now!" said the guy who used to sneak me out when I was grounded, chuckling.

"That's me. Uberhack to the stars."

"Ever write for *Vanity Fair*?"

"Not so much. But I met Tina Brown at a party once. Tina has a teeny mustache."

Ronnie has his own IT consulting business, and a wife and kids who spend all his money before he ever sees it. He was the brother I should've had, but didn't. We went through school together. We dated each other's friends, and swapped gross stories about them afterward. I tried to fix him up with Nat, but she was on to us. There was a song Ronnie and I always sang, to the tune of "The Eyes of Texas," except we switched "flies" for "eyes."

Now we were batting them away in the oppressive heat, seamlessly reconnecting as we drank Pearls from longneck bottles and recounted history.

When I split for Cooper Union, Ronnie went off to the University of Texas at Austin, just like most of our friends did. He became a very popular 1970-style guy. Ran the radical student newspaper, vended pharmaceutical refreshments on the side. When he claimed he knew all 50,000 people on campus, I believed him. I asked if he remembered a diminutive Yankee musician named McCarthy.

"Well," he said, trawling his memory bank, "I do remember one McCarthy. Kinda pushy. Black-haired, like an Injun. Music student, yup. Claimed to be from some New England town, but sounded like a hotdog vendor from Canarsie. Some kinda smokin' blues guitarist, I'm tellin' ya. Whew! Used to jam over to the Armadillo and Threadgill's. Boy, those were fun times!"

He popped the cap off another Pearl. "There was this blues club, the One Knite," he stopped and spelled it, "all the big drug deals were goin' down in the poolroom and the john. You hadda go, you went out back and peed over the side of a ravine. One time they heard there was gonna be a raid, so they bolted all the doors shut with everyone inside still drinkin', and the band just kept playin'."

Today Ronnie's most radical activity was sweat production. He ran his icy beer bottle across his dripping forehead, then continued in the same drawl Nat and I used to laugh at.

"Yup. I knew your McCarthy, alright. Wanted to play in bands real bad but couldn't catch a break. Things were real different then, ya know?"

I thought he was talking about Lane v. Rednecks, the epic Civil War drama about an undersized Yankee in King Shitkicker's court. I was wrong.

"Now I remember," said Ronnie. "Name was Elaine. Elaine McCarthy. No bands let chicks play guitar back then. Wasn't cool. Too bad. She totally had it goin' on."

Elaine McCarthy?

I drove the 1,589 miles home like a maniac on dexies. There were no museums or biscuits with gravy. The West Virginia highway patrol tried to pull me over, but I wouldn't stop even for them — they could mail their crappy summons to me. I screeched up to my house to see two of my front windows shattered. Damned kids. They'd have to wait, too.

I nearly ripped the four locks out of my front door. I raced up three flights of stairs, two stairs at a time. Out of breath, I frantically dug up the cigarette case I'd stolen from Lane's house. I whipped out the Polaroid. Holy shit.

Sure enough, it was Lane. Twilight Zone Lane. A much younger, pre-mullet Lane, dressed as Susan Saint James in *McMillan & Wife*.

Wow. How long did it take me to accept that he's no different from every other musician who dissed me, even if he was the best guy singer I ever heard? Damn! Now I had to rethink even that.

Chapter 28

You're traveling through a crazyass wormhole. A wormhole not only of sight and sound but of wackjobs, a journey into a twisted land whose boundaries are that of unleaded premium. Your next stop: The Weasel Zone.

As soon as I got my wind back, I got my windows fixed. Otherwise rats and squatters would move in, and the way the tenant laws are in New York, you can't chase out either one.

One of my windows had fought a Night Train bottle and lost. The other one got it with an eight-track tape deck. Brooklyn — I swear, they'll steal anything here.

I assumed the tape deck was commentary from the neighbors on my taste in music. I checked inside it to see if they left me any playlist suggestions. All I found was a note: DROP THE MACARTHEY STOREY OR ELSE. The big mystery was, where the hell did they find an eight-track?

I didn't say anything to Darryl or anybody else for a week. No one would believe this shit anyway. Had I even *wanted* to talk about it, where would I start? *Hey, Darryl, check this out — some editor who hates my stuff hit me with an eight-track, and Lane is Sally McMillan.*

I was still recovering from all this weirdness — enough for a lifetime, thanks — when more of it landed.

Here's what happened. My personal stash of the Elixer of Youth had run dangerously low. If ever a week required lubrication, this was it. So I was on my way to the liquor store in Brooklyn Heights that has air conditioning and canned R&B. I'd just pulled onto the Brooklyn Queens Expressway, having decided I wasn't up to taking the surface route that runs past the projects, the Navy Yard, the prison, and a junkyard where they sometimes don't lock up the dogs. Directly behind me was a pickup truck with Texas plates.

I watched in my mirror, annoyed, as he tailgated me. Maybe he was just a bad driver. Wouldn't be my first. Or maybe I'd lunkheadedly cut him off because I was so distracted by my other problems, and now he was going to teach me a lesson. I'd heard about Texas motorists shooting each other dead over lesser slights. His big black steel push bar got closer and closer to my taillight.

Well, if there's one thing Nona detests, it's strange men up her butt. I goosed the throttle and vroomed away. Presently he approached my behind again, and was accelerating. If he didn't pass soon, I'd be smushed.

It quickly became clear he had no intention of passing. We were overtaking a car in the lane to our left. I passed it, and as soon as the car and the truck were dead even I swooped into the lane with the car, cutting it off. Then I braked in an attempt to force the truck to pass, inconveniencing what turned out to be an unmarked police car.

I was very successful in shaking the truck. As the police car flipped on its dashboard light and siren, the truck guy panicked and scrammed for the nearest exit. I watched him disappear into the slums of Brooklyn.

On the shoulder of the BQE, I patiently explained everything to Bozo the Cop.

"Right," he said, "and I'm the Sultan of Brunei. Pleased to meet ya." He wrote me four tickets totaling $280, lectured me on speeding and the evils of motorcycles, and tacked six points onto my license.

I guess I should've been angry, or grateful, or some combination thereof. But all I could feel was sorrow that the liquor store had closed.

* * * *

Darryl and I heard that Joan Jett was appearing at Irving Plaza, so we decided to go. I thought it would get my mind off things. Last time we went, a misstep involving a mic cord and a studded harness launched her butt-over-heels into the mosh pit. Sweet!

Tonight's show would sell out for sure. We'd never get tickets at the door, so I tried to reserve some by phone. The Ticketmaster dode demanded my phone and credit card numbers. Then he said, "Oops! Too late to mail tickets" and hung up. The next day someone charged an eight-ball jacket and roller blades on my credit card.

So Darryl and I resorted to the convenient walk-in ticket outlet on lower Broadway. It took forty-five minutes to drive the four miles because of all the traffic jams. Then we had to park ten blocks away and fight our way through unruly throngs of NYU students to reach Ticketmaster's state-of-the-art computer, which was out of paper. *That* clerk directed us to another outlet, two blocks away. That outlet didn't accept plastic, which was all we had.

We walked five more blocks to the only cash machine in the neighborhood, and waited on a long line with other grumpy people and the fragrant bum who lived in the vestibule. Instead of money, the ATM kept giving me receipts saying "Your bank is not responding." Damn it, I was *in* my stinking bank! We gave up and left. Lou Reed walked past us carrying a watermelon, and I didn't care.

"When are you gonna tell me what's bugging you?" said Darryl.

"Would you believe me if I said it's the tedious minutiae of everyday New York commerce?"

"No. Is it boy trouble?"

"I don't wanna talk about it."

"Okay, boy trouble it is. You know, Nona, finding Mr. Right's a whole lot like buying a guitar." I couldn't wait to hear how. "First, you stumble onto the Ray Whitley of your dreams! You're pissing yourself because it's perfect, except for it's got the wrong tailpiece. But that's nothing — eventually you'll replace that. The guitar costs as much as a Miata, so you sell all your other guitars so you can take it home. While you're rubbing it down lovingly, you notice a scratch you didn't see before. A big one. You wonder how it got by you. But what the hell, the action's great! It's just a scratch, right? So you ignore it. But for some reason, the thing keeps going out of tune. You look at it closer, and you see the headstock's busted..."

"Is that the part that's like marriage?"

"Nah. That's when you call the dealer and make him give you your money back."

"If only. It's no use, Dar. Life sucks. I wouldn't even know where to start."

"Good, 'cause I got my own problems."

He then proceeded to weigh me down with all of them. His band was falling apart, he said, because its members weren't taking their careers seriously enough. Their gigs were drying up. He missed being bullied by club owners and drinking free beers.

"Damnit!" Darryl said. "Why can't I play out? Peter Frampton gets to play out. Adam Ant gets to play out. I wanna play out!"

Darryl started making loud noises about playing with real musicians. I don't know any of those, so I suggested he ask Love Dinghy. They were working The Guyland that night, a gig I forgot about the second I heard Joan Jett was in town.

I knew Lane tolerated occasional guest players, as long as he could show them up and they weren't too tall. Why not Darryl?

Many reasons came to mind as soon as I volunteered to introduce Darryl to Lane so that Darryl could jam.

"I'll brain him if he says no!" Darryl yelled, and kicked a street trashcan, hard. "If he messes with you again, I'll beat him to death with that shitty Jap tinderbox he loves so much!"

Darryl's concern for me was genuinely touching. Also, kind of scary. I had no idea he could get so angry.

I reminded him of his own advice to me: Never pass up an opportunity to sell a psycho an overpriced guitar. He allowed as how such an event might mitigate his pique, especially since he still had a 1959 Les Paul fake nobody wanted.

My personal motive for this enterprise wasn't so noble. I intended to show Lane I could be as moderne and detached as he was. I would orchestrate a detente in a nuthouse. If he ruined it, I'd shove his face in it. If he laid a hand on Darryl, I'd bludgeon him with his fucking protocol. He was an amateur at antisocial compared to me.

If there's one thing all three of us were good at, it's turning a pile of dung into a bigger pile of dung. What could possibly go wrong?

A few hours later Darryl and I were leaning against a hospital-green wall in a windowless, stuffy anteroom in O'Toole's instead of fist pumping at Irving Plaza. A smell permeated the air, like something had died inside the wall. We were waiting and waiting to be presented to Lane, and aging fast.

"That revolution thing we fought was a total waste. Some democracy we got," said Darryl. "Why couldn't we just have one main queen and be done with it, instead of a bunch of little ones? Who does this guy think he is? Princess Diana?" He was batting a thousand tonight.

As much as I hated to admit it, Darryl appeared to be correct about Lane's delusions of holiness. I wished I'd believed Darryl on his roof, back when he was trying to convince me. Now I was sorry I'd dragged him here where he had to endure Lane's posturing at close range. This stunk worse than the bridge-and-tunnel line outside Studio 54.

Darryl scratched his head and looked around morosely. A hair drifted to the shoulder of his Brooks Brothers buttondown. He wanted to play guitar pretty badly to put up with all this.

All the time we were waiting, no one went into or out of the dressing room. We figured someone more useful than us had gotten to Lane first and monopolized him, or vice versa. I just hoped he'd get tired of whoever it was before Darryl and I started collecting Social Security.

Larry once told me that Lane loved to pontificate, but not before he had to sing. He had to conserve his adenoids before caking them with nicotine and grinding them into chopped meat. So maybe the holdup was something else. Maybe it just took Lane forever to put on jeans and a tank shirt, like it does women. God forbid I should see a middle-aged man in his underwear. I stifled a tranny joke that was fighting to get out.

Darryl sighed. "He must be in there with Mellencamp. Or Dion. Someone important. Wait, I know — it's Springsteen!"

He couldn't have picked a worse time to perform "Darkness on the Edge of Town." Being Darryl, he had to be all the instruments, too. Loudly.

"Ba ba BOOMP. Chaaaaah..."

"Shut up!" I hissed at him, my fist balled up in his face.

He was extra emphatic about the secrets people just can't face, lowing the dragging-around part like a cow.

"Mwaaaaaaaaaaah!"

"Stop it!"

I looked nervously at the dressing room door, hoping no one heard.

He was just warming up. The part about losing his money and his wife was a symphonic stampede of barnyard sounds.

I reached to throttle Darryl. He just ducked and giggled and kept moohing lyrics as I chased him around the anteroom, my arms outstretched toward his neck.

And that's what we were doing when the dressing room door finally opened.

Alvin poked his head out. "Sssh," he said, and motioned us inside. I punched Darryl in the shoulder and we went in.

The anteroom decorator had also worked his magic on the star's domain. There was the same tan, no-wax flooring curling up at the edges, the green walls, a torn orange vinyl couch, some hard chairs with the arms broken off, and a plastic laminate coffee table with the corners gone and a half-eaten pizza in the center.

Amidst this splendor stood Lane. Two blank-eyed roadies hovered nearby. Larry and the sound man were in a corner, going over last-minute set changes. Larry waved.

Lane needed a shave. His eyes were bloodshot. He held a pump bottle of Chloraseptic in his left hand, a smoldering Camel in his right. He was wearing his Village People of the Damned costume and a leather necklace I kept looking at because I couldn't figure out how it fastened. Plus I needed something to focus on, because he wouldn't look me in the eye.

I glanced around the room for the throngs who adored him so much he needed bodyguards to control them, the worshipers for whom he made us wait until they finished paying homage. There was only me and Darryl. My temperature rose a notch.

"This is Darryl Colletti. He plays R&B," I found myself saying politely to Lane, who still wouldn't look at me. "Darryl, this is Lane McCarthy." *He plays songs about stranglers in drag.*

Lane transferred the cigarette to his face and they shook hands. Where's a camera when you need one?

I still couldn't believe I was doing this. There was some "Yeah, yeah, good to meet you" type jabber between them, but not much. Lane's golden vocal chords, you know. Lane pretended he'd never seen Darryl before. Me he treated like an encyclopedia salesman.

"Where've you played?" said Lane to Darryl around the cigarette.

"I was lead guitar with Migraine for a few years," said Darryl. "Played a Delroy Prince tour. Sat in with Albert King a few times."

I didn't say anything about the Delroy Prince tour that wasn't. Darryl stifled a cough induced by Lane's cigarette.

Even if Lane hadn't seen Darryl with me a million times, sometime in the last fifteen years he most certainly saw Darryl burn down some East Coast beer hall as only Darryl could. Lane would choke before he'd admit it. But he'd never forget it, either.

He exhaled a plume of smoke at Darryl and squinted at him through the cloud. "You wanna sit in with us?" he said. "We're doing blues for the encore."

Blues? Love Dinghy? They always played one of their freakish pop originals for their encores. Either I was witnessing the new birth of Love Dinghy Mark II, or Lane was being unnaturally solicitous toward Darryl, who he'd just gone out of his way to prove was nobody to him.

Whatever. Darryl had come too far to say no. Lane just turned and left wordlessly to go on stage.

Darryl and I fidgeted through two sets of Love Dinghy sturm und drang, during which he drank a couple too many. When the encore was imminent, Darryl moseyed casually — a little too casually — toward the stage. Whistles and gongs blasted in my head, but it was too late.

There was an unmanned Gibson SG on the stage, but someone handed Darryl an Ibanez instead, a cheap Japanese Strat knockoff he'd have plenty to say about later. Lane decided they'd perform "Rock Me Baby," a song we saw him play the bejesus out of in Harlem. He then gave orders to the band about exactly how he wanted their blues odyssey.

Lane gave a countdown and they started playing. Darryl sort of goofed along innocuously on his borrowed ax, being extra careful to not overshadow Lane. Until he got the nod to solo.

That's when it all exploded. Darryl wailed through that warhorse like a firestorm. He pulled out every chop he had. The audience went crazy. He totally blew Lane out of the water and wouldn't trade the lead back to him. Darryl was playing like Nero, and howling.

Lane was furious. He counterattacked with licks that astonished even the band he'd been tyrannizing for twenty years. But he couldn't keep up with Darryl. His hands were shaking too much. His final act of defiance was a cut signal to the band before Darryl was through, but the Dinghies kept pumping until Darryl was good and done.

The audience screamed for Darryl and charged the stage, hugging him, shaking his hand, calling him a genius. Darryl didn't discourage them.

I was sure I knew every expression in Lane's catalog of meaningful looks, but I'd never seen the one he had on his face now. He threw his new Prodigy violently at the floor and stalked off as fast as his little legs would go.

No one had spelled it out, but I was pretty sure this was all my fault. Being the root cause of a studly duel was an utterly foreign — and unexpectedly nauseating — experience.

After Darryl's fans dispersed, I ruined his night by giving him a lecture on manly honor. "You're very bad," I wrapped up. "Now go apologize to the Red Queen."

We found Lane in a fine mood out back, exercising his precious vocal chords on everyone within range. He was ragging Wizard, who was completely blameless for once, calling him a no-talent he could replace in two seconds flat. He threatened the roadies that he was going to hire Girl Scouts next time, because they work harder and drink less. He threw heavy equipment into the rental truck recklessly, muttering to himself. Charlie once told me Lane never handled equipment, because he didn't want to mess up his delicate hands. You know, the ones that were lashed to Bob's mast.

Wizard and the roadies were still deciding whether to interfere or back off when Lane aimed his frustrations at a six-foot, 250-pound Ampeg speaker cabinet. He muscled it around unsuccessfully inside the truck, cursing at it.

Unlike his toadies, his equipment didn't know when not to fight back. The Ampeg won. It toppled over on him amid a brief shower of epithets, and then there was silence.

Chapter 29

"Get it off him!"

"No. *You* get it off him!"

"No way! He'll just say I broke it! You do it!"

Eventually Wizard and Alvin and the roadies pulled the cabinet off Lane together. They threw a Beacon blanket over him so he wouldn't go into shock, though Lane's been in a fugue state so long all the blankets in Siberia wouldn't help him now.

Charlie and Larry heard the commotion and came running outside. Larry was being as authoritative as a man could in a fishnet tank and sparkle tights.

"Don't move him!" he commanded everyone. "Something might be broken. Charlie, call 911." The club manager was pacing and chain-smoking, more worried about a lawsuit than about Lane.

We all stood watching Lane drool on the truck bed as we waited for the ambulance. An interminable amount of time passed that turned out to only be fifteen minutes, and still no EMS.

"I was hit by a truck once," I reassured everyone, "bleeding all over a major intersection. It took them an hour to come wipe *me* off the road. These New York ambulances don't hurry unless there's a TV camera." There were groans from the conscious. "I'm taking him to a hospital myself."

Everyone thought this a wise plan, especially since they couldn't possibly leave without their equipment or their money. Darryl and I collected Lane and installed him delicately in Darryl's back seat as everyone watched. We told the band to meet us at Long Island Jewish, and we took off. I don't know about them, but we never got there.

Darryl hung backward over his bucket seat, poking at Lane. I drove leisurely. The oldies station played on the radio. Lane was completely out of orbit.

"Only thing looks broken to me is his nose. Like anyone's gonna notice *that*," Darryl pronounced. "In my expert medical opinion, he just got his head squeezed between a quarter-ton piece of furniture and a U-Haul."

"Good thing they didn't crush anything sensitive."

We headed straight for my house, more or less, after crawling through a series of traffic tie-ups and stopping for Chinese takeout. At one jam-up I hit the brakes hard; Lane flew forward and thudded into the backs of our seats, coming to rest with his head on the floor and his feet in the air. We looked at him, then at each other, and left him that way.

It was during this trip that I couldn't hold back anymore, and finally spilled what I'd learned about Lane's secret life as a skanky girl.

"Hey Darryl — you know all those psycho tranny songs Lane wrote?"

"You mean all his dumb fantasy crap the Neldaheads love so much?"

"Yeah. Well, that's just it. The Nelda part — not so much fantasy there as we thought."

When I told him about Lane's adventures in Austin, Darryl was as far from scandalized as you can get. In fact, he couldn't stop laughing. So I just bulldozed right along, telling him about Lane trading me in for a dude, and the music-loving illiterate who was going to poleax me if I didn't quit the story I wasn't writing about Lane.

"*What* story?" Darryl asked incredulously as he searched through Lane's jacket pockets. "You mean that spec soap opera you bagged a year ago?"

"I guess so. When Leatherface comes back to kill me, I'll be sure to give him an update."

Darryl surfaced from Lane's jacket with half a twisted pack of Camels and a busted A string. "Jesus, Nona!" he said, shaking Lane's bottle of Sally Hansen Hard As Nails. "Where the hell'd they get an eight-track?"

He wasn't nearly as impressed with the threat part. "Well, you better find out who it is that wants to kill you, so you can show 'em where to get on line!" He howled all the rest of the way to my house.

We extracted Lane from the car. Laughing uncontrollably, we hoisted him up three flights of stairs with all the care we'd give a free sack of bad apples.

Stinky the cat was thrilled to have so much company. Her visitors were pretty much limited to meter readers and sheetrockers. She shadowed us merrily as we deposited Lane on my pencil post bed.

"So whaddya think?" said Darryl, eyeballing Lane, and the bedposts, and Lane. "Tie him up?"

"Nah. Let me think a minute."

Contemporary dating practices was a subject Darryl and I discussed infrequently. His is not an anthropological mind, and mine doesn't want to know where it goes. However, we were inclined to boast about occasional exploits that especially banged our gongs. That's how I knew Darryl's notion of convivial bondage differed from mine, and I wanted Lane to stay in one piece.

We stood at the foot of my bed, our arms akimbo, each with one foot tapping as we considered Lane's immediate future.

"Boy, he's gonna have one helluva headache tomorrow," said Darryl. "D'ja check out that melon on his temple?"

"What if he wakes up and kills us?"

"He won't be moving too fast. We'll just run."

And without further discussion, we began peeling off Lane's clothes.

We started with me at one end of him and Darryl at the other. I removed things gently, then tossed them across the room. Darryl yanked off Lane's trademarks violently, then folded and stacked them neatly.

Darryl practically ripped Lane's feet from his legs while stripping off his pants. "Don't hurt him!" I ordered. "I want him alive."

"Hey, look!" Darryl said, pointing with both hands at Lane's business. "His hair's really this color! I thought he had a beauty school dye job. First year."

A cartoon lightbulb exploded over Darryl's head. "Hey, Stretch," he said to Lane, "I'm cutting your hair!"

We dropped Lane face forward on the bed. Stinky perched atop his storybook ass, looking to see if he brought kippers. Lane's jeans, socks, and boots were neatly arranged on my cedar chest. His wifebeater shirt dangled from the radiator. His Levi jacket was in the flue. All he had on was his leather necklace, because we couldn't figure out how to get it off.

Like slingshots, I expressed his wristbands to Stinky, who was beside herself with good fun. She attacked Lane's white crew socks with special zeal. Darryl went off to the bathroom for a comb and hair scissors.

When he returned, we uprighted Lane and propped him up against the headboard. I held his head. We said ciao to his hair and sideburns like a hat with flaps. Scissors clacked while Darryl raked Lane's ridiculously thick locks with my Afro pick.

"Jeez," Darryl said as most of it hit the floor, "it's all real!" He was jealous. His own hair had been falling like autumn leaves all by itself since 1980.

When Lane looked sufficiently like Ed Grimley, I did his makeup. Initially there was some general disagreement over shadow (I thought he was a winter; Darryl thought fall) until we reached a selection: Amethyst

Passion and Moonglow. And with that artistry complete, the beauty segment of Lane's appointment was over.

Primp Daddy was sweeping up clippings when something caught his eye.

"Nona..." He couldn't believe what he was looking at. He peered harder into Lane's boot. "Nona, this bitch keeps money in his *shoe*!"

"Leave it there. We gotta get busy, before he wakes up."

"You sure you wanna do this?"

"You're kidding me, right? The Hair Wax Nazi of Jackson Heights is backing out of the get-even opp of all time? C'mon, Darryl — let's be bad!"

"Could we not, and just say we did?"

"Where's the fun in *that*?"

He thought it over for half a second. "Okay. Let's do this. Show me what ya got!"

We started with the closet in my spare bedroom. It was full of artsy tailored clothes from my ex-life in advertising. I'd battled armies of argumentative tailors to get the sleeves right, and browbeaten countless dry cleaners to get the blood stains out. I can't afford cleaners or tailors now, nor do I actually need these outfits anymore, but I don't have the heart to throw them away. They cost a damned fortune, and anyway they're still good for funerals.

"This first!" Darryl said, obscenely fingering a fine black knit Kenzo dress. He gave a dramatic reading of the content label. "Seventy percent wool, twenty percent silk, ten percent cashmere. Oof!"

We loaded Lane into it. It didn't look as sexy on him as it did on me, but it had its charms. Lane's nipples were quite perky.

"That's one good thing about not needing a bra," said Darryl, removing the V-backed Kenzo. "No straps showing. Next!" I couldn't believe Lane was sleeping through all this.

Darryl hauled out a peak-lapeled, pinstriped Ralph Lauren dress with mountainous padded shoulders. Lane tried it on. This was a landmark in rock'n'roll history: the closest anyone would ever come to seeing Lane McCarthy in a suit.

"Too corporate," said Darryl, standing back with his arms folded and his head tilted.

"Right. It needs something..." I agreed, and ran downstairs to the coatrack. I came back with my Stetson and plopped it on Lane. It swallowed his head.

"Looks like you aced the interview, pal!" Darryl said admiringly to Lane. "You da man! Or something." Lane would shit if he knew.

But so far, he didn't. In fact, he was looking a little too green and lifeless for my taste. I touched his neck below his ear. I felt no pulse. His skin was cool. Now I was the one having second thoughts.

"You think he's in a coma?" I said. "Or dead?"

"No way. He's just out. See?"

Darryl tugged up Lane's eyelid roughly with his thumb. The pupil barely dilated as his iris rolled back.

"Turn me on, dead man!" said Darryl.

"God, Darryl! Don't be gross."

Darryl laughed. "You know, Ralph Lauren would shoot a model with this much hair."

I went to get a razor, and we shaved Lane's legs. His eyelids didn't even flutter.

We stepped back to admire our handiwork. Then Darryl disappeared again, talking all the way down the hall. "Too Wall Street," I heard him saying to nobody. "Lane McCarthy, carpetbagger to the stars."

He returned with another armload of mothballed fashions.

"Your office twat gear wasn't his style," he said. "These are *much* better."

He'd raided an even older stash, the one with my struggling artist wardrobe. It was all secondhand junk I bought the first time I was broke and stylish. Now stores call stuff like this "vintage" and charge lots of money for it. It's amazing the garbage you save when you have a four-story house.

My bedroom looked like an earthquake zone. We pored over the mess together, arguing about what music to listen to and which colors complemented Lane's complexion. We started with the Ronettes and a turquoise silk cheongsam. On deck was a Juliet minidress from Paraphernalia, circa 1966. We were at it all night, me and Darryl and Lane. We took turns dressing and posing with Renaissance Faire Lane and Annie Oakley Lane and Flashdance Lane, taking snapshots with the throwaway cameras I buy in bulk for documenting accidents.

"I haven't had this much fun since I blew Lane away on the guitar," Darryl said at dawn, tying a pert bow at Lane's waist. "But I really gotta go. Band's got rehearsal tomorrow." He looked at his watch. "Today, I mean." Darryl glanced at Lane wearing a pink lace teddy. "Don't forget. When he wakes up..."

"I know. Run."

Darryl burst out laughing and left.

A golden glow permeated the room as the sun fought its way out of Crown Heights. I continued playing with Lane, my personal giant Barbie doll. I bet this was the only time anyone ever called him giant.

That gave me an idea. I looked around. Ken's Corvette might fit Lane's foot. Luckily, I had two!

I rooted around the wreckage for the orange plastic ragtops, singing along with a Joan Jett CD in my best out-of-key voice. That's when he woke up.

"What the hell's going on?" he croaked, startling the crap out of me.

Lane rolled off the bed and stood woozily, squinting around. The sunrise bathed him in a smog-tinged light.

I could only watch, frozen, unsure what to expect. Once a crackhead came at me with a knife, and this was way scarier.

I knew Lane was going to kill me. Grab the nearest blunt instrument, run at me with a crazy tranny face, and flog me to death. I could see tomorrow's headline: BROOKLYN HACK SLAIN WITH KEN'S CORVETTE.

But that's not what happened. Instead, he took off the oven mitts and rubbed his eyes, looking only mildly annoyed. Then he brushed right past me and tottered — in my ruffled Victorian peignoir that on him mopped the floor — straight to my stereo system. Anyway, that's what I call it. It's actually a crazy jumble of mismatched components that fell off trucks. I'd networked it myself. My CD player was hooked up wrong and sounded like it. I'm great with mechanical things. Internal combustion systems? No problem. Electronic ones? No way.

Within a minute, Lane had dragged my cabinets all over the room, exposing the backs of the stereo equipment. He began taking all of it apart and rewiring everything, staying well away from the Voice of the Theater.

"Get me a screwdriver" was all he said.

I brought him a whole tool kit. "How's your head?" I said.

He didn't answer for a long time, just sat on the floor with my CD player apart in his lap, puttering intently. At length he finally did say something. It wasn't any of the things I expected.

"Why do I get the feeling you know about Austin?"

None of the responses I'd rehearsed for this moment seemed appropriate now. I tried not to panic, or laugh.

"Jesus, Lane," I eventually replied. "I finally get you to come to Brooklyn, and all you do is whine."

Chapter 30

"My head feels like a soccer ball at halftime," Lane said ten minutes after I asked him about it. He felt his temple where the knot was from the Ampeg.

"I have Empirin with codeine. You want that? Extra good for cramps and other excruciating pains."

"If I take some, will it make you go away?"

I shook my head.

"Just get me some aspirin," he said. His nose looked more lumpy and red than usual, but I didn't ask him about that.

After I brought him the aspirin, I fell into a deathlike sleep among mountains of outdated fashions. Served me right for going twenty-four hours straight on nothing but tequila and adrenaline. He finished up his electronics project while I was blotto. Then he put everything back where it came from and rounded up his own clothes.

They say agave is a hallucinogen. While I dreamed Lane was fronting Love Dinghy in a purple drape suit and a beehive, Ed Grimley Lane went to the bodega.

A few hours later I awoke and went downstairs to the kitchen. There was an empty tin of Albo sardines on the counter that I didn't buy, and Stinky was washing her face. Lane had made a pot of coffee, too. Guy got more done with a concussion than I ever did on a good day with a clear head. I wondered if he could cook. And why was he still here?

Amazingly, there he was, sitting quietly at my kitchen table in the outfit he'd arrived in, with Stinky in his lap.

I was never happy about anyone seeing my kitchen, with its general lack of walls, appliances, and other homey accoutrements. The sink was always full of dishes, the table piled high with papers and magazines. I figured Lane would've run away or killed me before ever seeing it, and either way I wouldn't care.

No such luck today. He pretended to be more interested in a two-week-old issue of *Variety* as he fumbled with the wrapper on a fresh pack of cigarettes. Apparently he'd never looked in a mirror the whole time he was roaming around unsupervised.

His hair was still saucily bouffant. There were big smudges of purple on his eyelids. I could just see him wandering along Fulton Street like this, asking junkies for directions. They must've been very confused at the bodega.

Suddenly I realized I'd never seen him in daylight before. His slate eyes took on a smoky violet cast as the noon light hit them. He didn't look like a kid anymore. His hair was greying; his smile lines were deeply creased. Before, he'd always come off like an arrested adolescent. The first time I got his pants off, I half expected him to be a satyr.

Now here he was, with his nightcrawler pallor and wrinkles, looking old enough to be someone's father. Theoretically he was old enough to be someone's grandfather. Quel buzzkill. Still, he was the only forty-something I knew who hadn't got the arrogance and ambition thwacked the hell out of him by the shitmill of life.

To be fair, the daylight wasn't doing me any favors, either. Like I always say: Everyone looks better in the dark. It's what I want cut on my headstone. Dorothy Parker would steal that. Anyway, there was nothing the three of us could do about the sunlight now.

Funny thing was, nobody ran. Me, I didn't want to. Dot, she was dead. And Lane, he was plain stuck. There's still no subway service from Brooklyn to Rhode Island. And in my neighborhood, when people see a cab, they take a picture of it.

We both knew he hated not being in control. You'd think something like that would have more entertainment value than what was happening here. Somehow, having the upper hand with him wasn't the prize I imagined it would to be. Now he seemed almost fragile to me. Almost human.

I poured the coffee he made into two Daytona 200 souvenir mugs. Then I sat down at my messy table with him. That's when he finally picked up where we'd left off.

"How'd you find out? About Austin, I mean?" There was no preamble. No "Your backline is as bad as your writing." No "Your neighborhood should be burned to the ground and salted." Not even "Answer me or I'll strangle you." It must've killed him to wait half the day to ask.

"It was completely unintentional," I said, guessing he'd doubt anything I told him, especially if it was true. "I'm not making this up. My cousin in Texas, he went to UT. We got to talking about the music scene there, and he said he remembered you. Well, actually, he remembers Elaine. I wasn't digging or anything." Yeah, right. When am I ever *not* digging? "For what it's worth, he commended your musicianship extravagantly. Said you were 'some kinda smokin' blues guitarist.' And I did *not* reveal your precious fucking secret identity, either. I *swear*."

I held my breath. Maybe that wasn't the best answer. But it didn't seem like a good time to explain I drove halfway across the continent to get away from him, only to accidentally exhume something he didn't want anyone to know about.

"Why be so polite?" he said to the coffee mug. "You're wondering why I was sashaying around Texas in skirts. You'd be insane if you weren't."

"Goes both ways. By everyone else's calculations, I should be in a straitjacket. Tell you what. If your explanation is as good as your musicianship, you win a cheese omelette."

"Good deal. Okay then, here's what happened. I graduated from high school in '69. My lucky draft lottery number was, like, five. So I got shipped straight to 'Nam. Somehow I managed to come back in one piece."

Oh brother, I was thinking. What I mumbled aloud was worse.

"Right. Chicken pox," I said, nonchalantly crushing his manhood as I poured cream in my coffee.

He shot me a look that would stop a train. I spilled cream all over the table. Stinky went to work cleaning up the mess.

Lane soldiered on. "After I got out, I went home and started looking for a job. Any job. There were no jobs. The economy sucked. All I got was the big finger from Little Rhody."

"Your father couldn't get you a government job?"

"No," he said testily and paused. "How do you know about my father? And the chicken pox?"

I looked around for the package of English muffins instead of answering him. He screwed up his face. "Be sure to stop me if I bore you with any more details you already know."

"Sorry. Do go on." I buttered a muffin and steeled for a borefest I thought I already knew.

"I had friends in San Antonio, so I went there. This was way before I started the band. Right away I met a girl there. We got married, pow, just like that. I didn't know her all that well. Didn't know anything about her past, her family. Didn't care. She was tiny and beautiful, like a doll."

Tiny. Beautiful. Doll-like. At last, perspectives in common! And a marriage record I missed! Damn!

He continued. "Guys fall in love, it's like, you know, they're drunk or something. I was crazy about her. You don't hang back and analyze things when your pants are on fire. I wouldn't have seen a bus coming at me."

He drew a filtered cigarette from the pack he got at the bodega and tamped it on the table, a habit of people who were smokers before filters were invented. Or who were poor for so long they rolled their own.

"I took all kinds of jobs to support us, whatever I could get — construction work, bailing hay, shoveling shit. We moved to Houston. They were looking for oil riggers there. The money was great, but the hours were long. I wasn't home much."

So far his story was remarkable for its ordinariness. He sounded like half the people I ever knew. I expected the story to end with his wife leaving him for Willie Nelson, or how she couldn't get off without an aardvark in the room.

He swallowed more aspirins and lit the cigarette. The matchbook read Caliente Couch Dancing, 227 Fulton. Stinky didn't like the smoke and ran away.

Lane balanced the Camel on the edge of a saucer, folded his arms over his chest, then never smoked the cigarette. I waited patiently for the aardvark part.

"So I came home late one day," he said very quietly, "and found her in pieces all over the living room. Someone had blown her to bits with a shotgun."

He stopped talking and looked at me. I stopped chewing my muffin. I stopped breathing. What happened to the aardvark story?

His face was utterly expressionless. At first I thought he was yanking my chain, trying to get back at me for yanking his. Not for nothing is he a world-renowned kvetch.

But not this time. His arms stayed folded. His hair kept pointing to the ceiling. His forgotten cigarette burned into a long cylinder of ash.

I was dumbstruck. Dorothy Parker would know exactly what to say, if she wasn't so dead. I certainly didn't.

"You don't believe me, do you?" he asked eventually.

I didn't know what I believed, except that Larry wasn't kidding about Lane's proclivity for pontification. But I didn't say it aloud, and I didn't say no, so he kept on talking. How long was it that he wouldn't even tell me to get lost, and now he wouldn't shut up?

"I couldn't imagine who could hate her that much, or me, or why," he said. "The police decided *I* did it. Of course, there was no corroborating evidence. The shotgun was gone, they couldn't place me at the scene. But I was all they had, and all I had was an alibi. Lotta good *that* was. So they booked me. Motive, they said, means, opportunity, all that. They said I was jealous, crazy. A damned Yankee. Whatever. Texas cops are lazy and stupid as hell. They'd arrest a cowpie if it got in their way.

"Anyway, my lawyer was golf buddies with the judge. He got the charge reduced to manslaughter. Things are really looking up now — only twenty-five-to-life for ol' Lane instead of electrocution. Yippie yi yo ki yay. Then the judge said he'd cut me loose if I could make bail. Only a hundred grand. My parents mortgaged their house and got me out. So I showed them what a good son I am. I ran."

I was suddenly finding out more about Lane's perspective than I ever wanted to know, not to mention his vocabulary.

"So it became kinda hard to get by, as you might imagine," he said.

Being the object of a statewide manhunt, Lane couldn't exactly walk into his bank and cash a check. He didn't have credit cards, either. This was pre-ATM Texas, the one that existed before BankAmericard spawned a nation of debtors. He didn't have enough money for a bus ticket. He couldn't even flee in his own car to hide at his parents' house in Rhode Island, because he had no scratch for gas.

So Lane hitched a ride out of Houston as far as he could get, which was Austin. He concocted what he thought was a brilliant disguise, got a fake

ID, and dissolved into the faceless swarm of drug-addled humanity that was UT.

"It was 1971," he said. "Turn on, tune in, drop out. Everyone could barely put one foot in front of the other. You think anyone noticed stubble on a hippie chick? Or an Adam's apple?"

My cousin Ronnie certainly didn't.

"I just wore my hair real long, over my face. Every mother's nightmare." He laughed, surprising me. "Besides, it's too hot in Texas for pants."

Hot is right. I was horrified and relieved simultaneously that he could joke about this. I definitely had problems seeing the humor in it, but then it was all new to me; he'd had two decades to process this mess.

I tried to imagine him wearing Birkenstocks and eating mung sprouts, the lively arguments he must've had with the manbabes running UT's library. *Ms. McCarthy, you've let* Our Bodies, Ourselves *go overdue again!*

Lane said the Houston police eventually turned up the real killer, by accident of course. He was an ex-con who was an old boyfriend of his wife's. When they picked him up for a minor parole violation, his fingerprints were all over a gummy shotgun they found in his car. The goo turned out to be blood from three or four different dead people.

"I saw his arrest on the news," said Lane, "between the car crashes and house fires. They showed him getting carted away and yelling 'I didn't do nuthin'!'"

Lane was exonerated and out of dresses in two shakes, but it was too late to get the bond money back. He scrammed to Detroit, where anyone could get work on auto assembly lines. He sweated out fifteen-hour days in the GM plant until he had enough money for music equipment, figuring music to be the short route to repaying his parents the ten percent they lost when he jumped bail. Then he went back East with his first truckload of uncooperative rock'n'roll hardware, started Love Dinghy, and got more payback than he ever bargained for.

All he really wanted was to make ten grand and forget — to stop seeing the mosaic of bits of clothing and human tissue that used to be someone he knew, the great swashes of blood on the furniture and walls. He tried to forget about the police calling him a liar, and his Texas-sized cellmates fighting over his perfect miniature ass.

"I threw myself into the biggest drug-and-drink songwriting binge of all time." The way all great bands start.

"I had definite ideas about the band's direction," he went on. "They wanted a sure thing, to just play bars and parties. Get cash from the door and cover Bread, like every other local band," he said. "But we had a bunch of original material, and I was willing to take a big chance. The way I saw it, we had nothing to lose. We were all broke. We were sleeping in our cars. I owed a lot of money. And it was my band, so that was that.

"The guys thought I was crazy because I wanted to record. Recording royalties wouldn't likely make them rich, so they didn't give a fuck. But here's the deal: *Songwriters* get airplay royalties, and a nickel per song per album sold. Cha ching, baby! Ten grand, two years, no problem.

"So we signed up with an indie record company run by a friend of mine. He gave us a four-record deal. We didn't know any better. Our first album did okay. Not great, not crummy. Bottom of the Top 100. Then the record company got bought by a big corporation. They tell my friend to take a hike, and they're down our shirts for another album."

He leaned back in his chair and ran his hand through his Ed Grimley quiff. He made a face and sighed.

"The first record had already shot its wad as a moneymaker, such as it was. We weren't Cream and never would be, so we suggested they just pay us off and we'd go away quietly. Went over great. 'Get in the studio or we'll see you in court,' they said. Real nice people. So we recorded this bunch of psycho-killer pop tunes I wrote when I was shitfaced. We'd already been playing them in bars for years. We're thinking, 'nobody's gonna buy *this* crap. Now they'll let us out of our contract for sure!' But no. We hadda be overnight sensations. My nickel turned out to be a nickel times eleven times six million. You do the math."

I already had, a long time ago: three point three mil.

"And that didn't include album royalties. Profits from our first and only world tour. Video residuals. Cover recordings by other artists. Nelda posters. Nelda T-shirts. Nelda bumper stickers. Nelda fucking action figures. Imagine GI Joe with big hair and a flowered apron, and you get the picture."

Lane paused. He swapped his empty coffee mug for my untouched one; I'd forgotten about it while trying to wrap my mind around all this. "No good cold!" he said.

"I heard 'What Are You Looking At?' in an elevator once."

Lane closed his eyes and rubbed the bridge of his nose. "My agent's fault. I lay this heartfelt speech on him about artistic integrity. Next thing I know, I'm Muzaked. Then he sells an option on 'Just About Impossible to Tell' to Playtex. Thank God they never used it."

"I'm sure he had your best interests at heart."

"I'm sure he had his kids' private school tuition at heart."

He stopped rubbing his nose. Stinky jumped back in his lap and stuck her tail in his face. He reached for the empty can of sardines and let her lap the oil out of it.

"You know, I wasn't shooting for immortality. It's just that I wanted us to play our own stuff. That's where the money is. Besides, we were good — too good to piss away a bunch of our dough on royalties to David Gates."

So even though the substance of *Itasca* actually predated *Nebraska* by a decade, nobody believed it because Lane didn't get around to recording it until 1983. When *Itasca* sprouted legs, the tabloids and teen mags were all over Love Dinghy. It was everything the record company could do to sweep Lane's youthful legal misadventures under the rug.

"I fended off media opportunists pretty successfully for years, except for you," he said.

Lane stopped talking and looked around. Who knew he could have a discussion this extensive, much less a bio so complex? I hoped he was finally done. But no, there was more.

"So there I was last year, quietly drinking my way to obscurity, when one of my old college roommates starts blackmailing me."

They'd shared a house off campus, during which time the roommate discovered Lane's secret. Something about a bathroom without a lock. Lane thought he could trust him to keep quiet and he did, until recently. Turns out the guy took some photos Lane found out about the hard way. Lane had to sell his house in Groton to pay him off.

Poor Lane. First his wife, then extortion, now the Beauty Shop of Horrors. I flashed back to the highway rest stop in Connecticut, the night I liberated the air from his tires. I remembered his hulking admirer in McDonald's. And O'Toole's. And the Gar. So much for my theory about Roger helping Lane with his career.

"What're you thinking about?" he asked.

I was thinking it was funny, now that I didn't care anymore what he thought, that I was getting the exposé of the century.

"What's your agent look like?" was all I said.

"You mean Shelley? He's a short, swarthy, middle-aged Jew. What do you wanna know *that* for?"

"A Pulitzer prize," I said. He look betrayed and confused. But mostly annoyed.

The knot on his forehead got bigger every time I looked at it. I leaned forward and ran my fingers gingerly through his hair, trying to eradicate Darryl's mischief. Lane didn't stop me.

This was arguably the weirdest part of all. I never understood why he felt threatened by mere conversation, never hesitated to attack like a rabid dingo over semantics, yet never flinched at a physical approach. Go figure.

"What about your blackmailer?" I asked. "Big blond hick who waves his hands when he talks?"

Lane didn't answer this time. He just squinted at me like I was a bank of floodlights someone switched on in his face.

Maybe he finally realized I'd blown off using him to get ahead. Or maybe not. I knew it was a lot to expect. I knew something else now, too. Lane wasn't screwing Roger at all. Roger was screwing Lane.

I gave up trying to adjust his hair and leaned back. He sat motionless except to scratch Stinky behind one ear, watching me for a really long time without saying anything. When I looked suitably uncomfortable, he swallowed some more aspirin.

"Forget the omelette. Just give me the cameras," he said, "and take me home."

Chapter 31

No way was I going to make Lane bounce on top of a worn-out monoshock for three hours with a five-pound helmet on his bashed-up head. Darryl was back from his band's rehearsal, so I drove myself to his apartment in Queens. I left my bike there, borrowed his car, went back to Brooklyn for Lane, and chauffeured him home, a project that shot the whole day.

The whereabouts he'd once so stubbornly refused to divulge turned out to be Point Judith, a fishing village famous for its many shipwrecks and useless but charming lighthouses. All the way there he talked a mile a minute. Some of what he told me — okay, most of it — I already knew, but I kept my mouth shut. I hoped if I didn't piss him off again, maybe he'd feed me once we got wherever the hell we were going. I was starving.

He told me all about a second brief marriage to a local beauty queen, after his first album charted and before Nelda hit the bigs. They were hitched by an Elvis impersonator at a Vegas drive-up chapel, which is why I never found the record of *that* nuptial. It ended as abruptly, if not as colorfully, as the first. Between auto shows, Miss Coffee Milk obtained a quickie divorce in the Dominican Republic and somehow stole all of Lane's cash from his first album.

In addition to the mistakes he married, Lane enjoyed the company of many other female admirers before, during, and after his fifteen minutes of fame. He claimed he had no official heirs, probably. "Grandchildren?" he said. "What're you, *nuts*?"

He also told me about Love Dinghy's third LP, the one nobody ever heard except for me, Darryl, two people who bought it at Crazy Eddie, and the suits at the record company. The band finally got their wish to be free from their contractual obligations and never recorded the fourth album — or any other — ever again.

So it seemed Lane did have good reasons to hide cash in strange places. Never know when your records will flop, or some dame will clean you out, or you'll get railroaded for a felony you didn't commit.

The revelations during the trip to Point Judith ran the gamut of unseemly to otherwise. Lane actually said he wondered sometimes about the meaning of life. I told him I never wonder about the meaning of life, because I don't think there is any. Then I told him about my theory that I'm actually dead.

"If you're dead," he said, "what does that make me?" He paused. "Don't answer that."

Eventually he asked why I knew so much about Texas. I told him how I grew up in Arlington and got arrested for driving a GTO I didn't steal. "So I ditched my court hearing, ran away to Cooper Union, and became the glamour hog I am today."

"Cooper Union, huh? Good school. My cousin went there. Said it was all pervs and fags. He barely lasted one semester before they whipped his ass and he ran home crying."

We discovered we both love pocket rockets. Since he was a lapsed Triumph fan, I got carried away about vintage Brit cafe racers and how I ought to be driving one, but can't afford to.

A highway sign announced an upcoming rest stop with a convenience store. Lane hadn't lit up since we left my house.

"You leave your smokes?" I said. "Wanna stop for more?"

"Nah. I'm trying to stop. I've stopped more times than anyone I know."

It was all real nice and polite and only slightly creepy, until Lane started asking about the guitar-playing sociopath responsible for his new look.

"What's with this Darryl guy? He's your boyfriend, or what?"

"No. We're just good friends. We used to make print advertising together. He was a retouch artist. I worked at an agency."

"An agency? What agency? I don't like him."

"Honestly, he's harmless. Think of him the way I do, as a girlfriend with a pecker."

Lane didn't think that was funny.

"Doesn't he live with you? I never called because he always answers your phone."

"No, Darryl lives in Queens. Sometimes he does answer my phone, when he's at my house, eating all my food and drinking all my beer and I'm busy getting him something else to hoover. He may look small, but he's a bottomless pit. And don't you *dare* give me a load of crap about not calling me. Did you really hang up a million times so you wouldn't have to explain yourself to someone who could give a shit?"

"What am I supposed to say to him? 'Remember me? I'm the guy whose balls you rattled in a bag in front of twelve hundred people. Lemme talk to your girlfriend.'"

"Why didn't you just ask if he had Prince Albert in a can?"

"Okay, I did call you from the Gar a few times, when I was sure you'd show up, and you didn't. I just wanted to see if you were okay. Bikes are dangerous."

"You sound like my mother."

"I'm sure she's a lovely woman, if she's anything like you."

I was trying extra hard to concentrate on the road, because I really wanted to punch him. He thought I wasn't looking and copped a feel of his own hairless leg.

"I saw that."

"So?"

"Didn't you get that out of your system during your girlhood?"

"You're kidding. Shaving? In the '70s? *So* not PC. What'd you do in advertising?"

I told him all about my previous professional incarnation. The high-profile jobs, the great money, the awesome perks, the big crash. How it all led to writing.

"It wasn't a matter of missing the career boat. I just keep getting on boats with a hole in the bottom. And that's how I became the bohemian cult figure I am today."

"Why don't you get an agent?"

"Had one, thanks. A hotshit New York agent. He tried to put his tongue down my throat. Now I don't have an agent anymore."

Lane gazed longingly at the rest stop whizzing by and reminded me not to miss our exit, still fifty miles away.

"My house used to be around here. Did you know where I lived in Groton?" he asked. "I always expected to find you in my bushes."

And lo he would have, had he ever bothered answering his door that day I brought the fake draft notice. "What do you think?" I said. "That if you don't give people your business card, they can't find you?"

"It always worked before," said the guy who had to hide from a whole state in a dress.

"Lane, that's just plain naive. I'm hardly your first muckraker. I can't believe you don't know this drill." Maybe he just wanted to see if *I* knew it. "There are a million ways to get someone's address. *Who's Who*. TRW. Dun & Bradstreet. Vehicle registrations. Legal notices — marriages, divorces, lawsuits, bankruptcies, incorporation filings..."

"Shit."

"...anyone can buy consumer mailing lists through the Yellow Pages. Then there are always big-mouthed florists. And caterers. And dry cleaners. In some people's cases, relatives. Lots of relatives."

"Yeah, I know. I'm related to half of Rhode Island. Sometimes it's a liability."

"Then there are crisscross phone directories. Police and FBI records. And if none of *that* pans out, I stake out the convenience store in your neighborhood and wait. You'll show up eventually. You're a smoker. I follow you home."

"Trying to be an ex-smoker. Okay, you can stop now. You're seriously creeping me out. But I don't get it. All the stuff you knew about me — it would've been front page. 'Rock Superstar's Secret Sex Change' and all that. Tabloids pay a fortune for that crap. You could've had a whole yard full of dented motorcycles."

I certainly could, Ollie.

Lane poked the bruise on his forehead again, then whipped out something from so far up his ass it's a miracle a search party didn't have to find his hands.

"How come you never used any of my dirt?" He actually seemed disappointed about me ignoring it. "Don't you even want a house that's not falling down, or a car?"

Now I was *really* mad. A million sarcastic replies flooded my mind. *Get over yourself*, and *I tried but no one would pay me for your personal baggage*.

He wasn't ready to hear the truth, and he sure wasn't getting any of that from me. I changed lanes to get away from the smelly Scenicruiser I should've put him on. There was enough shit going on in that car without diesel fumes in the mix.

"Listen," I said, "I like the house I have. I don't need a car, I'm a New Yorker. And there's nothing else I wanna buy bad enough that I gotta wreck your miserable life to get it."

"My life's not that miserable," he said, laughing.

"Coulda fooled *me*. What happened to your rant about all journalists being sharks?"

"Just because I'm paranoid don't mean they're not after me."

"Ha ha. You funny man. Find someone else to get you into the *Star*. I'm an investigative reporter, not a sniper. Why risk my hard-earned bohemian cult figure status throwing lawn darts at mini targets?" Why let him know I gave a shit about him, once?

"I just meant..."

"Look, don't flatter yourself that you're notorious enough to earn my journalistic spite. All you did wrong was pretend to like me a lot."

"What do you mean, I pretended to like you a lot?"

"Admit it. You're the one who needs hacks like me. I don't need *you*, you little..."

"Wait a minute..."

"... dipwad. The world is full of bigger career assholes I can exploit. Wanna know where Ronald Frump hid 1,700 truckloads of PCB-laced dirt from the West Side railyard?"

"No, no, I don't care about that. Wait..."

"Okay. It's in a landfill in Staten Island."

"No, back up. To the other thing you were talking about..."

"Big-mouthed florists?"

"No, after the florists and before career assholes."

"Being dead?"

"NO! Oh man — you mean that night on Bob's boat, don't you?" It was getting *very* loud in the car. "Goddamn it! I —"

"Hey — being dead, having sex with you — what's the difference?"

He grabbed the steering wheel and yanked it hard to the right. I hammered the brake. The right fender careened into a steel railing as the car fishtailed off the highway, finally stopping at a forty-five degree angle on the shoulder. I hoped Darryl had insurance.

"Why'd you do that to Darryl's car?" I said, very calmly for a potential murderer. Men never think women will hit them, do they? Nelda had nothing on this.

"Why can't you be normal?" Lane yelled.

"Define your terms."

"Define *this*!" he sputtered and sprang from the car. He slammed the door behind him and started marching away on the shoulder, fifty miles from nowhere.

I drove alongside him with Darryl's blinkers flashing, a parade of angry honking vehicles accumulating behind us.

"Get in the car, Lane!" I yelled out the window. "You're tying up traffic real bad. It's not rush hour yet."

"Leave me alone!" he yelled back and kicked a hubcap in his path. With his head down and his hands rammed into his jacket pockets, he stomped toward Point Judith. I only had one card up my sleeve.

"Hey, Lane. Want your faggy cigarette case back?"

His fingers were around the door handle before I could stop the car.

Chapter 32

The only way I could stop Lane from bailing from the car again was to confess I invaded his house in Groton and stole the cigarette case.

"I just wanted to get even after you hosed me," I said. I looked away from the road long enough to see if there was a reaction on his face. There was. Total shock.

"You did a bang-up job. Congratulations," he said dejectedly.

There was a long silence before he spoke again. "When I put the house on the market, I was worried about strangers going inside. One look at the awards and pictures and all, they'd figure out real quick who lived there. But that runaway boxcar Agneta goes, 'Not to worry! Won't take long to sell!'" Lane pulled an imaginary railroad whistle and tooted. "She said anyone with enough bread to buy it wouldn't be the type to mess it up. Next thing I know, my cigarette case is gone."

Turns out my little travel souvenir belonged to his dear destructed first wife. The case and the photo in it were the only mementos he'd kept from his Texas adventure, besides the clothes. "I just liked the way they felt," he said. It wasn't exactly a time of cherished memories. He didn't make any more jokes about Texas.

"All this time I was worried about who had the Polaroid," he said, "about what would happen if they put two and two together."

"Earth to Lane. If people find out about Elaine, the *worst* that would happen is you'd get your own TV show. And that asshole Roger couldn't blackmail you anymore, either."

"How the *hell* do you know his name?"

I didn't answer.

"Listen, you stay away from him! He's trouble. He's been tailing me everywhere, bugging me for more money. I figured when I moved, he'd never find me again. Ha! He probably just called half my family, like you did. Now he shows up everywhere I play. Know what *else* that bastard did? Broke into my house. Stole a file cabinet. A whole file cabinet! Got all my bank and insurance stuff. Business papers. Letters."

Hmm. Maybe Lane's stolen file cabinet contained unanswered interview requests from pesky Brooklyn hacks, on letterhead conveniently printed with their address and phone number.

A stupid theory, perhaps. Angry recluses rarely keep letters they don't intend to answer. And I'd met Roger. He didn't seem bright enough to find Brooklyn on a map of Kings County. But then I thought about the semiliterate Lane-related death threat, the non-Lane phone hang ups made from bars.

"I'm tellin' ya, it's not like the old days when all you had were street gangs and the Mafia," Lane said. "You just can't make handshake deals with crooks anymore."

I cracked up.

"What's so funny? It doesn't bother you? The Elaine stuff, I mean?"

"Lane, I went to art school. I lived in Greenwich Village. I was in *advertising*, for christsake. Hell, I've been cross-dressing for thirty years. No, the Elaine stuff does not bother me. Anyway, the whole world already knows you're a little off-kilter."

"What do you mean, 'off-kilter'? I'm not gay."

"I didn't say gay. And I'm qualified to know. I was referring to the Hit Parade ditties you wrote about serial sex murders."

"Oh. So, what, then? You were mad at me 'cause I'm off-kilter?"

"No. I find your off-kilterness charming."

"Then what?"

"Nobody ever reneged on an interview with me before."

"You were a pain in the butt."

"It's what I do. Lane, your house in Groton was weird."

"How do you mean, 'weird'? You think *your* house isn't?"

"I mean, it was so sterile. There were no tchotchkes, no plants, no toys. *Everybody* has toys. And half of it was decorated like a gypsy tea parlor, but the other half was like a church basement."

"Tchotchkes?"

"You know — memorabilia. Refrigerator magnets. Useless gifts from loved ones. Dumb personal stuff. Knickknacks."

"Oh. I had knickknacks. Knickknacks collect dust. You have dust, you hire help. The help steal the knickknacks. I wasn't home much. Ate out a lot. Mostly just used the studio. The people I bought the house from hired a decorator who died halfway through the job, thank God. I didn't have anything to sit on, so I bought their furniture along with the house. And I have tons of junk. It's all in boxes at the new place. Anything else about me keeping you awake nights?"

"Yeah. Why'd you treat me like shit after we had so much fun on Bob's boat?"

He didn't miss a beat. "I wanted you to go away."

Away. Right. I let this sink in.

"Wanna tell my *why*?"

"Because I had a maniac threatening to kill me and I didn't want anyone else involved."

"Do I seem to you like someone who needs protecting?"

"I'm sorry," he actually said. "But the last time I had that much of that kind of fun, I ended up in jail, in debt, and in dresses. And she ended up dead."

Chapter 33

We had the windows down, the marsh smells blowing through our hair. The only conversation was Lane giving me careful directions to the house he hadn't wanted me to find.

The Galilee Escape Road glowed bronze in the fading sunset, abandoned except for a flock of geese with no reason to feel threatened until we invaded their space. There was a great honking and flurry as they piled noisily into Point Judith Pond, leaving us alone in the jewel-toned sunset.

Directly we arrived at a weatherbeaten farmstead so old, it made my Victorian look like new construction. What I noticed first were the rain gutters, which were jammed with leaves, and the windows. Lane had gone off and left every one of them open.

The place sat in the middle of 11.4 acres of mostly marsh. There wasn't a whole lot of farming going on anymore, seeing as how the fields had turned into bogs. The house was way too big for one person. But it had obvious advantages if you have the loudest band in the smallest state.

The Range Rover no one ever drove but me was parked in the yard. The old sports cars were gone. Too bad. They were the only cool thing about Lane. His van languished on Long Island somewhere, unless one of the Dinghies had had the presence of mind to drive it home. They were probably still looking for him at Long Island Jewish.

"What happened to your cars?"

"Those old crates? Belonged to a friend of mine, a record producer. He was between wives. Asked me to hide them for him 'til after the prenup. I made him take them back when I moved. Good riddance."

"They were nice."

"Sure. Everyone was impressed. What's the point? Can't drive 'em, can't park 'em anywhere. They just get stolen and break down. No one can fix 'em right anymore. All they do is take up space and make messes on the garage floor to clean up. Meanwhile, my car's outside getting rained on and covered with bird crap."

We approached the front door. He retrieved the key from underneath a garden statue of Saint Swithen. I wondered why he bothered locking the door at all, what with all the windows screaming "Rob me!"

He started to turn the knob, then stopped. His eyes closed and he swayed slightly. When I put out my hand to steady him, all his weight fell against it. Without even thinking I gathered him up, kicked open the door, and carried him squirming over the threshold like a punk bride from hell. I poured him into a Barcalounger, of all things, that was parked in his entry hall.

"Don't ever do that again," he said. He jumped up and took off down the hall.

I was right behind him. It was quite a house, a vast warren of interconnected rooms accessible only by one to another. If I lost him now, I'd never find the food.

Lane's nonchalance about exterior details was mirrored in his interior decor. Only the few rooms he actually used were furnished, a descriptor I use reluctantly. Most of his belongings were in boxes that filled half the first floor. To his credit, none of the Groton dead-designer pieces had made the trip. The wood floors were bare and splintery. There were holes in the plaster he'd never get around to fixing, which is why I laughed when we got to his kitchen.

"What's so funny?" he asked.

Unlike the rest of his house, the kitchen was handsomely appointed with expensive modern appliances and lavishly overstocked, like a fat millionaire's bomb shelter.

"Oh, yeah, all this. People keep sending me food," he explained. "I don't know why. Guess I look hungry. Business associates, the record company, fans, my mother — they've all been sending me stuff, crates of stuff, mostly to my agent 'cause no one could find me. Shelley called and said, 'Get this crap outta my office, you little momser.' Check *this* out."

He took me on a tour of his walk-in larder. It was like a stroll through Dean and DeLuca, without the glaze-eyed tourists. He even had a curated exhibit of historic fruitcakes.

"I *hate* fruitcake," he said, laughing, "but I can't throw 'em out. People get insulted. And each one has a story, you know? And look — they make great doorstops." He picked up a mummified loaf and held it out. "Go ahead. Take it with you!"

"You wish!" I yelped, backing away. "Got any real food?"

"Whatever you want."

There was a massive, fake antique Lane Company farmhouse table in Lane McCarthy's massive, real antique farmhouse kitchen. When I pointed out this suspicious coincidence, he just said, "Came with the house."

For the next several minutes he commuted back and forth from the oversized Sub-Zero to the table, until it was covered with the most glorious spread I ever saw — pate, roasted venison, deep-fried mudbugs, artichoke hearts, Italian prunes, pumpernickel, chevre, almond butter, Greek olives, pumpkin ravioli, a chocolate Bundt cake with a molten center. He dragged over a whole case of chilled Chandon Blanc de Noir, a make-nice present from John Mellencamp. Lane popped the corks off two bottles and set them on the table. Then he left the kitchen momentarily, returning with a worn deck of cards.

We swigged champagne from the bottles, ate like starving castaways, and played pinochle for hours. Meat bones and fruit pits were everywhere.

We shuffled and dealt and played and shuffled. We scrapped over the last crawfish, the last slice of raisin black bread.

I play cards a lot, and owe my embarrassingly marginal success at it to card counting. Lane didn't know that, plus he had a concussion. We played until midnight, me winning, he losing, until he finally staked his Broadcaster and lost it to my first streak ever. The only graceful way to stop the carnage was to send him to bed.

"You should get some sleep," I said. "You're a mess."

He quit shuffling and looked up. "You're going home now?" he asked, confused.

I was going to, until he said that.

"How 'bout I take the couch? You have a concussion. Someone oughtta stay with you. And look at me — way too drunk to drive home. So, tag — I'm it! Now go to bed."

"No, really, I'm okay."

"No, really, you're not. Listen, damned if I'm gonna feel bad because you fell down a flight of stairs after I left. I already kidnapped you and tarted you up like a Ziegfeld girl. I feel guilty enough." I wasn't about to tell him about the flat tires, the junk bonds, the stolen Strat, or Tipper Gore's $3,000 bracelet. "Seriously, I'll be fine down here. Go."

"You gonna wake me up every ten minutes?"

"Only if you look dead. Like *that* would ever happen. You're like a jack-in-the-box with a busted latch. But someone should be here in case you have bad dreams, or wake up disoriented or something."

"I do that every day."

"Okay. So go to bed. Have bad dreams. See you in the morning." I started to carry dishes to the sink.

He had a different idea. "Let me show you something." He took the dishes away from me and set them down. "Over here," he said.

He grabbed my arm and hustled me into his living room, a warehouse of stereo equipment and recorded music. He put a Patsy Cline album on the Thorens, pried off his boots, and pushed me to the middle of the room in his white crew socks. Then he put his arms around me and stood on my feet. We languidly scuffed up the splintery parquet while Patsy yodeled about being treated like dirt.

Lane's face was covered with Sonny Crockett-y whiskers. He'd been having too much fun the last couple of days to shave. It was all silvery down now; I couldn't resist nuzzling it. He pulled his head back and looked at me.

"Wait a minute. How come it don't bother you that I gotta stand on a box to make out?"

"I can't resist a man in a pompadour."

I wished he'd stop thinking. I pulled his head toward me again and put my nose back in his cheek fuzz.

Gently with two fingers, he pushed my face away from his and licked a fish egg off my collarbone. Then he kissed me. His mouth tasted like Bundt cake.

With his other arm still around my waist, he unbuttoned my shirt with his free hand. My free hand followed right behind his, buttoning it back up again. This went on for a couple of tracks. Whenever I felt I was losing, I'd tug gently on what was left of his hair; he'd fall off my insteps, grab my wrist, and go "Ow! Don't touch my head!" I'd pull him back onto my feet by his belt loops, we'd resume dancing, and he'd start on my shirt again.

"How about this then, can I do this?" I'd ask him, laughing, barely laying the pad of my index finger on the tip of his purple nose.

"No! Don't touch that!" he'd say and pull my hand away from his face, then bite my shoulder or arm or neck or whatever else was currently unguarded.

To make him stop biting, I'd say "Well, can I touch this then?" and put my hand down his stuck-in-the-'80s pants, and we'd struggle for control of his stiff-in-the-'90s stuff. This went on until the needle ran off the vinyl and I'd been transformed into a half-naked Broadcaster owner.

"So let me see if I got this straight," I said. "You're through with fun, and I've sworn off musicians. Now what?"

As usual, Lane had an idea. Of course, there are special technical requirements when fooling around with a concussion. Pirates of the Caribbean are out. No choreography lessons, either. And definitely no rushing. Otherwise, screw the rules and do it in the middle of an 11.4 acre marsh, because you can make all the noise you want.

Chapter 34

The light in Rhode Island is blue. Even the night sky is blue. Not black like in Texas, or orange-red like in New York. At noon it's a luminous aqua with white wisps, like an Italian ice; at night it's velvety and jewellike. At the end of summer the sky turns periwinkle at dusk, then violet, then indigo.

That's what I was remembering as I lay awake in the dark, unable to sleep. This was a hell of a place to be restless. No books, no TV. I didn't have the heart to wake Lane. He was far away. Not in Ampegville again, just dreaming. He kept stamping the bed in his sleep and saying things like "Key of G, idiot!"

For a while I entertained myself by looking out the window at stars. There are no stars in Brooklyn, only smog and glare and tall buildings blocking the sky. Here there were zillions of stars, all sparkly and winking.

Lane's windows were curtainless, the sashes thrown open. The symphony of bugs outside was raucous — cicadas and crickets and locusts, all looking for dates. We don't have bugs in Brooklyn, except for cockroaches, and they don't make music, only doodoos.

When my knees started to hurt from kneeling at windows, I crawled back into Lane's bed and played with his hands. They were small and strong and always knew what to do, even if his brain didn't. I sucked his callouses until his fingertips wrinkled. "Stop! No more Crazy Glue!" he shouted in his sleep. I crawled back out of his bed and prowled around.

There was a pile of something in a corner that I inspected the only way possible in the dark, quickly determining it to be laundry. I pulled out a denim shirt that smelled like he'd worn it for a week. I put it on and curled up in an overstuffed chair opposite the bed, where I could watch Lane sleep.

His shimmery outline appeared and disappeared as he breathed. There was just enough pale moonlight to distinguish his body from the mess where he lay tangled up in more blankets than anyone needed in August.

He looked like a lunar surface with a couple of rain forests. Earlier I'd confessed he was the first man I'd known biblically who had hair on his chest. He thought I was calling him a throwback and got mad, until he realized I found it exotic and he calmed down. He said I was the first woman who hadn't presented him with an instruction manual or read him the riot act before her clothes were off.

I couldn't imagine him getting a rough time from any horny women, especially if they were drunk. On the other hand, I'm so culturally disconnected, maybe that's what passes for courtship in the '90s and I just never learned the rules.

Me, I was on him like a rash. The only thing I could think of to improve what he was doing was to whisper "slow down, Stretch, I ain't goin' nowhere," just before plunging over a waterfall of blinding colors and ten thousand spark plugs firing in sequence. Moderne and detached, my ass. But if it ain't broke, I say don't fix it.

It was strange to see him motionless now, unguarded, utterly quiet. I'd gotten used to all the noise and flashing lights that always surrounded him, his following of costumed halfwits, the air redolent of smoldering hemp and cheap beer, the phalanx of foldback monitors barricading him from the undead of the world.

Now it was just Lane surrounded by the night. The loudest sounds were trees swishing and a gate swinging in the breeze. The air was soft; it smelled of cut grass and honeysuckle. The brightest light came from lightning bugs on the window screens that were old and rusty and full of holes, and always would be. Lane mumbled something crude about a bounced check and rolled over on his stomach, dragging his *Star Wars* sheet across his perfect tiny ass.

I wanted to stop time. I wanted to put him in my pocket and carry all this away with me. All I could do was sit there watching him, transfixed, holding his shirttail to my nose until long after the sun rose.

Eventually the sky turned gold and mauve, then gradually an intense turquoise. The outdoor noises changed to seagulls, the drone of private planes, ferry horns: E-flat, F-sharp.

Lane woke up and we got dressed. In the kitchen he pinned me to him with one arm and licked my neck while making French toast. We ate it with Kentucky sweet sorghum, and then he kicked me out because he had to go "finalize a business deal." He wouldn't say what it was, which is how I knew it was Roger.

Chapter 35

When I got back to New York, I dropped off what was left of the Toyota at a body shop in Flushing. I was safe at home before I told Darryl what happened over the phone. It was just what he wanted to hear after I didn't return it the same day I took it, like I promised. He was slightly less furious about me hooking up with Lane, only because I brought home the Broadcaster.

A couple of days later he got his car back looking better than before I borrowed it, and the screaming noises from Queens gradually died down. I sent the mechanic's bill to Lane, along with unwashed lace panties and a pale blue cashmere men's sweater from Paul Stuart. The note read: Couldn't find my straitjacket, just this.

I spent the next week in Connecticut, where I'd been hired by a vintage motorcycle magazine in Darien called *Classic Trend*. Thanks to a miracle of modern medicine, I was tapped as their fill-in editor (by which I mean the regular editor contracted mono and they told him don't come back).

In fact, I owed some of my good fortune to a well-timed twist of fate named Nancy Delgado. Overnight the whole bikesphere was abuzz about this delicate little thing from Bolivia who raced big Ducatis and Harleys. She was the only woman competing in the H-D Twin Sports series and ranked eleventh in the AMA/CCS championship points standings. She even wrenched her own bikes. For one shining moment guaranteed to crash, even mortal bike chicks like me were regarded more seriously than before Delgado whipped twelve dudes' asses in her first H-D pro race.

"You'll have your own desk here. And a Mac," said my new favorite editor. "Oh yeah, and we got a shop. With tools."

His name was George Clifford. I called him Cliffie. He hated that. I was supposed to be the token placeholder until they got a real male editor, but they were so impressed with how fast I got there after they called, they just went ahead and gave me the job.

On my first day at work, Cliffie told me that due to a unanimous board decision between him and the assistant editor, they were putting my name on the masthead.

"Did you *read* my résumé?" I asked him. "Every magazine I ever worked for tanked." I assured him that putting me on his masthead guaranteed bankruptcy, but Cliffie refused to reconsider.

"I'm doing it," he said. "So stop calling me Cliffie." Cliffie didn't forget to pay me, either.

My assignments for *Classic Trend* required prying into the restoration efforts of hapless rescuers of stubborn antiques. I interfered with their projects and took blurry pictures that Cliffie was thrilled to have, because the publisher was too cheap to let him hire a real photographer. Being a classy guy, Cliffie just told me he was confident his readership would appreciate a woman who knew the difference between an F-stop and a G-spot. He said he liked my style of cutting through all the bike-jockey chestbeating that was skunking up the industry.

Whatever. I just like crawling around under bikes, getting grease under my nails, and getting paid for it. At *Classic Trend* there were bikes apart all over the place. And writing about machines is way easier than writing about people. If a bike cops an attitude, you can fix it with a wrench.

I was spending as much time at the office as possible, feverishly inventing new projects. Everyone there was thinking: *wow — Nona's so dedicated!* Nona was thinking: *wow — how long can this last?*

For my first hardware shootout, I talked Cliffie into letting me resuscitate a rusty 1970s Jap superbike. "Lemme rebuild that CBX in the junkpile," I told him, "then we'll test it against your Benelli Sei."

"You can *do* that?" he asked.

"With a rock," I said. "Watch me."

I always go to Darien on the Merritt Parkway, a twisty road built right after the stock market correction of '29 for driving the automotive equivalent of bathtubs on wheels. There are no buses stinking it up, no trucks to avoid. I revel in sweeping its pristine blacktop at 95.

The ride to Darien is my narcotic. On the Merritt I'm a sine wave of chill, impervious to any siren. The wind is all that's left of the Connecticut on the map. Soon even the blacktop is gone. All around me are Lane's *Star Wars* sheets covered with cake crumbs, comic books, CDs, globs of whipped cream. I think about Lane kissing my palms, about stroking him all over like some feral creature that came for scraps and stayed; Lane wrapped around me like a Chinese finger puzzle, his hair like fur against my neck.

And then I'm in Darien, underneath a shop project. That's where I was when Lane got tired of not finding me underneath him instead and materialized on the other end of a phone page.

In addition to its pantheon of moldy rides, *Classic Trend* also has an outstanding collection of obsolete office technology. Someone handed me a giant 1980's-era cordless receiver as I lay on my back on a greasy concrete floor, ecstatically deconstructing a seized Honda six-cylinder engine that should've been on a locomotive. We had a really romantic conversation, me and Lane.

"When do I get my cigarette case back?"

"When I get through dismantling this CBX."

"I should live so long. How 'bout tonight?"

"Okay. But I gotta go home first and get it. It's not like I carry it around with me. Plus I need a shower."

"I have a shower here. You can borrow it. Just get my cigarette case and get over here."

Yes sir. Right away, sir. You little prick. I couldn't wait to see him.

First I drove all the way back to Brooklyn, stopping at home long enough to pick up the cigarette case. I didn't even change my work clothes before driving half the night to Rhode Island. It was 2 a.m. when I rolled into Lane's bog, making my cranky entrance in denim jeans and a jacket covered with grunge and dead bugs. None of this phased Lane, who stood in his yard, waiting patiently for me.

We stayed outside for a while, pinching each other and roughhousing. "Where is it?" he asked over and over, twisting my arm behind my back and copping feels and laughing.

I pulled the cigarette case from my map pocket and pushed it at him. He checked that the Polaroid was still inside and I hadn't drawn a mustache on it. Then he snapped the case shut and put it in his jacket pocket. "C'mon, let's go in." he said. "It's late."

We went into the house through a side door I never knew was there. His house had lots of doors like that, that went to parts I hadn't been in yet. Lane's Haunted House of Fun.

"C'mere. I wanna show you something," he said over his shoulder as we walked and walked. All his guitars were back, strewn everywhere in their secondhand glory. And one was a new addition.

"A Gibson Moderne!" I gasped and stopped dead. "*Nobody* has one! They're only rumors! An urban myth. Is it real? Where'd you get it? *How* did you get it? What'd you pay? Can I touch it?"

I knew it was real because he said nothing and dragged me away. Hot damn, a Moderne! Wait'll Darryl sees *this*!

I followed Lane's backside better than his patter as he trotted down the long hall, rambling on about business stuff — something about contracts and showcases at clubs with table service. He seemed especially happy. Who cared? A real Moderne!

He finally stopped at a doorway that looked familiar. It was the bathroom by his bedroom. How we got there, I didn't know. It felt like we'd walked in circles. Would I be able to find the Moderne again after Lane conked out? Damn! Should've left a trail of crumbs.

He went inside the bathroom, leaned into the tub, and turned on the taps.

I must've had a look on my face, because the next thing he said was "Thought you said you wanted a shower?" It was more like a challenge than a question. He'd already disposed of his clothing somehow. I never knew anyone who could get naked that fast.

While I balanced on one foot, trying to get my sock off, he plucked a South County slug off the floor and escorted it to the toilet, singing "Sea Cruise" to it.

Meanwhile, the bathroom filled with steam. He picked up something that looked like a can of shaving cream in all the fog. It wasn't. By the time I realized what it really was, I was covered with Silly String.

There ensued a protracted skirmish with lots of squealing and dodging, out of which I emerged victorious with the can and returned the favor until it was empty. We never made it to the shower. It was still running, filling the house with vapor.

I backed into the bedroom, popping Lane with a Hilton towel as he came after me with a loofah. He was laughing and grabbing at the towel when suddenly he froze. He was staring at something over my shoulder.

I whipped around. Through the dense cloud of steam I saw someone across the bedroom, rifling Lane's drawers. He'd been stuffing handfuls of their contents into a bag when he heard us and spun around. I recognized him.

"Roger," said Lane, betraying no emotion other than exasperation, "didn't the check clear?"

"Spent it all," said Roger in his full-tilt Austin drawl. "Came for some more. I know ya got it."

Money — that I could understand. But Lane didn't keep money in drawers. What kind of leverage did the Dumbest Man on Earth expect to gain from stealing terry wristbands and white socks?

I'd never stood this close to him before, only sat next to him in a darkened bar, looking away and hoping he'd shut up or leave. Same as I was hoping now. He was huge. Easily 6'4", maybe 250 pounds.

"Ya know, I like ta never found this place," he said. "Ya weren't tryin' ta get ridda me now, were ya?"

Lane didn't answer.

The whole scene was straight out of *All My Children*. The only thing missing was a Polydent commercial. I didn't know whether to laugh or run. I watched Lane, trying to gauge what to do by his reactions, but he wasn't giving me much to go on. The other times I saw them interact, he didn't exactly score high marks. So I waited, in case someone had to deck Roger.

"Hey," said Roger, squinting into the mist at me like an idiot. He was long overdue to notice I was wearing aerosol confetti instead of clothes. "Hoo wee! You're that writer gal, the one doin' that big magazine story 'bout Elaine!"

Lane and I looked at each other. I rolled my eyes. This would definitely require an explanation. Later.

There were a lot of things I wanted to tell Lane: that I never interviewed his college roommates; that Roger and I only ever talked once, in a bar, and *he* was pestering *me*; that there *was* no story about Elaine, never had been a story about Elaine. But Roger just kept yammering away.

"Ya'll know, don'cha, if that there story gits out I won't be able ta make my truck payments no more? Ya'll ain't gonna make me find another cow ta milk, are ya'll?" He scratched his head. Tectonic plates shifted. "How'm I gonna pay for my swimming pool?"

Roger's inflections turned everything he said into word chowder. *How muh gonna pay fer muh swemmin pooh?*

But his tenuous grasp of the national language wasn't uppermost in my mind. Losing him was. And I knew the perfect way to do it. He'd just given me the idea himself: convince him the ride was over.

Unfortunately, there was one problem with my brilliant plan. I'd probably lose Lane along with Roger. But Lane already thought I'd sold him out anyway. Couldn't last forever, right? *La vie suce.* At least he wouldn't have Roger hanging around his neck like a boulder.

"Roger, go home," I heard myself say. "You're *so* too late. The cow's beyond milking. It's in the meat case." He just stood there, blinking. Damn! Too many metaphors. New plan.

"Dog, my story about Elaine is done. Over. *Fin.* Turned in. Sorry about your stupid pool, but whatever happens, happens. Understand? I got my own career to think about, and this is the story of the century. Guys in dresses are hot news. Dame Edna Everage. Divine. Harvey Fierstein. J. Edgar Hoover. Dana Carvey. RuPaul. Ed Wood, Jr., Hitler..."

"Shut up!" snapped Roger. "We got us a serious problem here." He shifted his weight from foot to foot, shaking the bag with Lane's things at us.

"Yo Roger, *you're* the problem. You watch too much TV." I was hoping he'd just get frustrated and leave. It worked on everyone else.

He looked at the door, like he might actually use it. I crossed my fingers.

"We'll work something out," Lane piped up, ruining everything. Damn! I should've known he'd cave.

"You and me'll discuss that directly," Roger said to Lane. To me he said, "It's right nice a ya to come ou'chere like this, hon. I was fixing ta drive all the way ta Brooklyn again ta do something 'bout the situation. Thanks for saving me the trip."

"My pleasure," I said. Hmm. Drive to Brooklyn *again*... So I guessed right about him authoring the eight-track note. Half those hang-up calls were probably Roger, too, checking for a good time to deliver his maim-o-gram. But what was the something he was gwanna to Brooklyn again to do? Terrorize me with *Dallas* reruns?

Roger was starting to bore me. He didn't know it yet, but he could threaten me all night and I'd probably just doze off. I grew up with a brother and a hundred cousins just like him — all big-boned, big-mouthed Texas wankers who talk loud and fall hard.

I considered enlisting Lane in a full body tackle on Roger. Alone, neither of us would've made a dent in him, but together we could turn Roger into rump roast. That is, we could if Lane could momentarily overlook the goddamned Elaine story.

There was no quick and dirty way to communicate my crazy plan to him, and he seemed determined to avoid physical contact with Roger at all costs. A clear case of been there/done that. I remembered the Leatherman tool in Roger's pocket. Lane wouldn't take his eyes off him.

"Okay, okay. Don't everybody get excited," Lane said. "Let's say I got cash for you. What's in it for me?"

"You get to live. But either way, the heifer's gotta go."

Live? Go? HEIFER?! That cinched it. The hell with both of them.

"Yeah right, Hoss. Milk *this*!" I yelled and started to dive for Roger, but Lane grabbed my wrist and held me there. He was deceptively strong for such a tiny man.

"What are you? *Stupid?*" he said to Roger, face straight as a two-by-four.

Roger got quiet while he decided. I must admit, I didn't know where Lane was headed, either.

"It's too late to shut her up," Lane said. "She's been trying to tell you, you big dork. She already filed the story."

I stopped prying back his thumb from my wrist and looked at him, aghast. He winked at me.

Roger turned to me in a panic. "Then call whatever magazine it is that's runnin' it. Tell 'em to stop the story!"

"I can't," I said, still staring at Lane. "It's at the printer's."

There was a brief scary silence before Lane answered the next question Roger would've asked, eventually.

"Look. There's not a damned thing you can do about it now. I already tried. You think I want people reading that crap about me?" Lane was gnashing the scenery to shreds. "Everything's in that story — you, me, the drugs, the clogs, all of it. I've seen it. You kill her, they'll just come looking for us. You wanna do time for nothin'? Is *that* what you want?" *I* wanted to boff Lane on the spot. "Now why don't I give you some traveling money, and you just take off? You don't wanna be around me when the shit hits the fan."

Roger shrank into himself. There was nothing left for him to do except nod, wait for Lane to get his money, and blink at two naked people covered with Silly String trying to buy time. And from where I stood, there wasn't much of that to be bought. Even someone as mongoloid as Roger would start to wonder why Lane was naked with someone who'd allegedly ruined his life.

"Put your clothes on," Lane said to me, letting go of my wrist. "Get out of here."

If all he really planned to do was pay Roger to go away like he always did, why make me leave? Obviously he'd made some other decision, and left me and Roger out of it.

I totally snapped. I'd had it with him leaving me out. I'd had it with men and their hormonal rampages. And for sure I'd had it with jumbo assholes and little dictators.

Lane flung handfuls of Silly String everywhere, then put on the clothes he'd dropped in a heap by the bathroom door. He was all business.

I did the same and left. *You boys have fun storming the castle*, I almost said as I looked back and saw them arguing animatedly, waving their hands in the air. The shower was still running.

Believe me, if I knew the fastest way out of that steam-filled labyrinth, I'd gladly have taken it. Someone was about to get sandbagged, and damned if it was gonna be me.

I took the only route I was sure of, down the long hall. I saw the front door and ran to it. When I opened it, there was the ass end of the hulking red Chevy SS 454 pickup we didn't hear Roger roar up in because of our infantile war games.

Funny. Or maybe not. It looked just like the truck speeding off that time Darryl saw someone stealing my trash. Now I could see it had Texas plates. Duh. Roger must've been looking for tossed drafts of that big story on Elaine. Hell hath no fury like a blackmailer with used tampons and kitty litter instead of proof.

Lane's rusty screen door slammed shut behind me. I walked to the front of the pickup and saw the big black pushbar on it. Now I got it. *Squash you like a blowfly* is what Roger was fixing to gwanna Brooklyn again to do.

For once, Lane wasn't overreacting. Half a lifetime in New York, and who knew I'd have to come *here* to get killed?

Get out of here. Lane's words echoed between my ears. Right, I thought. I'm gonna leave a guy who just saved me from a homicidal nut having a bad day.

I turned back around toward his house. Even if Lane had a cannon in there, he was still no match for someone who'd casually bulldoze a motorbike with a two-ton utility vehicle. But if all that folklore about his thugster youth was true, he could handle Roger short term. And he'd probably stay wrapped as long as he was the one giving orders, or thought he was. Fascism was his specialty. I'd never tell him this, but I'd clean his floor with my tongue if he ordered me to.

I couldn't imagine what kind of gladiatorial two-step was going on inside the house. I only knew I'd be in the way if I went back in, and I'd already trampled Lane's manhood enough times. He needed elbow room to try his plan, whatever it was. I'd be more use to him as a backup when it failed. I decided to give him five minutes and went looking for a sledgehammer.

As I hurriedly surveyed his yard, it soon became obvious he was tending a saggy, double-centenarian, 10,000-square-foot rattletrap with a Weedwhacker and fifty pounds of road salt. I shook my head and went to my bike to unbungie the helmets. I've used them for street weapons before — they're big and hard and have nice handles if you fasten the chinstraps. You can break someone's face with one, easy.

I was just fastening the straps and checking my watch when Lane bounded out of the house.

"Start the bike!" he barked, flying toward me. I fumbled for the keys. "Do it now!"

As he climbed onto the bike, he said he'd told Roger the money was in the fuse box. Anyone who knew Lane would believe that. So they went to the basement door. He pushed Roger down the stairs, slammed the door shut, and blocked it with a loaded amp rack. It wasn't going to hold him long.

Lane was right. In my mirror I could see Roger running from the house to his truck. I also saw something that looked like flames shooting out the kitchen windows. Then I stopped looking and redlined it the hell out of there. Roger was right behind us.

Chapter 36

All the way from the Galilee Escape Road to Route 1, Route 108 is four straight flat miles of speed trap on which I hoped to attract the notice of the local constabulary. I ran six lights to ensure this. Much to my dismay, we did see them — zealously pursuing a Porsche in the opposite direction.

I was surprised at how hard it was to shake Roger. He possessed driving skills inversely proportioned to his intellect. Being conceived and born in back seats, Texans learn to drive early. For the next twenty-one miles I ran all eleven traffic signals on Route 1 until we hit Westerly without benefit of law enforcement.

By then I was convinced Lane wasn't taking the situation all that seriously. Every time we'd pass another fleabag motel, the same guy who yelled at me to run from Roger would punch my shoulder and signal me to pull over.

Now Roger was like toilet paper stuck to my heel. We blew through a construction zone with a Be Prepared To Stop sign knocked to the ground. I could hear Lane laughing hysterically inside his helmet. I don't think he knew his house was on fire.

We barreled crazily through dark and abandoned downtown Westerly, Home of Guild Guitars. Until that point, Route 1 conveniently had been a limited-access four-lane highway. In Westerly I had to slow way down as the same road degenerated into five hard right-angle turns in quick succession. It's a bitch if you've never done it before, and even worse at night with limited visibility, an enraged arsonist chasing you, and an unhinged passenger slipping sideways in every turn. Roger handled the course fearlessly, bird-dogging us like the zombie thrillbilly he was.

At the intersection where you cross Mechanic Street and you're in another state, I turned onto Route 2 in Connecticut and headed for I-95. Two more more miles of red lights and no cops later, we climbed onto the interstate with nobody but Roger interested in us.

Someone with more sense would've headed for Providence, a big town with lots of side streets to hide on. It was only forty minutes away. Or twenty, if you're in a big fucking hurry. But for once I wanted to go home to my crappy house in Brooklyn, with the big gun under the bed.

On I-95 South there was no traffic except for a few trucks, giving Roger a clear view of us. We sped down the highway swapping lanes like ribbon streamers until New London, where he almost succeeded in running us into a rock embankment. ("Did you not *see* the giant flaming wall of death?" Lane screamed helpfully at my cortex.)

All my brilliant plans to lose Roger failed — getting off the highway and getting back on, hiding behind moving vans — all the way along the great nothingness between New London and East Haven.

As we approached New Haven at dawn, we got waylaid by rush-hour traffic. A sea of brake lights appeared before us as everyone slowed for some distant unpleasantness we couldn't see yet. With Roger temporarily separated from us by many unhappy commuters, we stopped in the middle of the world's biggest parking lot and pushed up our face shields.

The good news was, Lane was still on my back seat. The bad news was, he needed to pee. "Not now," I said. "I gotta tell you some stuff."

"Are you *shittin'* me?" said Lane. "What's he gonna do — run across car roofs and catch us?"

"Shut up," I said, and took the opportunity to educate him on the fine art of ditching. Just in case. Might be my last chance. He could pee later. Or during.

"It's a three-part operation," I said to him over my shoulder. "Don't panic. Kick the bike away as you go down. Try to land on something padded."

"When we get to New York," he said, "let's go for Chinese."

It was hopeless. He was all sinew and muscle and roughly no percent body fat. We'd both left his house wearing ultra-unprotective denim jeans and jackets. I skipped the part about how, if we did spill, we'd be putting some plastic surgeon's kids through college.

"We can't stay here. Let's go," I said, and pushed his visor back down over his face. I seized the chance to split lanes, something Roger couldn't do unless his Leatherman had a Jaws of Life, and tried to put some more real estate between us.

We were the only hardware moving. Soon we saw the messy five-car pile-up that was stopping all the other traffic for miles. This is hardly an unusual occurrence in the New Haven metro area. It was just the first time I was ever glad to see one.

The crash scene was a circus. The totaled cars were in positions so crazy, I couldn't imagine how they ever got that way. A hundred people buzzed around them. Victims, cops, firefighters, paramedics, tow truck operators, media crews, sightseers. The wreck choked two whole lanes and the shoulder. Nothing I couldn't get around, and did, and stopped at its westernmost end.

I had an idea. It didn't involve eating food or eliminating it. Lane wouldn't like it. I didn't care.

I lifted my visor and twisted around toward him. His throat was covered with goosebumps; he had to be freezing, and he'd never said a word about it.

"Get off," I told him.

He looked perplexed and didn't twitch a muscle.

"Go. Circulate. Meet your public. Pee."

"You're *leaving* me here?" he said, incredulous.

"Well, yeah."

Whether he liked it or not, a circus was the perfect place for him to be right now. He could hide from Roger, and I could do what I had to do without worrying about him becoming airborne. I'd come back for him later.

"Where are *you* going?"

"Got some business. Hurry up, get off."

"What does that mean, 'business'?"

I wasn't about to tell him I was low on gas. I needed to do something about it, fast. Something risky, illegal, and alone.

"Big sale at Bloomingdale's," I said. "Gotta go. Get off now."

"I'm not getting off. You can't make me."

"No? Watch me. Listen, Roger's dimwitted, not braindead. Even *he* knows we don't have to sit in traffic with all these leadbutts. He probably bagged this mess at the last exit and went surface. He'll get back on the highway down the road and look for us."

"I don't get it. Why do I hafta stay here?" I wished he had a dial I could turn to speed him along on the uptake.

"Because if Roger got off the highway, he'll never find you here. And if Roger *didn't* get off the highway, this is the last place he'll look for you. Thank me later. Now get off."

Lane thought about it a moment longer than I wanted to waste.

"Why don't you stay here, too?"

"No place to stash the bike. Check it out."

As he scanned the scenery, we shared a quality moment of perspective: no foliage, no buildings, no billboard polluting the view that we could hide the Beemer behind.

"You know Roger. Eternal optimist. Thinks he can still save his meal ticket if he catches me. Let him try. Gives you a chance to go the other way. Hide out at Larry's for a while. Have a party. Go pee. Now get *off*."

"This is stupid," he said, and sat like an anvil.

"Fine. Let me rephrase it: I'm dead already, remember? And you're not. Yet. Wanna keep it that way? *Get off my bike!*"

He got off. All he said was "How will I get back?"

"You've got more brainwave activity than Roger, and he's doing alright. You figure it out."

I blew him a kiss, gave him a wink, and popped a wheelie as I sped off toward Brooklyn.

Chapter 37

I wish my wackometer worked as well with editors as it does with drivers. Sure enough, at the first highway entrance past the pile-up, there was good old Roger, waiting. He saw me whiz by him and burned rubber.

When not fleeing insane blackmailers, I read all kinds of automotive magazines. I knew a Chevy 454 was good for 137 mph. The best my bike could do was 110, downhill with a tailwind. It was only a matter of time before Roger either pulverized me or got bored, and went back to pound on Lane. For now, heavy traffic enabled me to evade Roger at modest extralegal speeds so Lane would have a fair chance of catching a bus or something.

Things got dicier when the road widened to three lanes — great for rush hour volume, not so great when a lone nut is trying to mow you down. I cut off a Corvette in the left lane and shot down the highway toward New York. Roger cut off a refrigerator van to the right and came after me.

I watched him in my mirror. His window was down, his left arm out; he was holding something. In my mirror it looked like a blurry lump of blue-black metal. I was sure it was the Sig Sauer I saw in Lane's drawer in Groton. And as I recalled, it was loaded.

The one day in my life I ever *wanted* police intervention, and where were those sons of bitches? Where's fog when you need it? Where were the Pacific Rimmers driving backwards to their exits? I gunned the throttle.

The only thing I had going for me was the statistical probability that Roger wasn't a lefty. If that was the case, he could shoot and miss forever. However, the only compelling evidence I had of that was seeing him smoke cigarettes right-handed. Anyway, Roger was probably mad and dumb enough to kick out his own windshield, so he could shoot clean with whichever hand misbehaved better. Lane could buy him a new windshield later.

For the moment, left seemed the right place to be. As I factored all the variables, my calculations were disrupted by a blast. Sparks exploded off a chain-link fence atop the highway divider at the very spot where I was a half second earlier.

I didn't much care anymore which hand Roger liked better.

The road narrowed to two lanes again. Up ahead were two semis riding side by side, one trying to pass the other. I slipped in between them, knowing neither could see me, and prayed. "*Noodle*," I could hear my father say, "*Left is the passing side. Right is suicide.*"

I got past both trucks a nanosecond before the one on the left made his move into the right lane. The draft of displaced air whooshed up my back. I heard the screeching of brakes and thirty-six tires skidding behind me as I jetted away.

But Roger, he had to slow down for the trucks. I was dusting him! That is, I was until an impenetrable knot of weaving, butt-dragging New Yorkers and Massholes got in my way.

Ordinarily I'd have made like a Rhode Islander and used the shoulder as an express lane, but this one was covered with gravel and impassable at any useful speed. My alternatives were diminishing as fast as my gas. I had just enough left to splutter to a halt pretty soon and get my head blown off.

I pulled in front of another big truck that Roger could shoot at while I considered my options. I wondered what Nancy Delgado and Dorothy Parker would do.

I decided to take my chances on surface roads, and sailed off the next exit. I'd find a place to hide in Bridgeport, Underworld of Connecticut.

It appeared I'd successfully buried myself from Roger's view beside a tanker truck on the exit ramp. So I was a tad perturbed to see Roger directly behind me.

The end of the westbound exit ramp intersected with a road that ran perpendicular to the highway. The light at the end of the ramp was red. Praying no vehicles were coming, I slowed to 55, threw down the Beemer, and cut a hard left under the overpass without looking. My left cylinder made a sharp bang as it smacked the pavement. The good news was, no one was coming. The bad news was, the cylinder dragged some macadam with it that was now burning and stinking like a tar truck. The other bad news was that the friction shredded my jeans when my knee scraped the ground, and the asphalt cooked my kneecap. Yo, thanks Roger. It's not like I use that knee for anything.

After the corner, I whipped the bike upright and looked back fast. Roger took the same corner on two wheels, not quite missing a car that had the right of way and wasn't expecting to clip a speeding pickup.

I had one more idea, a very bad one. I hooked a right onto the highway's northbound off-ramp. I didn't think he'd have the balls to follow, but there was Roger, still up my rear end like a heat-seeking missile.

Even though it was my first time at something like this, I was pretty sure what to expect upon entering an interstate going the wrong direction. If there was a wide, unoccupied shoulder, I'd be fine. If not, I'd win a breathtaking prize selected from a vast and colorful array of codas.

As usual, my optimism was premature. Coming directly at me was a semi. And as if that wasn't bad enough, it was hauling *a house*! Christ, I was *not* having a good day.

The ramp was barely wide enough for that truck; there was no shoulder at all, not even room for a little motorcycle to squeeze by. The driver hit the air brakes hard, but no way was he ever going to stop in time. Goddamn it, Lane — first my car, now my bike. You asshole.

I stood up on the pegs. I pushed myself off the Beemer as hard and fast as I could, launching myself into a graceless somersault down a weedy slope as the semi collided with my former bike. Then I heard the Beemer bounce onto Roger's hood with a great sickly crunch just before he, too, connected with the semi. It sounded pretty final. I was grateful I couldn't see shit.

I waited for the pickup to land on top of me. And waited. It didn't. Instead there was distant banging, followed by a big sploosh, and then nothing. Which could only mean Roger rolled off the other side of the ramp, down a seventy-five-foot drop into the scenic Housatonic River.

Everything went eerily silent. Lying in a patch of weeds, I tested the viability of my appendages and wondered whether standing was a smart idea. My head pounded the inside of my helmet like it was trying to get out. I couldn't peel the thing off because something was wrong with my arm, and I couldn't unhook the strap of my German-made helmet with one hand. Fucking Nazis.

My vision was fuzzy. I rubbed my eyes. My vision grew fuzzier. Everything hurt.

I'd just started examining myself for blood, of which there was plenty, when I heard arguing. I stopped poking myself and looked up.

The truck with the house on it had stopped on the ramp. The distraught driver was outside the cab now, fighting with someone. Just what I needed today, one more goddamned argument.

The driver and the visitor were screaming at the same time, making it hard to interpret the finer points of their discussion. One thing I heard was the second person saying, "Where'd ya learn to drive, OJ? On a *golf course*?"

That was followed by more unintelligible shouting as countless cars got stuck on the ramp and the highway beyond, and a great din of honking and yelling welled up. I wondered how I was going to get up and go home.

Then I heard the visitor tell the truck driver, "I don't care if ya gotta get this house to *China* by four-thirty! You fetch your damn radio and call an ambulance *right now*! Git!" The truck driver started crying. Of the two of us, he needed a Valium more.

Her car was blocking his truck, so he didn't have much choice in the matter unless he wanted to flatten three vehicles that day. And then the woman came half sliding, half running down the grassy knoll, toward me. She had on a pink pillbox hat. This was not good.

"Goddamnit! Goddamnit!" she yelled all the way down. "Goddamnit! I'm comin'! Don't you move!"

I looked up at her car blocking the truck, expecting to see a vintage black Lincoln convertible. It was a late-model blue muscle car with a strobe going on the dash.

As its driver got closer, I was relieved to see it wasn't a pillbox hat on her head at all, just a baseball cap turned backward. As she slid into focus, I had either my two-thousandth epiphany of the day or a more serious head trauma than I thought. It couldn't be. Could it?

"What the hell kind of friend are *you*?" I said to the USPS regional security manager. "You can't call? You can't write? Don't tell me you can't pilfer stamps at that dump where you work."

I was never more glad to see anyone in my life.

"Jeez, I've been chasing you since Groton," Nat said. "My boss sent me there to check out a body rotting in a metered mail box, and you blew by me with that dumb sodbuster in a cowboy Caddy up your butt. Just like old times! Cool, I'm thinking, we'll have breakfast! That was one hell of a traffic jam you made me get around in New Haven."

I squinted at her car. The entire length of it was a parti-colored stripe of other cars' paint. One headlight hung by a wire.

She carefully took off my helmet. Then she held my shoulder in place and told me bad jokes, so I'd stay conscious until the ambulance came. "Why'd the pervert cross the road? Because he couldn't get his dick out of the chicken."

EMS came and went with me in the meat wagon screaming "No needles!" And that's the last thing I remember about my day in Underworld.

Chapter 38

According to Bridgeport Hospital I was hardly a mess at all, if you don't count my collarbone being cracked and my nicely braised knee, or my dislocated shoulder and a few thousand gaping wounds requiring stitches.

"You'll be a little stiff for a while," the ER doc pronounced in the understatement of the millennium that was, thankfully, nearly over. It's hard to believe hospitals charge money for this.

They gave me a ton of painkillers I could fence and promised to send me a big bill. I kept telling them my head was broken and to x-ray it. All they did was call me a cab, among other things. I was taking up a bed sick people needed, they said. Plus I'd been threatening everyone there about transfusions. The story made the *New York Times*, and the hospital switchboard was paralyzed by media vultures and anyone with an opinion about women drivers. The hospital couldn't wait to get rid of me.

The cab dropped me at the Amtrak station in Bridgeport. I stumbled onto a train that took me to Penn Station. Many bums and escalators later, and with my right arm in a sling, I beat out some suits for a Yellow cab. Then I won a fight with a Palestinian cabbie who didn't want to drive to Brooklyn. "No go! Get out!"

I came home to a billion phone messages — from Darryl, Cliffie, Don DeRosa, Nat, my mother, and sixteen editors and three literary agents who wouldn't return my calls before but who all wanted to talk to me now. Oh yeah, and Lane.

"See?" Mom's message said, "I told you bikes are dangerous." Darryl said he knew of a good body shop. DeRosa said he was glad he never let me road test any of *Motorhead*'s bikes. Nat just wondered if I was okay and hung up; she didn't want to run up Bob's phone bill. Cliffie said *Classic Trend* got a ton of free publicity from his dainty female editor mixing it up with two trucks and a house. He offered to pick up my hospital tab if I stopped calling him Cliffie.

The longest message was Lane's. He found out what happened to me the same way everyone else did.

"By the time I knew you'd gone to a hospital," he said, "you'd already checked out. Holy shit, are you okay? Can I see you? When?" I didn't return his call.

My phone kept ringing, but I waited a few days to answer it. The happy pills they gave me at the hospital made me zone out, and I was still too miffed over my bike to be civil about it if it came up in conversation. When I finally did answer the phone, it was Lane.

"I'm at Larry's," he said, and gave me the number. He told me how he swiped a cell phone from one of the wrecked cars where I left him on I-95, and used it to call Larry to come get him. "Larry wishes I'd go home." Who wouldn't? "The catch is, I ain't got one."

When he got back to Point Judith, his house and everything in it were a pile of charred sticks. "All I got left are the clothes I had on when we split, and the cigarette case 'cause I forgot to take it out of my pocket. Still got the van, though, and the Rover. And the cell phone. Always wanted one of these."

The firefighters uncovered evidence that someone torched the house, but then they found out who lived there. They were big fans, and they didn't know about Roger.

"They put in their report that the gas company screwed up," said Lane, "so it never got reported as arson. It wasn't like there was anyone to prosecute anyway. I didn't own the house, either, so it isn't a total loss. I'll clean up on my renter's insurance. You have to come out here."

"Here's an idea. Why don't you come to Brooklyn?"

"Because there's something here I have to show you."

"Lane, I have a broken collarbone and no way to get around." Eternal asshole.

"Look, what if I come and get you?"

"I don't think so."

"Okay. I'll be there at five."

At 6:15 he pulled up in the Rover. I got out of bed to answer the door, an act I intended to be my major physical exertion for the day. I met him with his Broadcaster and handed it to him. I'd planned to sell it to buy an MV Augusta, but he needed a guitar right now more than I needed another crotch rocket. It wasn't like I was going anywhere.

Lane's hardly the sentimental type, but he looked ecstatic to see the Broadcaster, like it was some old friend that changed its mind about dumping him. He checked it out, turning it over and over in his hands, while I checked out the haircut he'd gotten to obliterate Darryl's mischief. It was more like stuff from a lint trap than hair. I could see the actual shape of his head, the velvety curve of his nape. He seemed somehow naked and vulnerable. Unfortunately, it would grow back.

The bruise on his forehead from the Ampeg had mellowed to a greenish-yellow spot barely visible through a fringe of short bangs. The outfit he had on was another story. He was wearing Air Jordans, a voluminous red turtleneck shirt, and floppy cargo pants. The pants hung like a deflated parachute from his hips, overwhelming all his best personality traits. He couldn't help seeing me giving him the once-over.

"Rhode Island Mall. Best I could do on short notice."

"I'm sorry, but those pants are so baggy. Who can tell what you're shaped like in there?"

"All my old pants went to the same place your bike is, and Sears was out of 512s."

He stopped looking at the Broadcaster and looked at me, to see if he'd said the wrong thing. I was too beaten down to chew him out. He winked at me and said, "We can go through withdrawal together!"

Lane held the tail of the guitar up to his nose and sighted the length of it, to see if the neck was still straight. What did he think, I used it for a tire iron?

I thought about all his snug, air-conditioned jeans that were now history. The blue cashmere pullover I was still paying for. The hand-knitted Fair Isle sweater he'd worn in Harlem that had probably been his father's, and his grandfather's. All those white crew socks. The Gibson Moderne. His platinum award. It was the first time since I got back that I'd thought about someone else's problems. I didn't like it much.

Funny thing was, the repercussions of the fire bothered me a lot more than they seemed to bother him. He reached into his pocket, pulled out a bumper sticker, and handed it to me. "For you," he said. It read Horn Broken, Watch for Finger.

Then he started talking, and talking. He blabbed a mile a minute, way too fast for me to follow in my diminished state. I lost track of whatever he was going on about pretty much immediately. But he must've said something very persuasive at some point, because I heard myself agreeing to go somewhere with him.

While I tried to remember where I put my house keys, Lane sat on my rickety stairs and played one of his ballads on the Broadcaster. I'd never liked that tune on his Strat, going blam blam blam through a twin Marshall stack. Now it sounded like a spiritual.

Eventually I found my keys and wallet, and crawled into the Rover with him and the Broadcaster knowing it would be way past my bedtime before I'd crawl out of it again. I was glad I never got around to leaving a chicken bomb in it.

We took off. I turned sideways so I could observe him driving. I'd never seen him drive before. A simple thing; everybody does it, it's like walking, except when Lane does it. This was to driving what Neil Armstrong boinging around on the moon was to walking.

I watched Lane like I'd watch gerbils mating. He planted his left foot on the edge of the leather bucket, with his knee resting against the window, his left elbow propped on his thigh. His left hand held his chin one moment, scratched his head the next, then ran through his hair, then tapped a rhythm on his quad to music only he could hear. It had a life of its own.

With his right hand he steered, more or less, while babbling away and swerving around mattresses and bottomless potholes and stalled Novas on the Brooklyn Queens Expressway. Periodically his head would drop back against the headrest and roll to the right as he checked to see whether I was still looking at him. A couple of times he reached over to push my bangs out of my face. Once he squeezed my knee, the one with no skin on it. I said "Ow!" and he stopped.

We got stuck in traffic in Greenpoint, a sprawling Brooklyn industrial neighborhood that seemed to have eluded the EPA. If something's vile, it's manufactured or stored or both in Greenpoint, and not very efficiently. There hasn't been any ozone over Greenpoint in forty years. The wind was up today, and the 'Pernt Perfume was strong.

Lane's idea of making the best of an unbearable situation was to say "Hey! Who cut the cheese?" and laugh uncontrollably.

I suppose it was nice that one of us was having a good time. I'd conveniently forgotten my pain pills, and the last one was wearing off. I was hoping the aches would go away if I ignored them. It worked with cramps.

"Please explain again why I'm in this parvenu excuse for transportation. I believe I missed it the first time," I said.

"You have to see something I got."

"Oh yeah, right. You couldn't just bring it with you?"

"Nope. Too big and heavy. You know, I'm not as strong as I look."

He wouldn't tell me what it was despite my best effort to pry it out of him, an exercise that wore me out. I looked out the passenger window and fought to stay awake.

The cell phone was on the console. It rang several times but he never picked it up.

Traffic started moving again. We passed through Queens and made quick work of the Clearview Expressway. Little Bay was clogged with small boats. A million people zigzagged into each other in their pleasure craft, getting away from it all.

We were halfway across the Throg's Neck Bridge before he spoke again. "Listen to this," he said, and popped a tape into the stereo.

Woke me right the hell up, that tape did. The voice singing sounded like his, but these were songs I'd never heard before. They were bluesy and introspective. They weren't covers of the worn-out standards beloved of his ilk. They were all new.

He had a very good stereo system; Alvin's bass came pounding through the Blaupunkt, directly into my stomach. I rolled down the window, just in case.

"What *is* this?" I asked.

"The new album I was just telling you about. Where were you?"

"Great to be back, ladies and germs. I'll be here all week. When did this album happen?"

"You like it?" He didn't wait for an answer. "Warner did. They bought out my old record contract because they wanted this. Can't say I'll miss my old label."

"Oh, you mean those assholes who Jewed you out of money, never promoted your records, and didn't care if you played in hellholes?"

"Yeah, them." He laughed. Stamford with all its cheap motels and prefab office towers passed by us like a bad dream.

The new material was better than good. It was way more mature and straightforward than his '80s stuff, with more edge and funk than anyone was used to from him, dismembered debs notwithstanding. No one would miss the old, puerile Lane. There were no fake jobs with fake fathers in these songs. Nobody got mutilated or pink-slipped. When he said he wrote all the lyrics, you could've knocked me over with a feather, although today a stiff look probably would do it. I could hear he'd played the leads himself, too, that haunting way he does. Darryl, who would run out to buy a copy and never tell anyone, was going to be inconsolable. And of course Lane sang every song himself, like a demented angel.

When the tape was over I made him play it again, then once more so I could listen to different things, and because when it was playing he stopped talking. The material was all nervy, earthy stuff about confounding relationships, lousy luck, spiritual redemption, and fortitude in the face of absurdity. You know, the way real music used to be, before disco and teen pop and Yanni.

One song was about not being able to see himself in the mirror. One was about losing a claim ticket to a locker where he'd parked a nice old Fender Jazzmaster. There was one especially interesting cut about some woman who made him furious, but he couldn't stop thinking about her. I rallied from my stupor sufficiently to fire a lot of nosy questions at him about that one, but he changed the subject. He was more interested in hearing about my fine adventure.

"Nothing much to tell," I deadpanned. "Roger chased me into a truck. I jumped, he didn't."

"The *Times* said he couldn't swim. I'll miss Roger."

"He was a piece of work. You know, he had your gun. You're gonna have to buy a new one."

"I gotta buy a new one of everything. How'd you know I had a gun?" He took his eyes off the road to squint at me while waiting for an answer he'd never get.

"Watch the road. *Please*," I said. "I've been in enough fender benders this week."

"Anyway," he said, looking at the highway again, "I don't need another gun. I only got that one to protect myself from Roger."

"Oh, good plan. Worked great."

"At least Roger doesn't have to worry about his swemmin pooh payments anymore. Hey — how do you feel?" Two hours into our first conversation after I'm in a hospital, he asks me this.

"Like roadkill. Got any more music?"

Of course Lane had more music, lots of it. May as well ask FAO Schwartz if they have more toys. He played another tape, full of rough tracks of new songs he'd recorded by himself with a computer and a Band in a Box program, when he was hot to produce but his band had to stay home to log family time. "Bunch of decrepit geezers," he called them.

The lyrics and arrangements on the second tape were fresh and stylish, mostly rock'n'roll with hip hop touches that would make anyone dance who hadn't just been hit by a semi. If these were unpolished versions, the finished cuts would be killer. Something had busted a whopping hole in Lane's firewall, and the oxygen was getting in.

I looked out the side window again while the music played. It was nice to be driven, to be able to look around mindlessly. It was a luxury I'd forgotten.

I watched strangers in their cars picking their noses, hitting their kids. Bridgeport and New Haven zoomed by, with their cineplexes and truck stops and discount barns. After Branford the street lamps stopped and civilization fell away. The rare exit sign suggested there might be human life beyond the access road, past the high landscaping, magical stuff you couldn't see from I-95. The exits had fairytale names: Goose Lane, Horse Hill Road, Four Mile River Road. I always meant to take them sometime, but had never gotten around to it.

The foliage aside the highway was lush. The wind blew the emerald leaves in waves, up and down, the silvery undersides peeking out before you saw their dark tops again. The trees shimmered like sequin dresses in the coral and turquoise sunset.

Lane filled the dusk with stories about meetings taken and deals done until New London was engulfed by the night, blue and starry as the Hayden Planetarium, and then Rhode Island disappeared under our wheels.

It was 11 p.m. when we got where we were going. Larry Ochowitz, who drives Hogs and two-strokes and subscribes to *Tatoo Review*, lives in a sweet little bungalow in a bucolic Massachusetts suburb called Seekonk. His station wagon was parked in the grass, which I thought odd since he had a garage. Probably he'd surrendered it to Lane's nonwaterproof van.

We pulled into Larry's driveway. Lane sprang from the Rover, sauntered to the garage, remembered I couldn't get out of his SUV by myself, came back, and opened the passenger door for me. Then he went back and opened the garage door, leaving me standing in the driveway.

Larry's car was in the yard, it turned out, because there was a large wooden crate living in his garage. It was sheathed in cardboard, with a Norton logo and cryptic code numbers stenciled on the sides.

Lane steered me to an out-of-the-way spot next to a workbench where Larry had left two radio-controlled model boats he was building for his kids. After hours of sitting in a car, my body felt like that stuck engine I was dismantling in Darien.

Lane picked up a crowbar and noisily attacked the crate. While he tangled with it, I sat on a five-gallon tub of joint compound with my chin in my hand and got depressed. The only production bikes made by Norton anymore are huge rotaries, luxury rides you couldn't get serviced in America if your life depended on it. I was flattered that he wanted to be a bike bum like me, but I wished he'd asked for advice first. I didn't want to be around when he found out his feet weren't going to reach the ground. And honestly, he could've picked a better time to show off.

Just then the side of the crate broke away, thudding loudly onto the floor in a cloud of dust as Lane jumped back. The first thing I saw was a glossy black frame, shiny red enamel, and lots of chrome. The tailpiece looked like a wasp's ass. The gas tank had the old-style Norton decal. The side cover decal read Commando.

I couldn't believe what I was looking at. It was a 1970 750 cc Fastback. And it was brand stinking new. At a fire sale, it was a $10,000 bike.

"You wouldn't believe how many calls I made to find this thing," said Lane, shaking the dust out of his hair. "Larry's gonna chase me with a meat cleaver when his phone bill comes."

"No shit, Sherlock? Well, you just knocked $6,000 off the market value by breaking the crate."

"That's *your* problem."

"Huh? Whaddya mean, *my* problem?"

He didn't answer, just stood there beaming like a child with an M-80.

"Wait a minute. You got a *Commando Fastback*, in a *crate*, for *me*?"

"Yeah. But you can't drive it in a box, so I gotta fix it."

Chapter 39

What can I say? I was shocked that Lane had considered my commuter needs before buying another guitar, or even before finding a place to live. I was especially touched that he'd noticed I craved something small and light to manhandle. Yes, I was fond of the Beemer. It got me around and it was paid for. But mainly it was a paid-for pig that I threw around heedlessly until the end.

"I can't possibly pay you back for this," I said to Lane when I regained my voice.

"No need," he said. "I got money stashed everywhere."

When he said he was going to fix the Commando, I didn't think he meant right now. Much to my dismay he finished dismantling the crate, commenced removing the packing restraints, installed the front wheel, and hauled the Fastback out onto the garage floor, gabbing loudly to me over the noise the whole time.

I wondered if the Ochowitzes were sleeping through all this. I hadn't forgotten I owed Larry a monster favor, and this seemed like an ideal time to repay it. But I just didn't have the juice to hogtie Lane with the clothesline.

Larry owned lots of useful tools and Lane seemed determined to use every one to prep the bike, a ritual I knew would take half the night. There were fluids to pour, accessories to adjust, a battery to fill and charge, bolts to tighten, functions to test. Lane had somehow gotten hold of a 300-page Norton workshop manual from 1970, and he was only up to page 42 by 1 a.m. I knew Lane. He wasn't going to let it rest until he declared it done.

"I gotta lie down soon," I said. I didn't want to seem ungrateful or ruin his fun, but I hurt all over, and I was cold. My hands were trembling, and probably my voice, which he didn't seem to notice.

"Okay," he said, and kept wrenching and talking.

I was still sitting there, shivering and holding my shoulder at dawn when he finally poured gas into the tank from an illegal plastic container. Electronic ignitions weren't added to Commandos until 1975, so Lane had to go old school to engage the engine. I watched with great amusement and genuine awe as he threw his full weight onto the kick starter. The sleeping motor exploded to life.

Until that moment I thought I hadn't a single maternal cell in my entire bruised anatomy. Now I thought it might be nice to clone Lane.

"Just gonna take it around the block!" he yelled gleefully over the raucous, primitive, pre-emission-control thumping. "Be right back. Don't move!"

Yeah, right? Like I was going somewhere. He shot his best obscene smile at me over his shoulder, then rumbled triumphantly across Larry's lawn on one of the most beautiful, unreliable bikes ever made. He aimed down the road, toward the crimson slash of sunrise where another day started.

I sighed and leaned back against Larry's workbench. I closed my eyes.

A door slammed. "Larry?"

"How many fingers?" said a voice that wasn't Larry's.

"Huh?" I thought I said.

"I'm telling you, this one's out," said a second voice.

"Beyond out," said the first voice.

"What the fuck's going on here? Hey — no transfusions!"

No one answered me. I opened my eyes. I was inside a van.

"Gimme a Rolo," said the first voice. "Never seen anyone survive a collision with a *house* before."

"And you ain't gonna, neither," said the second.

They pulled the sheet over my face and silently passed the box of Rolos.